Wolfheart

also by
Hallie Lee

Paint Me Fearless

Wolfheart

The Shady Gully Series
Book 2

HALLIE LEE

WordCrafts Press

Wolfheart
Copyright © 2021
Hallie Lee

ISBN: 978-1-952474-87-3

Cover design by David Warren.

Published by WordCrafts Press
Cody, Wyoming 82414
www.wordcrafts.net

"Everyone thinks they have the best dog.
And none of them are wrong."
~from *The Canine Commandments*
W.R. Pursche

For all the *best* dogs who crossed the Rainbow Bridge
this year...especially, my Lucy Belle.

T he good folks of Shady Gully wouldn't be surprised by my actions. Not on a night when the moon drooped hazily over the swamp, and the air dripped with pre-storm humidity. As usual, the folks of Shady Gully would assume I was up to no good.

And they'd be right.

As the irony caused me to stumble, I stilled my body, and slowed my breathing. Within seconds I became one with the animals who guarded the night. The snakes that slithered along the cypress trees. The owls that hunted for prey. The cicadas oblivious and intoxicated by the sound of their own symphony.

On this night, I felt a kinship with the shadows that wandered in the suffocating heat. Like ghosts, they seemed to cry out, desperate to be remembered. I tipped my head in recognition of them all, even as blood stained my own hands.

I shifted the lifeless body in my arms, carefully lowering it to the ground. I stood slowly, my back aching with the strain. It took me a while to find the shovel, as my legs were awkward with arthritis. Regrettably, I was no longer young.

The shovel was in its usual place. Always four clicks behind the cypress tree festooned with umbrella shaped moss. Not everybody could find the shovel. Only my people. The Creek People. Or who some in Shady Gully referred to as—the Creek Freaks.

My gaze swept over the sticks, rocks, and feathers strewn amid the dirt. I understood the purpose in their placement, appreciated the

1

memories and reverence in each trinket. I shook off the unwelcome emotion as it rose within me, focusing instead on the dig.

Within minutes my brow grew moist with sweat, and the gore on my shirt dampened the skin on my stomach with blood. Probably where I'd tucked the body close against mine on the hike to the sacred land.

When a sudden flicker of lightning created a floodlight across the ground, I realized the hole I'd dug was big enough. Too big, in fact.

"Stop putting it off," I hissed loud enough to wake a snake from its slumber. The water moccasin slipped into the marsh, deciding I wasn't worth the effort.

I picked up the body, gently placing it into the grave. Why gently, I wondered? Gentleness had never been a word used to describe him. And God knew he hadn't been gentle tonight.

I shoveled dirt atop the grave at an emotional, feverish pace. Anything to temper the memories that threatened. The emotions that came uninvited.

Fury.

When the hole was nearly covered, I knelt next to the grave. Mumbled a prayer.

Regret.

I pulled a ragged blue wolf from the pocket of my jeans, and cradled the worn, scruffy material against my forehead. The stuffed animal's eyes seemed to skewer me with disappointment. I mumbled another prayer.

Grief.

I carefully placed the blue wolf into the grave. The hell with the consequences, I thought. At least now the torment was over.

I allowed myself one more glance, one more memory.

A flash of jagged light lit up the southern sky, and thunder pounded the ground. I watched as the storm descended on Shady Gully, Louisiana.

Because it had come to rage.

PART I

Chapter One

HOLED UP IN SOME KENTUCKY HOLLER
Luke

W hile I wasn't actually present when my sister Micah was born, I'd be willing to bet she came into the world talking.

"I can't believe I wasted all those years in school." Micah sighed dramatically. "And for what? A stupid job I hate. I mean, I'm only twenty-three, and my life is ruined."

Because I felt her eyes on me, I did what every big brother would do when faced with an emotional, *I-hate-my-life* meltdown. I resisted eye contact, remained focused on the road, and gripped the steering wheel like a bull rider latches onto a flat braided rope. Anything more, or less, would have surely inflamed her tirade.

"And I'm not even getting paid anything."

"You're getting paid—" Too late to swallow my words, I accepted my fate like a washed-up bull rider.

"Not enough. I have to live with my parents. How embarrassing is that?" Micah ducked her head forlornly. "I spend my whole day with my face in somebody's mouth. It's so gross. I don't think I can take it anymore."

"Your face? Really?" I side-eyed her. "If that's the way you're doing it, I think the dental hygienist school ripped you off."

Unamused, she glared. "They overbook me. I barely have time to eat lunch. My patients are always grouchy."

"Before or after they see you?"

She ignored me, pointing toward a sign. "Remember to take a right up here. By the pharmacy." She carelessly twisted the cap off a bottle of fingernail polish, and proceeded to touch up her glittery nails.

"I know where to turn." I eyeballed the wobbly bottle. "Be careful with that. Don't get that on my seats—"

"I'm not. Right here," she pointed. "Luke, turn." Although a thick sheet of rain and wind obscured the street sign, I managed to turn before annoying the driver behind me.

I blamed my parents, who'd encouraged her incessant babbling at infancy. And my brother Petey, who'd rejoiced when he met a lively, animated spirit to match his own. While my whole family romped in their own playground of gaiety upon Micah's birth, I, at the young age of four, had been forced to become the serious one.

I'd had no choice really. Someone had to look out for them.

I glanced at my sister, who still looked like a child with her petite frame and bouncy blonde hair. Even with her endless chatter, I enjoyed her cheeky personality. "You sure are bossy for somebody needing a ride to work."

"Just trying to keep you out of traffic." After the required amount of nail-blowing and hand-waving, she shrugged. "Especially with the bad weather today. Did you hear the thunder last night?"

I nodded, let her prattle on about the weather as I surveyed the flow of cars heading in and out of Belle Maison. Despite the scattered limbs and debris from the storm, the roads looked well maintained. Tall pine trees the color of evergreen framed either side of the highway, giving the city a quaint, small-town feel.

"Mama and Daddy lost their electricity."

"I used to think Belle Maison was so big," I mused. "When I was a kid anyway."

"It's bigger than Shady Gully."

"Not really," I said. "And yet, look at all this hustle and bustle. It's what happens when you incorporate. Businesses come in. People build houses. You get more firemen and police—"

"And somebody lost a tree by the crossroads. Lightening sliced it clean in half."

"Stop trying to change the subject. In fact, to both hold your interest, *and* make my point, let's take a trip to Micah's world. As scary as that might be—"

"Oh please," Micah rolled her eyes. "You do know everybody in town avoids you because of your obsession with incorporating Shady Gully?"

"I'm serious. How great would it be to find a good job right at home in Shady Gully? And not have to drive all the way to Belle Maison to go to work?"

"First of all," Micah jabbed one of her pink nails in the air. "I'm not driving. You are. And don't get me started on my stupid job again."

I hesitated, wavering between a variety of lectures, weighing out the risk and reward ratio on each. I opted for the more pressing, obvious pickle. "Well, if you hadn't wrecked your car, I wouldn't be driving."

"I didn't wreck it," Micah said defensively, turning her attention to her phone.

"You backed into a patio table at the Cozy Corner."

"Charlie Wayne moved it," she argued. "It wasn't supposed to be there."

I sighed, exasperated. "You're right. How dare Charlie Wayne rearrange his furniture."

As she tapped her glitter tipped fingers in agitation, I tried my best to ignore the sparkly pink smudges that dusted the gray interior of my car. "Micah, you just need to be more careful. More aware of your surroundings. This time it was a table. Next time it might be something—bigger."

I turned left on Medical Plaza Way, a long tree lined community that led to the dental clinic where Micah worked, as well as several Urgent Cares and Physician offices. As a flash of lightning brightened the early morning gloominess, I glanced at Micah, whose fascination with the weather had been replaced by the tantalizing allure of social media.

"The good news is, Bubba said your car is almost ready. He and Daryl are painting the back fenders today."

"I can't believe you hired those two." Micah scrolled on her phone. "Much less Petey, who's never in town."

My thoughts drifted to the auto body shop my Aunt Robin helped me buy after I graduated business school. Since it was the only one in Shady Gully, and I priced competitively, folks seldom ventured into Belle Maison to have their cars repaired. I employed a few people, like Bubba and Daryl, who were my parents' age, and until now had never had health insurance, or held steady jobs.

I also hired my brother, Petey—or inherited him—since he'd worked for the failing body shop before I bought the business. Petey was a decent body man, but he was an even better public relations man. He was good with the folks who came in, forever dazzling them with his infectious smile and his memory of family particulars. "How's your Aunt Edna?" he'd ask with genuine concern. "Is she still battling the flu?" Or "I think I found the perfect puppy for Joey," he'd say as he keyed up a picture on his phone. "This little fellow is at the humane society. I reckon he'd take Joey's mind off losing Rascal."

"Bubba and Daryl do good work," I told Micah.

"Luke, you can't fix everything. Or everybody." She twisted in her seat. "I wish you'd just chill out and get a life. Instead of trying to change the world."

"I'm not trying to change the world," I countered. "Just Shady Gully. And speaking of Petey, how long is he going to stay in Lexington? What's going on with him?"

Micah shrugged, "For all I know he's holed up in some Kentucky holler drinking moonshine."

I suppressed a chuckle.

"Mama said he's visiting Aunt Robin. Hanging out with Violet and Sterling while his shoulder gets better." She looked up from her phone. "I wouldn't come back either if you were still paying me."

"It's okay. He needs some time to rest his shoulder." Petey had had his own fender bender under the hood of an ancient Ford Mustang.

"Maybe if I injured my hands, I could go to Kentucky and have fun with my Aunt and cousins and drink moonshine."

Robin wasn't really our aunt. And her twins, Sterling and Violet, weren't really our cousins. Not technically anyway. We'd all grown up together, as had our parents, and we thought of one another other as extended family.

"You think the dentist would still pay me?" Micah asked, "If I hurt my hands?"

"Doubtful. You'd still have your face."

I tapped my blinker as we approached the Medical Plaza. A few employees wearing scrubs sipped coffee under the awnings of their respective offices. One looked particularly familiar.

"Maybe I could work at the post office?" Micah tugged her rain slicker over her shoulders. "I could deliver mail like Bella and her mom."

"Who?"

"Bella. My friend from across the creek. The one with the voice."

It was impossible to keep up with the random rhythms of my sister's conversations. "I have no idea who you're talking about," I said.

"Remember Mama was all worked up because Brother Jesse wouldn't let Bella try out for the church choir? Which is just crazy, because she has the most amazing voice. If he'd let her sing, his attendance would skyrocket—"

"Is that Tammy Jo?" I asked casually. "The girl in the scrubs?"

Micah glanced up from her phone. "Yeah, she works at the urgent care now."

Petey's ex-girlfriend. When had they broken up? A year ago? Two years ago? Sometimes I marveled at the way my brother flitted from one project to another. One passion to another. One girl to another. He'd casually offer up a humble grin and a flippant explanation about how things had run their course, with the added assurance that it had all ended well.

"Anyway, Mama gave Brother Jesse a piece of her mind at the church fair. I think he'll live to regret his decision," Micah went on. And on.

I envied my brother his easy-going manner, as well as the way people were drawn to him. Sometimes I even wished I could bounce from thing to thing, without purpose or direction. Just happy to be on the journey.

"They're done," quipped Micah as I pulled to the curb. "You should ask her out."

I felt my face heat up as she eyeballed me. Flustered, I scrambled for a comeback as a text sounded on Micah's phone. She glanced at it as she opened the door. And then she stopped.

"What?" I asked, unsettled by the stillness of her usually frenetic body.

When she turned back to me, she appeared stricken. "I'm not sure. Something happened last night across the creek."

"From the storm you mean?"

I waited as she read the text again.

"No," she said finally. "Somebody was murdered."

Chapter Two

Enlighten Me
Sheriff Rick

When I arrived at the crime scene the ground was wet, and a light mist dripped from the trees, but the hellacious wind and rain had stopped. The lifting of the storm provided me with a perfect sightline to my knucklehead deputies. All two of 'em.

After removing the wrapper on a nugget of strawberry taffy, I popped the morsel of heaven into my mouth, and moved to confront whatever version of hell had descended upon my town.

"Here he comes." Max pocketed his phone. "Magnum PI."

"No," disagreed Quietdove. "That's Sam Elliott."

I slipped on a pair of latex gloves, and peered at them both. "I'm younger and better lookin' than either of 'em." I snapped the latex. "Now tell me how you two maintained the integrity of my crime scene. Go on, impress me."

"We got here about the same time as the paramedics," began Quietdove. "Once we realized the victim was deceased, we set up barriers. We did a walk through—"

"Touch anything?"

"No sir," he answered. "Not a thing. Just documented our initial observations. Talked to the witnesses."

"Witnesses?" I stopped. "Enlighten me."

When Quietdove seemed hesitant, Max stepped in. "The victim's daughter, Meadow, and her granddaughter—"

"Bella?" I asked, disheartened. "Who called it in?"

"Meadow did, but she was pretty upset, so Bella talked to the operator."

I muttered an expletive, followed by hollow words of regret. "Poor Miss Peony." I glanced at Quietdove. "I'm sorry." I patted his shoulder.

Regardless of how well Quietdove knew Miss Peony, her daughter Meadow, or her granddaughter Bella, these were his people. This was his side of the creek. And violence against one was an affront to them all.

I resumed my interrogation. "How'd y'all know she was deceased?"

"Well, I checked her pulse. But—" Quietdove glanced at a group of EMTs gathered around the ambulance— "Patty and her team confirmed it."

I nodded at the EMTs as we approached the weathered shotgun house, dodging random chickens and stray cats and dogs along the way.

"Hey Ricky, how's it going?" A female paramedic with a serious expression greeted me as she exited the home.

"Good. How ya doing, Patty?"

She tipped her head, eager to get down to business.

"Go on, enlighten me."

"It appears the victim, a sixty-year-old female, died from blunt force trauma to the back of the head." Patty pointed to her own head to demonstrate. "She was severely beaten, but I believe what killed her was the head injury. Either from a fall…or she was hit with, or pushed, into something. The coroner should be able to tell you more."

I sighed, already missing the sweetness of my taffy.

Patty glanced at the small house. "The two witnesses are okay. Meadow is bruised, roughed up. She was likely involved in the altercation.

"And Bella?" I asked.

"A little better. Likely in shock. But they wouldn't go to the hospital. They refuse to leave Miss Peony, the deceased." With nothing left to add, we both turned our attention to the aimless chickens, pecking and clucking about the yard.

"Thanks Patty," I waved goodbye. "Say hi to Denise for me."

Max and Quietdove followed me toward the old, gabled front porch. While the front steps were uneven after years of wear and tear, someone had made the effort to plant fresh flowers in colorful hand painted pots.

Before we walked inside, I asked Quietdove, "Any sign of Wolfheart?"

"None. Which is strange. He and his sister were close."

Max scoffed, "And no sign of Madhawk either. Who, if you ask me, is the likely suspect—"

"Nobody asked you." I gave Max a stern look. Part of my deputies' training was learning to consider all the evidence before making assumptions. That being said, Peony's disreputable boyfriend was on the top of my list as well.

"Oh, and one more thing," said Max. "There's a significant amount of blood pooled around the back exit of the house. And drag stains. Like something, or someone, was dragged into the woods."

My boots made a squishing sound as they plowed to a stop. "Next time, numbskull, try leading with that."

After calling in reinforcements from my office in Belle Maison, I indulged in a little rant. "It's bad enough we got all this rain making my crime scene soggier than buttered grits, but now, I got an extended scene that hasn't been taped off—"

"We roped off the back as soon as we saw the blood and—"

"Max, that's wonderful. You want a trophy?" A beat. "Go widen the barrier. And when backup gets here, I want y'all to start searching. There could be someone in the woods who needs help."

When Quietdove moved to follow Max, I held him back. "I need you with me. I know these two witnesses and I think a lot of 'em, but you speak their language. I wanna know about nuances, tells… anything you see that I don't. Got it?"

"Tells?" Quietdove raised an eyebrow.

As we entered the house, I scanned the upended furniture, the broken dishes, and toppled picture frames that held ragged photos of family and friends. Jagged hints of elders, kids, dogs, cats, and even chickens peeked back at me amid the broken glass.

Although there were splashes of blood throughout the kitchen and living area, the house didn't smack of the metallic odor associated with violent crimes. Instead, oddly enough, the place smelled like Christmas trees.

Meadow and Bella sat on the floor next to Peony, whose body had been carefully covered with a brightly colored quilt. The kind of quilt old ladies circled around for months, armed with only fabric, needles, and a lifetime of stories. Somehow, over time, a miraculous patchwork of art materialized, seemingly enriched with the experiences and wisdom of its makers.

As an EMT gathered his equipment and spoke softly to the women, I scanned the home, noticing the candles displayed precisely around the body. Curious as to the symbolism, I glanced at Quietdove.

He remained solemn, giving nothing away. Despite his lack of help, it seemed I'd at least discovered the source of the pine tree smell.

Once the EMT left, I approached Meadow and her daughter, Bella. "I'm very sorry about what happened to your mama, Meadow. She sure was a fine lady."

Without looking up, Meadow acknowledged my condolences with a curt nod.

Bella however, squinted at me. "I know you." A streak of boldness broke through her haunted, stricken face. "You're friends with Micah's Mom, Desi. And her Dad, Lenny."

While I'd seen her a few times when she was younger, and was aware of the unfortunate story of her conception, I was taken aback by Bella's beauty.

"Yes, that's right."

"And you used to play football at Shady Gully High with Lenny." It wasn't a question.

But I answered it anyway. "I did." Surprised by her ability to carry on a random conversation in the middle of a traumatic event, I mumbled, "He threw the ball. I caught it. We had some success."

Her eyes flitted about the house, finally settling once again on her grandmother.

Quietdove cleared his throat. "If y'all are up to it, we—I mean, the sheriff, would like to ask you a few questions."

I frowned, unused to my deputy steering my focus. "That's right," I said. "We're gonna do everything in our power to find who did this. But we're gonna need your help."

Bella and Meadow glanced at one another, offering nothing.

"Can you tell us what happened?" Although distracted by the sound of several car doors slamming outside, I pressed. "Meadow, what about your uncle? Where's Wolfheart?"

"Micah is my best friend," Bella announced randomly. "We're the same age." She and Meadow traded furtive looks. "Did you know that, Sheriff?"

"No, I didn't." Disconcerted by the obvious attempt to distract me, I tried again. "And what about Madhawk? He has a reputation for… being unkind to Peony. Can you tell me where he is?"

Meadow marked me with unexpected ferocity.

She'd had a hard life, this remarkable, self-assured woman closing in on forty. As I met her cynical stare, there was no doubt in my mind she knew exactly what had happened to her mother. But for the moment, she seemed resolute, so I decided not to push.

My attention drifted once again to the rising hullabaloo outside. "What's all that racket?" I complained to Quietdove.

The door opened, and in walked Luke, whose family was at the center of Bella's diversion strategy. The kid was decked out in foot booties, goggles, and latex gloves.

"Good grief," I muttered.

"Uh…hi." Luke's eyes flitted around the room, and crash-landed on Bella. "Uh…looks like you've got visitors, Sheriff."

"Yeah," I snapped. "Too many. And I don't need you traipsing on my crime scene. I got enough problems—"

"But I've got these slippers on my feet, and I'm not touching anything." Luke removed a couple of bulging water bottles from his khakis, and presented them to Meadow and Bella. When he spotted the quilt strewn over the body bag, he reminded me of a squirrel frozen in the middle of the road. Staring down the headlights of a truck, tail fluffed up, wide-eyed, and uncertain which way to flee.

A few more car doors echoed from outside. "Surely that's the crime scene techs," I said to Quietdove.

"Yeah, they're here." Luke dragged his googly eyes off Bella. "But those aren't the visitors I meant. There are a bunch of…creek…uh, citizens out there." He glanced awkwardly at Bella and Meadow.

"It seems the word is out," Quietdove said. "I expected they'd come."

"Yeah," Luke nodded. "And they're pretty upset. They just slit the sheriff's tires."

Quietdove assured me he could deal with the crowd. "It's better if you stay here and keep an eye on the mayor there." He indicated Luke with a tilt of his head.

"Mayor?" I grumbled at him.

Sometimes I thought Quietdove and Max had the potential to make good deputies, but the other ninety-nine percent of the time, they carried on like kids on a playground, cracking themselves up pitching goofy nicknames back and forth.

He moved for the door. "I got this. Tells. Remember?"

Once he left, I turned to Luke, whose earnest face kicked up my blood pressure a few notches. "Don't you have something better to do? And don't start in on that incorporation nonsense either. I'm about on my last nerve."

"Just wanted to help, Ricky. But you must admit, if you had the funds for more deputies in situations like this—"

Whether it was the glare on my face, or the steel in my eyes, he stopped talking. "It's Sheriff," I scowled. "Sheriff Rick to you. And that's only 'cause of Desi and Lenny. Speaking of which, if you wanna help, why don't you call your mama and find out if she knows where her buddy Wolfheart is, huh? Can you handle that?"

Luke reached for his phone, holding it high to get a better signal. "You got it. Sheriff Rick." He glanced at Bella as he pushed a button. Unfortunately, the distraction caused the poor mutt to hit the wrong icon, and he ended up calling some distant relative on his daddy's side. It was painful to watch him apologize to Aunt Edna, and then awkwardly try again.

I leaned close to his ear, lowering my voice. "I reckon this is the first time you've seen her, huh?"

"Who?" His face turned redder than boiled crawfish.

"Pretty little Bella there. She's been rattling on like she's part of your family. Trying to throw me off."

Luke jabbed at his phone. "I've seen Meadow at the post office. And I think Micah is a friend of—what was her name again?"

If the mounting noise was any indication, the ruckus outside was escalating. "Stay with them," I barked at Luke.

When I stormed onto the porch, I encountered a large, angry mob who prevented my forensic team from entering the house. Quietdove was nervous. And Max was useless. Even worse, I didn't fancy the way his hand rested on his gun.

"All right. That's enough," I gestured broadly. "Everybody just calm your britches."

"Where's my boy?" A woman who looked about a hundred years old besieged me. "What'd y'all do to him? He in there?"

"Who's your boy, ma'am?"

"Madhawk is my boy. And he ain't showed up this morning to check on me. He comes by every morning at sunrise. Is he the one the ambulance came to fetch?"

"No, ma'am. He's not. But—"

The throng erupted again, this time rattling off questions and accusations.

"Who's dead?"

"Why are the cops here?"

"What are you trying to hide?"

After a few minutes, I gave up trying to answer questions and simply stood there and let them holler at me. I eyed my deputies, imploring them to keep their hands away from their guns.

I hated to admit it, but there was only one person who could calm these folks down. He was the one they trusted. He was their unspoken leader. And if anybody knew where he was, Desi and Lenny would.

"Luke!" I hollered. "Get out here. Get your mama on the phone."

Hesitant, Luke walked out, followed by a teary-eyed Meadow and Bella.

When the gathering got a glimpse of Meadow and Bella's troubled expressions, they exploded again.

"What's going on?"

"Where's Wolfheart?

A particularly rugged, angry young man, flanked on either side by two equally rugged men, pulled out a knife. He flicked it open with a twist of his wrist. As he strode toward the forensic van, marking the tires, the mob spurred him on. "Cut 'em! Redflyer, cut 'em!"

Just as full-fledged pandemonium set in, a sudden hush fell over the crowd. The tough guy with the knife paused, and the hundred-year-old woman quieted. Even Meadow and Bella's demeanor changed.

A familiar figure stumbled from the woods, his shirt covered in blood, and his face etched in misery. He held his hands out to the crowd. To the authorities. And to his people.

Tall and wiry, his once blue-black hair now dusted with white, Wolfheart's green eyes locked onto mine.

"Wolfheart," I breathed.

Chapter Three

PEOPLE RISING FROM THE DEAD AND SUCH
Wolfheart

"Wolfheart," the sheriff repeated.

I nodded respectfully, and then moved with purpose toward Meadow and Bella. I focused on breathing and standing up straight, even as dried blood speckled my shirt like a beacon of guilt. Everything had changed. In just a few hours, the whole scene *had changed*. I saw his blood at the back door, only *he* had disappeared.

Meadow reached for me, her face bruised, and the life gone out of her eyes. "Did you?"

"Yes," I whispered as I heard the shuffle of Sheriff Rick's cowboy boots closing in on me. "What happened? Where did he go?"

Before she could answer, Bella crashed into me. "Uncle Wolf." She wrapped her arms around my waist. When she released me the blood from my shirt had tainted her skin. I felt ashamed.

"Are you okay, Bella?" My voice was hoarse, raspy. I didn't recognize it. Behind Bella stood Desi's oldest son, Luke.

"Wolfheart," the sheriff repeated, this time more insistent.

I offered him nothing more than an empty stare. What did he expect? In the middle of so much grief. And so much evil. "Ricky, just give me a second. Please."

I glanced at the crowd. Saw them waiting for me. They were on edge. Confused. Riled. They were waiting for reassurance and direction. "Let me talk to them."

The sheriff's bushy mustache twitched. I took that as a yes.

As I gingerly made my way to my people, I refused to look at the steps at the back of Peony's house. Like I didn't know what was there less than six hours ago. Like I didn't know *who* was there six hours ago.

I reached my blood-stained hands out to Madhawk's mother first.

"Wolfheart," the ancient woman frowned at me. I saw her confusion as she grasped for the appropriate reaction. Accusation? Mercy? I murmured soothingly into her ear, making it easy for her.

"Redflyer." I moved to the young man with the hidden rage, his knife open at his side. "Shush, give me your anger," I told him. "Be peaceful now." I placed my hands gently on his shoulders, and the tension in his body eased. As he relaxed, so did Moonpipe and Youngblood, his buddies, who held vigil on either side of him.

I considered all of their faces. Somber, tearful, but better now.

"Wolfheart, if it's not too much trouble," the sheriff said sarcastically. "I'd like a moment of your time."

I lingered a second longer, taking the time to nod at BlueJay, a wise and level-headed elder, and pat the head of a small boy, who as I recalled, went by the name of Littlefire.

"Brad, let's go." The sheriff was annoyed now. I'd pushed too far. The *Brad* was payback for my calling him Ricky.

Some sneered at the sheriff's use of my first name, but I nodded, and held up my bloody hands. "Lead the way, Sheriff."

I caught Meadow's eye as I followed the sheriff, but she lifted her shoulders, as bewildered as me. My mind raced. I needed to think. I needed to stall. I glanced at Bella, who was composed. On the outside at least. She held a bottled water while Desi's son, Luke, hovered. For the first time I noticed his goggles, foot booties, and khakis.

"You can stop cutting your eyes at them," the sheriff snapped. "They told me everything. Now I want to hear your side."

He stopped at the back door of Peony's house. Stared down at the blood pooled around the steps. And then back up at me. "I'm sorry about your sister."

His unexpected sincerity disarmed me, which was likely his plan.

"She was a good woman. Everybody liked her."

"She was." My voice still sounded unrecognizable. I tried again. "She'd want me to go to her daughter. And her granddaughter. So, if we could—"

"What happened? Whose blood is this, Brad?" Again, with the Brad. When I didn't answer, his exasperation increased.

"See, you might be some kinda king with your tribe here, but we go way back, and I remember you in a different way. You were the predator that circled the high school looking for prey. Gullible, pimply-faced kids who just wanted to make all the bad things go away. Remember that? Selling dope to them? Introducing them to chemically induced happiness?"

"I remember. And I remember your being one of those pimply-faced kids."

His mustache twitched. Bullseye. "That's true. But now I'm on the right side of the law."

"Me too. Even I'm redeemable, Ricky."

He said nothing. Gazed into the woods. His ears perked to the echoes of deputies scouring in the muck. They would find nothing.

"Madhawk didn't go see his mama this morning." He bent down, leaned closer to get a better look at the blood-soaked dirt. "Is this his blood I'm looking at?" He stood up, and pointed at my soiled clothes. My hands. "Is that his blood I'm looking at?"

I closed my eyes. Tried to think.

"Everybody's redeemable." Sheriff Rick cocked his head. "You. Me. But I'm not so sure about Madhawk. He used to beat on your sister all the time. You know how many calls we got in the middle of the night after he set in on her? And by the time we'd get out here she'd swear she fell. Or she burnt herself cooking. Or she tripped over her dog."

I flinched. "I tried to always be there for her. For the girls."

"But that's the thing. You couldn't. And now she's gone, and I wanna get to the bottom of it." He glowered at me. "The crime scene techs are about to finish on the inside. They'll be here in a minute. Whose blood is this gonna be? Come on, Wolfheart, enlighten me."

A few deputies came out of the woods. Wet. Weary. Empty handed.

Sheriff Rick whipped his head in my direction.

I shrugged my shoulders.

"'Cause see, it doesn't add up. Let's just say, for the sake of argument, that there was an accident last night. You okay if we call it that for now?" When I didn't respond, he went on. "So, you're in the middle of this big, horrible ruckus at your sister's house. This accident." He paused for an exaggerated beat, glancing at the blood smeared across the ground. "I gotta wonder, did somebody meet their end here? 'Cause it kinda looks that way to me."

I held his gaze.

"Was it Madhawk? 'Cause if that's the case, I'd like to know where he moseyed off to, considering his condition and all."

Again, I refused to take the sheriff's bait. "Why would you run off to the woods? What could be so important that you'd leave your beloved niece and her daughter here alone? That's puzzling to me."

He glanced at the ground and back at me in disbelief. Under better circumstances, I would have enjoyed his befuddled expression, but the moment passed as Luke rushed over, phone in hand. "Sorry Sheriff. Uh, Mr. Wolfheart."

"What is it, Luke?" Sheriff Rick snapped.

"It's Mama," Luke handed him the phone. "She wants to talk to you."

The sheriff snatched the phone out of Luke's hands, cramming it to his ear. "I can't chat right now, Desi. I got big things happening here. People rising from the dead and such—"

Sheriff Rick's expression changed as Desi interrupted. It grew angrier as he listened, and was livid by the time he spoke again. "That's ridiculous. Don't go and do that. I'm just asking him a few questions."

Luke tapped my elbow, wide-eyed. "What do you think that's about?"

"She's *your* mama," I shrugged. "It could be anything from world events to Southern Living recipes."

Luke considered. "She's got a range, that's for sure,"

"Désireé," Ricky's mustache twitched at a furious pace. "You do realize I'm your husband's best friend? And you do realize I set my sirens a'blazin when you went into labor with Micah? Got y'all to the hospital in Belle Maison in plenty of time, didn't I?"

"It's ridiculous to go all the way to Belle Maison for healthcare," Luke mumbled. "We should at least have an urgent care here in Shady Gully."

I pivoted to Luke, trying to get a read on the kid through the absurd goggles.

"If we could just get enough signatures on the petition, we could vote on incorporation in the next election."

It was hard to believe he came from Desi and Lenny. Since he seemed to be talking mostly to himself, I let him go on. I had enough on my mind.

"Dad blasted, Desi." Sheriff Rick cursed. "You got just enough money to be dangerous." As an expression of resignation spread on his beet red face, he acquiesced. "Fine then."

With an angry jab he disconnected the phone, pressing it into Luke's hands. He scowled at me. "She hired you a lawyer. She said to tell you not to say another word."

Madhawk watched, mesmerized, as the blood pulsed out of his shoulder and neck. He should feel pain. But he felt none. He should feel fear, but instead, he felt exhilarated. He was still alive. The blood that leaked from his body proved he'd beaten death. What had the sheriff said about people rising from the dead?

The look on Wolfheart's face! The Big Chief. The so-called Leader of the Creek. Mr. Bible Thumping Holier Than Thou. Stunned, shocked into silence when the sheriff questioned him at the foot of the back steps. When he found nobody there.

When he found...no body.

Madhawk swallowed back a laugh, bubbling over because he'd outfoxed them.

Camouflaged in the underbrush behind a cypress tree, Madhawk spied the deputies as they fluttered in and out of the house, trailing one another like clowns. Like insects. Like little ants in uniforms, with their goofy hats and their shiny badges. And oh, the bright lights and bleating sirens! Caution, they screamed! Warning, they announced!

He pitied his ancient mother, the old bat, as she gawked at the clowns, and then reluctantly spoke to Wolfheart. Not only had he escaped the deputies, but he'd also escaped her clutches as well.

During the search, one of the uniformed clowns had almost tripped over him, but Madhawk hadn't felt threatened. He could have easily elimi-nated him. If it had been Quietdove, Madhawk wouldn't have hesitated. Quietdove was a disgrace to everyone on the creek. A traitor to his people.

The only real threat to Madhawk were the dogs. And so far, only the clowns hiked through the woods looking for him. With their sticks, their chatter, and their lights. The dogs wouldn't be so stupid. Their noses would sniff him out.

Madhawk hated dogs.

Madhawk also hated Meadow. Hard. Judgmental. Unappreciative.

And Bella. Always trying to be something she wasn't—trying to be like them.

And Madhawk despised Wolfheart, who had planted doubt into Peony's heart long ago. Wolfheart had come between them. And worse, he'd brought the Spirit Warrior into their lives.

Of them all, Madhawk loathed the Spirit Warrior most of all. They'd all fawned over the Spirit Warrior. Especially Peony.

Not any longer. Meadow, Bella, and Wolfheart all deserved to die. They'd soon realize they'd placed their bets on the wrong warrior.

Chapter Four

B*ut I D*idn*'t S*ing
Luke

I tapped my brakes as I neared the four way stop sign in Shady Gully. I'd made it all the way from the creek to the center of town in a little over thirty minutes. Impressive. And yet, I found I didn't want to abandon the thoughts rattling around in my head.

It was the girl. This Bella, whose existence I didn't even know about until this morning. Micah's friend. *The one with the voice.* It was true her words held a melodic, lyrical tone, and were careful in a thoughtful, measured way, but it was her wild, unpredictable nature I couldn't shake. She was stunningly gorgeous as well, with her long, shiny hair, so black it reflected light. And her eyes, strikingly blue. Unusually blue. Not green like her mother's, or her great Uncle Wolfheart's, but the distinctive blue the sky turns just before a storm. Just before it morphs into gray...and the storm descends.

A familiar cackle and a blast of a horn shook me out of my reverie. Bubba and Daryl, in a red truck adjacent to me at the four way stop, waved their hands out the window. They pointed to the Cozy Corner, one of the four businesses occupying the crossroads of Shady Gully. My auto body shop took up one of the corners, the town's gas station another, and finally, Jesse's and James's churches (they each had their own) shared the other.

"You want us to get you a bacon cheeseburger?" Bubba raised his meaty fist in a cheerful gesture. "Charlie Wayne's got 'em two for a dollar."

Daryl, riding shotgun, bobbed his head enthusiastically.

"No, go ahead," I waved them off.

As delicious as Charlie Wayne's cheeseburgers were, I knew I wouldn't be able to eat. Not after seeing all the blood, the body bag, and beautiful Bella's streaked mascara. Once again, I couldn't seem to move past her eyes.

The thought prompted me to text Micah, who I considered calling several times on the way back to Shady Gully. Afraid she'd have her hands, or her face, as she put it, in some grumpy patient's mouth, I'd put it off. I didn't want to share the news via text, so after I parked at the shop, I typed, *Call Me!*

Within minutes Bubba and Daryl returned with their hot burgers. Oblivious to the life changing events of the day, they pulled their truck to a stop beside me.

"What's cookin', Mayor?" Daryl, the taller, skinnier of the pair, scratched his neatly trimmed, sandy-colored beard. "You on a diet?"

The three of us headed into the shop. "You're the second person to call me that today."

"What?" Bubba took offense. "That's our pet name for you. Who else called you that?"

"Quietdove."

"Oh yeah, he helped us come up with it." Bubba chewed, "Speaking of which, where's our lunch buddy? He always eats with us on two-for-a-dollar day."

The sheriff's substation sat just past the gas station, and Quietdove and Max loved to conspire with Bubba and Daryl. "Oh man, that's right," Daryl held up a fry. "Something happened across the creek, right? He and Max got a call. Like, a legit call."

Bubba nodded in agreement, taking a bite out of his second burger. "What happened? The storm knock a tree on somebody's house or something?"

"No, it's worse than that." I wasn't sure how much I should say, but since the sheriff authorized an extensive search of the swamp and woods surrounding the victim's home, I figured it was only a matter of time before the whole town knew anyway. "Miss Peony died. Got killed. I'm not sure really how to say it, but there was an... altercation of some kind."

"Meadow's mama?" Daryl asked. "That's terrible." The post office stood just past the Cozy Corner, so as a mail carrier Meadow was well known among the crossroads businesses.

Bubba put his burger down. "That ain't right. I reckon she was one of the nicest ladies I ever met. Wolfheart would bring her in sometimes to get her old jalopy looked at," he glanced at Daryl. "Dang thing was falling apart, but she loved it so much, we'd patch it together to make her happy."

"Yeah, we were always glad when Wolfheart brung her in, and not Madhawk. Meaner than a snake, that one. Did he kill her?"

"And is Meadow okay? And Bella?"

My stomach did a flip at the sound of her name. Was I the only one in Shady Gully who hadn't known Bella? Maybe Micah was right, and I needed to get a life.

"Yeah," I mumbled, then reached for my phone as it vibrated. It wasn't Micah. It was Mom. One of her usual cryptic texts. Just a question mark and an emoticon of some kind. I had no clue what it meant, only that it wasn't a smile. "I gotta go. I'm being summoned."

Bubba chuckled. "Tell Desi we said hi."

"And tell Micah her car is ready," Daryl said. "We'll warn Charlie Wayne."

For some inexplicable reason I turned my radio on as I headed to my parents' house. Even more out of character, I turned the volume up as Bob Seger and The Silver Bullet Band sang about finding "Real Love." I opened my window at the notion, and stuck my head out, mumbling along with the song.

But I didn't sing.

Instead, after a glance at my disheveled hair, I slowed past Dolly's Diva Dome. Unforgivably shaggy, I couldn't have made a good impression today. But I came to my senses when I saw a blue-haired old lady exit the salon. No way I could go into Dolly's Diva Dome, even for an emergency haircut. Mama would have my hide.

I had no idea what had caused the falling out between Mama and Dolly, only that it had happened when I was a kid and had something to do with my parents buying Dolly's house. As happy as my parents were in the home now, a scandal involving Dolly's ex-husband had been the nexus to the disastrous purchase.

I pulled into the Piney Lake subdivision where I grew up, coasting down the windy road that led past the lake to my parents' white siding house. The setting was perfect and picturesque. It was home. I couldn't conceive of a scandal, a disaster, or anything unpleasant about this place or my parents.

But as mama often said: "Luke, I know it's hard to imagine, but we were your age once, and we weren't perfect. And neither was this town."

I smelled the roast beef as soon as I entered the house. The savory aroma of stewed carrots and potatoes combined with the buttery scent of rice made my stomach growl. I was suddenly glad I'd passed on Charlie Wayne's two-for-a-dollar special.

"Luke! In here, it's hot," called Mama. I turned the corner into the kitchen to find the table set for three and my dad pouring iced tea. Ginger and Mary Ann, Mom and Dad's rescue dogs, rushed me with excited yaps and wet kisses. Ginger, a multicolored Papillion bounced on her hind legs to get my attention, while Mary Ann, a floppy-eared black and white cocker spaniel, collapsed on the floor and threw her paws into the air to receive her affection.

"Thank goodness you're here," Dad said. "I'm starving." Lately he was packing a little extra around the waist, so I shot him a dubious look. Still handsome, even with the added paunch, Dad towered over Mom, who was barely five feet tall. Despite her diminutive stature, she ran circles around my dad, who would have been content to live out the rest of his days with his family, his dogs, his detective novels—and his beloved Desi.

As I bent to give her a hug, I felt the frenetic energy charging through her body. "Sit, sit, Luke. I made your favorite. I hope you didn't eat already."

"No, I'm hungry." Although it was only three in the afternoon, I'd grown accustomed to my parents' early dinners. I knew they'd be eating ice cream by eight o'clock, as they'd somehow gained a meal in retirement.

I took my usual chair, enjoying being fawned over, pampered, and served a hot meal, all of which I should enjoy while Petey was away. "What about Micah?" I asked when I noticed there were only three place settings.

"Oh, they'll be leftovers. Now," she looked at me expectantly. "Tell me what happened this morning? I want to hear every detail."

I shook my head. "I should be asking you. You hired a lawyer?"

"Oh, I didn't hire any lawyer. I just told Ricky that."

"What? Are you serious? I'm pretty sure that's illegal, Mom." Horrified, I glanced at Dad, who appeared amused. These two. No wonder I had to look out for them. If I left them to their own devices, they'd wind up in jail.

"Oh, it's fine," Mama said. "Try your potatoes. I experimented with some herbs from my garden. Rosemary, for instance. I'm not sure I like it." She squeezed her eyes in distaste.

"I think it's great," chimed Dad, who thought everything Mom did was great.

"I'm pretty sure interfering with an ongoing investigation is some kind of crime." I ate a potato. "I'm never going to get this place incorporated if people don't abide by the law—"

"Oh, come on, sugar. You're overreacting." She shushed Ginger, who pranced beneath the table, begging for scraps. "If you're going to beg, go see your Daddy," she told the dog in mock irritation.

"I'm not overreacting. You can't do stuff like that, Mom. And I like the rosemary."

"Don't be silly. Ricky knows Brad didn't do anything wrong." Mama ladled some gravy onto Dad's potatoes. "I was simply trying to buy him some time."

"I think the sheriff was trying to get him to be honest about what happened."

"So, what did happen?" Dad slipped Ginger a piece of meat.

"I don't know." I gave Mom the eye. "He stopped talking."

We ate in silence for a few minutes. "Ricky was pretty hard on him," I finally said. "I mean, Sheriff Rick. He's kind of intense."

"Oh, he's just doing his thing. Trust me, he's a teddy bear. Just wait until Robin gets here."

"What? Aunt Robin is coming?"

Dad nodded as he glinted at Mom. "They've been yacking on the phone all day about Peony. And Wolfheart. I think your mom is excited about having reinforcements. And seeing Violet and Sterling."

"And Petey," Mom added with a smile. "My baby boy has been gone so long and I'm worried about his hurt shoulder and his state of mind."

She trailed off, no doubt fretting over the prodigal son.

"He's fine," I told her. "Probably holed up in some Kentucky holler drinking moonshine."

My mother was not amused, but Dad chuckled. "How's the duplex? Need any handyman work done? I can bring my tools—"

"No, thanks Dad."

"Your father and his tools," Mom quipped. "I wouldn't be surprised if he names them. Sometimes I think he loves them more than me."

I glanced at Dad. "I just got the carpet cleaned for the next tenant."

"You're up to six now? Not counting yourself, of course. That's good, son." He pushed away from the table, rubbing Mary Ann's snout. "Between that and the auto body shop, you've got your hands in a lot of things these days."

I nodded, pleased by the success of my duplex investment, despite one rather ornery tenant.

"Dinner was good, Desi." Dad meandered toward the living room. "I got some work to do over here." He settled in his recliner. "Just gonna rest my eyes."

I helped Mama pick up the plates, and stack them by the sink. "How's he doing? Seems a little slower than usual."

"Oh, he's just tired." She scraped the plates. "All those years on that oil rig took its toll. The back surgery helped, but he'll never be able to run a marathon."

"I can't picture Dad ever running a marathon."

She shot me a look. "I'll have you know your father was quite the quarterback back in the day."

"No way. Seriously?" I teased because she recounted Dad's accolades on a regular basis.

Mom made Micah a plate, and I covered it with foil, helping her tidy the kitchen while Dad snored in his recliner. Afterwards Mom gave me a spontaneous hug. "You're such a good boy. Let's go sit on the patio and have a cup of hot tea."

Mom exuded good health, sporting her characteristic bright lipstick, flashy earrings, and perfectly coiffed pixie haircut. She seemed happy with her life now that Dad had retired. She, Aunt Robin, and Dad had the freedom to travel from state to state, flitting from one artsy community to another, showcasing my nana's paintings. Sometimes Dad accompanied them, and sometimes he stayed home with Ginger, Mary Ann, and his whodunit books.

Showing Nana's art had become therapeutic for my mom, a way to grieve and celebrate her complicated relationship with her mother. Aunt Robin had invested in *Sunny's Place*, their first gallery in Lexington, and it had paid off as Nana's paintings were a huge hit. Now they floated, on loan, from gallery to gallery, gaining much deserved recognition. My parents made good money through the sale of giclee prints, which were digital prints made on canvas with a jet ink printer. They sold by the hundreds, and my mom never had to part with the originals.

"When's Aunt Robin coming?"

"This weekend. Come with us to the airport," she urged. "And after we'll have a big party." She picked up her tea. "I'll invite Ricky."

I squinted at her. "What's the deal there? You don't mean he like—*likes* her?"

She threw her head back in laughter. "Oh, I do. He's been oh-so-casually bending your Daddy's ear, asking how she's doing, if she's ready to—date again." She sipped her tea, suddenly thoughtful. Undoubtedly thinking about Uncle Dean.

"That's not going to happen. She loved Uncle Dean too much. And Ricky? I mean, Sheriff Rick? I don't see it."

"You never know, Luke. We all loved Dean, and I know you had a special bond with him." She looked at me. "Robin once told me that at times it hurt to look at you because you're so much like him."

I swallowed some tea. Even though I hated the stuff.

"It's been five years," Mom said. "Hard to believe, isn't it?" She set down her mug. "Are you okay? Today must have been hard."

"Yeah. All the people out there were angry. They don't like the sheriff, or his deputies. Except for Quietdove maybe."

"They need Brad. He'll help them through this. I worry about him though. I know he's heartbroken. And angry."

"You called him Brad. The crowd got upset when Ricky called him that today."

"It's the custom. Only family and close friends use their first names."

"Why is that? I've never really understood their culture. Are they American Indians?"

"Probably a combination of that, creole, and some Cajun mixed in." She nodded, "Nobody knows for sure. Not even them. But they hold tradition very dear, and the names are part of their history, passed on from one generation to another."

I thought of the tight knit crowd I saw today and wondered how my mom had become so familiar with their ways. With Wolfheart.

"What an amazing gene pool though, right?" She grinned. "Some perfect combination of DNA that created gorgeous green-eyed people with olive skin and luxurious hair."

My thoughts drifted to Bella. *Blue-eyed* Bella.

"They're wonderful people, but they don't trust outsiders," Mom went on. "That's why they need Brad."

"How did y'all become friends?"

She fidgeted with her tea bag. "Long story. For another time."

Because she seemed uncomfortable, I didn't press.

"How were Bella and Meadow?" she asked.

"They were okay." Now I was uncomfortable. "Sad."

Mom considered me for an agonizingly long moment. "She's quite something, isn't she?"

"Who?" I asked too quickly.

"Bella. Micah's friend."

"Micah!" I slammed down my mug. "I forgot! I've got to get to Belle Maison to pick her up from work."

Glad to be Micah's chauffeur for once, I rushed off before falling victim to Mom's intense scrutiny. Unfortunately, the ambiguity of her familiarity with the people across the creek would remain a mystery. For the time being.

Chapter Five

A Good Pair Of Khakis
Sheriff Rick

I made my way to the kitchenette and put the coffee on, hoping a little java might help make sense of the upcoming day. The hot shower hadn't helped, but I was optimistic. When the coffee grumbled to a full brew, I heard footsteps sound from the bedroom.

I saw her cynical face peek around the corner. Uncommunicative, a little grumpy first thing in the morning. Orange all over, white-socked feet, green eyes. "Mornin' Gertrude, you sleep well?"

She jumped onto the counter, watched as I opened the can. Tuna, meaty morsels, her favorite. Even after I placed the bowl on the floor, she continued to stare. With a sigh I turned on the faucet over the sink. When I got it to a favorable drip, she lapped it up.

Gerty and I had been living together about three months. It was a mutually beneficial relationship in that I didn't have to tell her how I felt or what I was thinking about, and she got to lay around all day, no questions asked. I think we were getting ready to take it to the next level.

My cell rang as I stirred sugar and half and half into my coffee. "Yeah," I snapped. "Anything new?" I listened as my chief deputy in Belle Maison ran through the night's activities. A breaking and entering in Lebeaux while a family was having dinner at the Shoney's. A nasty barfight in Toulouse that left two rednecks in the hospital, and one in the drunk tank. And a car accident in Azalealand. No fatalities.

"What about Naryville?" I asked.

"All good," said my deputy chief.

Thank God for Naryville, the easiest community in my jurisdiction. While I spent most of my time at my headquarters in Belle Maison, I floated between Toulouse, Lebeaux, and Azalealand. While I maintained a small apartment in Belle Maison, I preferred to end my days in Shady Gully when possible.

A little over five years ago, right about the time my girlfriend, Ashley, left me, the duly elected sheriff went and had a heart attack. I, as the longest serving member of the sheriff's department, found myself the acting sheriff. The timing wasn't bad, since it kept my mind off the fact that I'd ruined yet another relationship, but the role itself set me on a path that changed my life forever.

I liked the gig. I was good at it. And truth be told, I did bear a striking resemblance to Sam Elliott.

When the time came to elect a new sheriff, I won in a landslide. The office gave me purpose, and filled a void I'd been trying, unsuccessfully, to fill my whole life. Through football. Through women. And countless other iniquities.

The downside was the loneliness.

"I'll check in at the substations later today," I told my chief deputy in Belle Maison.

"Copy that. And you? I hear you've got your hands full there?"

"Boy, do I."

"Let me know if you need me to send in the cavalry."

After I ended the call, I regarded Gertrude. She'd jumped from the counter, eaten her food, and now groomed herself with lazy pleasure. I opened the shade so the sun would shine on her cat bed later in the day.

"See ya later, Gerty." I grabbed my keys, locking the door behind me.

I hurried through the parking lot, and had almost made it to my department assigned Ford F-150, when I ran into my annoying landlord.

"Good morning," Luke said with a pleasant smile. The kid wore his usual khakis. Crisp, white button-down shirt. Freshly shaved. He needed a haircut, but at least he'd lost the foot booties. "You're up early, Sheriff. How's your day going so far?"

"Not good," I grunted. "My hot water isn't hot enough."

"I'd be happy to take a look at that for you."

"Good." I moved toward my vehicle.

"But I'd hate to let your cat out."

I stopped. "What cat?"

"Oh, you know, the cat you didn't put a deposit down on."

I raised my eyes to the sky, swallowing back the rant on the tip of my tongue. As I ducked into my truck, he followed me, tapping on my window. "For the love of God, what now? I'll pay the dang deposit."

"Great," he said. "By the way, I talked to my parents last night about Wolfheart. If you want, I'll stop by the station in a bit and fill you in."

"Wait, what? What in the world are you going on about? Wolfheart himself is coming in with his lawyer later."

Luke waved, made like he was walking off, and then turned. "Oh, one other thing. I thought you'd want to know. Aunt Robin's coming into town this weekend."

"Oh. Is that right?" My hand twitched as I put my key into the ignition.

"Yep. I bet you're looking forward to that, huh?" The kid grinned at me.

I forced some casualness into my voice. "It'll be nice to see her." I offered a cocky salute as I quickly exited the parking lot.

But the smug little whippersnapper just stood there, staring after my truck...almost as if he'd seen the vibration of my heart pounding underneath my shirt.

I could have used a few minutes to process the news, but unfortunately, the Shady Gully substation was within walking distance of the duplex. Not ready to turn on my usual charm for the likes of Max and Quietdove, I drove past, deciding to stop in at the Cozy Corner. I'd grab a donut, eat it in my car. Take some time to clear my head. Develop a strategy.

The gravel crunched beneath my tires as I brought my truck to a park. Distracted, I moseyed over to the order window. "Hey Charlie Wayne, what's fresh?"

Charlie Wayne peered at me through his coke bottle glasses, orneriness falling off him in waves. "What kind of dumb question is that? Everything is fresh. What kind of place do you think I run, Ricky?"

The old coot had been running this joint since I was in high school, so I bit back my knee-jerk response and let the *Ricky* pass. Still, he was a cranky old goat with a rotten disposition. "What would you suggest, Chef Charlie Wayne?"

By the look of him, I'd pushed too far. Eventually he meandered over to the warmer and pulled out a bear claw. Wrapped it in paper, tossed in a few napkins. I watched him closely in case he decided to accidentally drop it on the floor.

"It's on the house," he glared.

"Well thanks, Charlie Wayne."

"I expect you and your boys to do a better job of keeping all those worthless young heathens away from my place in the middle of the night. All they do is drink beer, smoke cigarettes, and dip Skoal."

"Absolutely. Will do."

His bug-eyes zeroed in on me. "That's the thing, Ricky. You say that, but I've yet to see y'all do anything. Take a look around. You see all the cigarette butts on the ground? And all the stinking beer cans?"

I took a gander around the picnic tables, which looked pristine. "Nope. Can't say as I do."

Charlie Wayne nodded with slow deliberation. "That's because yours truly gets here at five every morning and picks 'em up." Even after he slammed the order window, I could hear him. "I'm too old for this nonsense. Do your job."

Not bothering with a rebuttal, I slid into my car, nursing my bruised ego with a freshly baked bear claw.

Things hadn't gone well the last time Robin visited, so I needed to come up with a better strategy. Regrettably, I had a lot working against me. Not only was I the exact opposite of Dean, who'd been all buttoned up and business-minded like Desi's kid, Luke, but I had a miserable resume. I made a meager living, and over the thirty years since high school, I'd wrecked my way through several failed relationships.

Meanwhile Robin was wealthy, and the mother of two beautiful kids. She was also gorgeous, energetic, and creative. She'd master-minded the whole plan to unveil Desi's mother's art in galleries across the country, which had not only kept her busy after Dean's death, but had made Lenny and Desi rich.

Basically, the young girl I'd had a secret crush on in school had grown into an amazing, smart, and generous woman, all of which made her even more desirable to me now. But even if she could one day move past Dean's tragic cancer and untimely death, what would she ever see in me?

I jolted as my cell went off. It was Max. I guess I could start by being nicer to her kid brother. I sighed, beleaguered, as I stepped out of my truck and headed once again to the order window at Charlie Wayne's Cozy Corner.

I entered the substation with a box of Charlie Wayne's assorted pastries, and coffee for my deputies. "I made sure Charlie Wayne put chocolate in the croissants." I handed Max the pastries. "Just the way you like 'em."

Max squinted at me for a long moment, then exchanged a glance with Quietdove. "Oh," he said knowingly. "You must have heard my sister's coming home this weekend."

I scowled, and headed to my office as the two knuckleheads tore into the box of sweets.

Quietdove meandered over, leaning his long frame against my door, his second Danish crammed into his mouth. "Nothing came from the search this morning. No tracks, no blood, no body. No wounded."

"And still no sign of Madhawk," Max chimed in from the lobby.

"And y'all got eyes on his mama's house?"

"In case he gets homesick. Or needs help." Quietdove confirmed with a nod. "But I wouldn't hold out much hope there. I'm hearing they weren't as tight as she made it seem."

"What about Bella and Meadow? Either of them talking yet?"

"We're letting them be—for now," Quietdove answered. "It's what I'd recommend. Let them mourn Peony."

I agreed. "What do you think happened? What do you hear?"

"You mean, like tells and stuff?" Quietdove held back a grin. "Seriously, most of the talk on the creek now is about Peony's funeral. People loved her, and they respect Wolfheart. It's going to be a big turnout."

"Max," I hollered. "Did you get the coroner's report?"

After Max smeared a napkin across his mouth, he hopped up to join Quietdove at my door. "Not yet, but I put in a rush because her people want a quick funeral. But I suspect it'll be like Patty said, blunt force trauma. Wood and debris from the fireplace mantel matched the wound on Peony's head, and the crime techs concluded the blood on the mantel is hers."

I leaned back, stretching my legs atop my desk. "Sounds like we've got a scenario where Madhawk is drunk, high, and mean."

"The usual," Max quipped.

"But on this night, it was a deadly combination. Meadow stepped in to try to protect her mama, and comes away with the bruises we saw all over her arms and face."

"But she can't save her mama," Quietdove added on to my scenario. "And as the situation escalates, Madhawk pushes Peony too hard. Whether it was intentional or accidental, Peony's head gets cracked against the mantel."

I sighed, draining the rest of my coffee. Feeling fidgety, I swept my fingers through the taffy bowl on my desk. Settled on a dark cherry. "It's not enough. Where was Bella? And where was Wolfheart? The only reason this hasn't happened sooner is because Wolfheart keeps a close eye on Peony and a tight rein on Madhawk. And, the big question, whose blood was pooled outside the back door?"

"Expecting those results anytime," Max said.

"Great. And when do we expect Wolfheart and his lawyer?"

Quietdove looked at his watch just as we heard the station door chime. "That could be them now."

Max groaned as he recognized the new arrival. "Afraid not."

Jesse, the least pleasant half of Shady Gully's Twin Preachers, stood before me now, bursting with outrage and indignation. Practically bald now, and as skinny as all get out, he fidgeted with his outdated gold wire-rimmed spectacles.

His henchmen, Thaddeus and Big Al, waited for him in their four-wheel drive outside the substation. I could see the tip of Big Al's John Deere hat, and Thaddeus's beady eyes peering at me through the lobby window.

"I hate to disturb your pastry party, Sheriff, but if you haven't heard, we've got a killer on the loose." He sat, uninvited, in the chair across my desk. "And I think we all know who's responsible. The same dark soul that's been a blight on this community for decades."

As often happened when I ran into Jesse, I found myself at a loss for words. His self-righteousness just sucked the air right out of me.

"Wolfheart's been slowly poisoning our kids for decades, and leading Lord knows what kind of shady happenings down there across the creek. And now, unsurprisingly, he's killed someone."

Quietdove lingered at the door, his face darkening.

"Even my brother, James, is weakening, showing signs of compromise. I will not do that, Sheriff, and I demand you make an arrest." Jesse had never married, which could be part of the problem. Then again, I'd never married, and I wasn't a lunatic.

Jesse, his twin brother James, and sister Dolly had been raised in their father, Wyatt's, church. Wyatt was a decent old guy, but he hadn't been able to control his family after Dolly's husband dragged them through a horrible scandal several years ago. Instead of coming together and supporting one another, they'd imploded. To the extent that Jesse and James each built their own church when Brother Wyatt retired. The identical churches sat side by side, occupying one quarter of Shady Gully's four way stop—an obvious reminder of what the failure to forgive looks like.

Quietdove cleared his throat, "I know you're awfully sorry to hear about Miss Peony—"

"Who?" Jesse asked.

"The victim. That's why you're here. Right?"

Max moved closer into my office, ensuring his partner of his support.

"All right." I stood, gesturing to Jesse. "I appreciate your visit. We'll take everything you've said into consideration. Now if you don't mind, we've got work to do."

Jesse didn't move. "You can't just kick me out. I'm a citizen. I pay your salary. And yours," he tilted his head at Max and Quietdove.

"That may be so, but unless you have evidence in the case, you're just wasting our time."

"Fine then. I'll get evidence. That shouldn't be hard."

My knucklehead deputies and I glowered as Jesse remained planted in my chair. Eventually, the pressure became too much, and he stormed out of the substation. I could see him through the lobby window, grumbling to his friends in the giant truck.

After a beat passed, I said, "Okay. On to other business. We need to keep the kids out of the Cozy Corner's parking lot at night. That is, if we want Charlie Wayne to keep giving us free coffee and donuts."

Max nodded. "Copy that."

By the end of the day, it had become clear that Wolfheart and his lawyer weren't coming. Angry that I'd been had, I called Lenny's cellphone. He didn't answer. Annoyed, I texted, *would you and your lovely wife happen to know why Wolfheart and his lawyer stood me up today?*

The delightful dots of promise danced on my phone. I stared. And waited. Nothing.

I texted Desi something similar, but the dots didn't dance at all.

I thought about calling Luke, who'd bragged earlier about stopping in and updating me, but I was so doggone beat I couldn't even work up a sarcastic text, much less a phone call.

"I'm headed home," Quietdove said. "I'll see what I can find out when I get to the creek."

"Good deal. Be safe," I noted the skip in his step as he strolled to his truck. A strikingly handsome young man, Quietdove had always been eager to assimilate. Becoming a deputy was testament to that, but I realized I didn't know much else about him. Was he going home to parents? A girlfriend? A cat?

The ding of a text dragged me from my curiosity. It was Lenny, chocked full of emoticons, *Sorry, things crazy here in anticipation of Robin's visit—party at our house after we pick her up at airport. Come!*

A blatant teaser, of course. But it had worked. I rifled once more through the taffy bowl on my desk, not fooling around this time and selecting coconut, my personal favorite. I glanced at the time, deciding a quick haircut at Dolly's Diva Dome might be in order. Then I'd go home to Gerty.

Dolly's hair was just as blonde as it had been in high school thirty years ago. Amazing how that worked. When I walked into the salon, she greeted me with a coy smile. "Hey Ricky, you handsome devil." Her comb paused over her client's head. "Don't tell me you want me to cut that gorgeous hair of yours?" I'd learned long ago that most of what came out of Dolly's mouth was either vague, untrue, or a sad attempt to either cause pain or gain approval.

"If you have the time."

"Have a seat. I'm almost finished with Mrs. Guidry here. Isn't she gorgeous? She's so skinny, she's gonna waste away to nothing." Case in point. Mrs. Guidry was about two-fifty on the hoof, but I reckon Dolly was just being nice.

No doubt she'd been dealt a bad hand, but knowing Dolly, she'd probably brought shady cards to the game to start.

Once Mrs. Guidry was coiffed to perfection, Dolly saw her out to the parking lot. When a vaguely familiar truck honked as it passed, Dolly and Mrs. Guidry raised their hands in a pointed wave. I squinted at the driver of the rarely seen pickup truck.

Curious, I asked after Dolly sent Mrs. Guidry on her merry way, "Was that Tom and Wanda?" I hadn't seen Desi's stepdad and his new wife in ages, and something about their gradual withdrawal from the community unsettled me.

Dolly's bracelets jangled as she responded dismissively. "Just Mrs. Wanda. Last I heard Mr. Tom was sick."

"Is that so? Something serious?"

Ready to fully devote her attention to me now, Dolly shrugged off my question as if it were frivolous, embracing me with a lingering full-on hug designed to remind me she was a woman. Which it did.

"When are you gonna take me to dinner in Belle Maison? I know you've got an apartment there." She smiled demurely. "You wouldn't even have to drive me back to Shady Gully."

I cautiously steered the conversation in another direction. "Too busy keeping the peace, Dolly." She wrapped a cape around my shoulders. "Just thin it out, a little off the ears."

She gently ran her fingers through my hair. Massaged my scalp. After the day I'd had, I could have closed my eyes and surrendered to my frustration and exhaustion.

But Gerty was waiting for me at home. And Robin was coming this weekend.

"I heard some bad karma finally caught up with those sketchy folks across the creek. Never trusted them, with their crazy names and all—"

"What exactly did you hear?" Actually, I rather enjoyed their creative monikers. It's what set them apart, really, since they looked and dressed like everybody else in Shady Gully. "Or have you been talking to your brother?"

She shrugged her shoulders. "It is what it is."

Some things changed over time. Improved even. And then there was Dolly...

I cleared my throat. "Say, you know where I can buy a good pair of khakis?"

Chapter Six

FIREMAN
Wolfheart

"Where should I put my keyboard?" Bella asked as she glanced around my tiny home, which was essentially an extension to my shop. A kitchen and a small table sat across from a living room big enough to hold a recliner and a small couch, while a loft upstairs provided me a bedroom and a bathroom. My shop, on the other hand, was large enough to house an array of supplies and equipment, ranging from large herbal tools to smaller necessities like measuring scales, grinders, and cutting boards.

"Anywhere you want, Bella. Your music makes me happy."

"Good," she grinned. "I'll set it up by your recliner." Bella's music grounded her in such a way that despite the trauma of the last several days, she radiated strength. Her brows knitted in concentration as she unfolded the keyboard, placed her iPad on the sheet music stand, and plugged in the microphone.

Peony and I had put our herb money together and bought her the electronic keyboard system a month ago, and she'd mastered it already. Her lofty aspirations and boundless confidence drove her to challenge the long-standing ways of Shady Gully. Her passion and determination to break barriers was admirable, but because that quest hadn't ended well for me, I worried.

"Look," Bella pointed out the window. "Some of Mamaw's chickens followed Mama. And some of the cats too. And she remembered my earphones."

A profound sense of sadness came over me as I watched the

migration of Peony's lost and displaced critters. "Let's go help your mama unload." As we padded onto the porch, I carefully scanned the yard, peering beyond to the dilapidated shed and the winter wood pile at the tree line.

As the dome light atop Meadow's old clunker slowed to a lazy swirl, I pored over the items from Peony's house, all crammed in the back seat amid haphazard mailing envelopes and packing tape. "Hey," she grumbled.

"Everything okay?" I grabbed a box. "You have any trouble?"

"None." She patted the bulge against her back hip, indicating the gun she carried. "Y'all?" Her eyes, fierce and protective, cut toward Bella.

"Safe and sound." I grabbed a sack of bird feed from the trunk. "Looks like we gained a few mouths to feed. "I don't even recognize some of these mutts."

"Just call me Pied Piper."

Bella grinned, putting her arm around Meadow's waist. "Nope. But I'll tell you what your name means."

When Meadow shot me an exasperated look, I implored her to be patient with Bella's recent fascination with spirit names and their meanings.

"Meadow means strong, happy, and graceful," Bella pronounced.

Meadow snorted. "I think you're off on that one."

"You're strong," I insisted.

"And graceful," Bella added.

"Two out of three then," Meadow shrugged cynically.

"Come relax," Bella tugged. "Uncle Wolf made soup."

"Yeah," I added. "We need to have a family meeting."

"About my taking your mail route next week," Bella piped. "I already talked to Claire at the post office and she said I could."

While the bruises on Meadow's arms and chin had faded to a churn of yellow and green, the shadows under her eyes remained etched with grief.

"Really?" Meadow was skeptical. "Who knew Claire was so nice?"

"She's not," I warned. "But we need to talk about more pressing matters than that." I gave Bella a look. "I won't be able to avoid Ricky much longer. He plans to be at the funeral tomorrow."

After we cleared the table, I grinded some lemon balm and hibiscus and made us each a mug of tea. I regarded Meadow as I set the tea down, relieved to see that some of the strain had eased from her face. She returned the scrutiny. "You look tired, Uncle. Drawn."

"I'm fine," I said. "Better now that you're both here, and safe. But we need to get our story straight before tomorrow."

"We can't stay here forever," Meadow said. "Eventually we'll have to go back."

"Why not? It's cool here," Bella added sugar to her tea. "Today Uncle Wolf taught me how to infuse olive oil with rose petals and flowers."

"You'll both stay here as long as necessary," I said. "As long as he's out there."

"I'm telling you, Uncle Wolf," Bella shook her head. "Madhawk was at the foot of the back steps." She stirred her tea. "Just like you left him when you went to bury—"

"How was he—at the end?" Meadow interrupted, wiping a tear.

"I miss him so much," Bella's eyes filled as she started to speak.

"Don't say his name." Meadow warned. "It's taboo to evoke the ghosts of the dead. Leave the lost one at peace."

Just as I'd done earlier with her mother, I silently pleaded with Bella to resist the eye roll.

"Whatever," Bella finally shrugged. "I just don't believe in all the old customs like you do."

"Oh, but the spirit names are all fun and games?" Meadow sulked.

After an uncomfortable, extended moment, they both looked at me expectantly. "He was a brave warrior," I told them thickly. "As always."

"How could Madhawk have just got up and walked away?" Bella wondered. "He was dead."

"I don't know. I checked his pulse before I left. I wouldn't have left you with him otherwise. Tell me again what you remember. Did you hear anything?"

"No," Bella answered. "When you left, we went in and lit the candles. We sat there with Mamaw until we saw the lights from the police and the ambulance."

"Okay," I sighed. "And you said nothing to them about Madhawk?"

"We didn't say anything to anybody," Meadow insisted. "We figured they'd find him right away. I don't understand how he could have gotten far."

"After the funeral, I'm going to get some men together and we'll do our own search." I reassured them. "We know where to look. Places the deputies don't know about like the old Indian mounds and the sacred places in the black lands. We will find him. Dead or alive."

"How could that devil not be dead?" Meadow wiped angrily at a tear. "While Mama and—"

I took her hand. "There will be justice. If not in this world, then in the next. But for now, we must be vigilant. In case he still walks among us."

"I think we should tell the truth," Bella said suddenly. "Sheriff Rick is nice. He's friends with Micah's parents—"

"Bella, you don't understand how things work around here," Meadow snapped. "We can't trust any of them. You didn't talk to Micah about any of this, did you?"

"I didn't, I promise. I just don't think we did anything wrong. Uncle Wolf?"

"We did nothing wrong, Bella. Madhawk was the wrongdoer." I reached across the table, taking her hand in mine. While I didn't want to taint Bella's idealism, I understood Meadow's point.

Meadow had been raised with the town's built-in prejudice, and years later, when she'd become a victim, she'd suffered the consequences of their bias. Her cynicism only increased when she'd been denied truth and justice, and surely hearing her daughter spout those lofty ideals now stung a little.

I too had experienced my share of the town's scorn, as had my sister, Peony. But nothing like Meadow.

I squeezed the hands of the beautiful souls on either side of me.

My true family. The only one I had left. My purpose now was to help them thrive. Contribute to their happiness. And keep them safe.

"Let me think on it." I eyed Bella as I rose from the table. "But now, I have to think about what I'm going to say at Peony's funeral tomorrow."

Bella's church music never failed to chase the demons away. As Meadow slept upstairs, the house was quiet except for the calming, melodic voice of my beautiful great-niece. While I watched her graceful fingers sweep lightly along the keyboard, I prayed for the words—and the strength—to eulogize my sister.

"What?" Bella suddenly stopped playing. "Was I too loud?"

"No," I signaled her to stay silent. "I heard something." Instinctively, my fingers clasped the handle of the weapon I'd used since I was a child.

I'd found the ancient knife while hunting arrowheads near the Indian mounds when I was seven years old. Immediately drawn to it, I'd claimed it for my own, and now the bowie with the distinctive double-edged blade was like an appendage to my body.

Although inclined to argue when I directed her upstairs, Bella disappeared without much resistance. I quietly made my way to the door, and listened. I heard small steps. Little strides. As if someone was slow. Or injured. I yanked the door open, positioning my blade to strike—

"No, wait! Please."

Not slow. Not injured. But a child.

"My granny sent me." The small boy I'd seen at Peony's the morning of her death presented himself. "She's hurting, and I didn't know where to go. Now that Miss Pe—" He stopped mid-sentence. Like Meadow, he was afraid of disturbing the ghosts of the dead by uttering their name.

"It's okay." I opened the door, inviting him in. "It's very late, and dark, for a young boy to be out."

"I'm not a boy," he raised his chin in defiance. "And I'm not scared."

"What's your name?"

"Littlefire," he said. "But some call me Littlefry."

"And which do you prefer?"

Again, with the chin. "Fireman."

"Very well. What's wrong with your granny, Fireman?"

The boy fought back a smile. "Her joints hurt. Around her knees.

They're big like this," he gestured with his hands. "And she coughs a lot too. But I'm mostly here because of her joints. They hurt so bad she cries." He paused, as if sizing me up. "And Miss…your sister… said your medicine was even better than hers."

The vestige of my sister's praise flooded me with a wave of pro-found grief. Healer, teacher, sister, grandmother, mother. Peony meant so much to so many, and she was taken from us in such a senseless, unfair way. "Have a seat, Fireman. I won't even have to go to my shop. I have everything we need right here. I'll show you what to do."

I pulled turmeric, burdock root, and ginger from my herbal cabinet. Showed Fireman the differences in the herbs, and the way to grind them. "All of these will help her joints. Do you know why?"

"Why?"

"Because they're anti-inflammatories."

He nodded. "Keeps the swelling down." Taking care of his granny had seasoned the boy.

"That's right. And this one has a funny name. It's called cat's claw." He grinned as I labeled the bags and filled them with the ground herbs."

We looked up as Bella tip-toed down the stairs, her eyes wide with curiosity. "Hello."

"Bella, this is Fireman. He's here to get medicine for his granny. Fireman, this is Bella."

Fireman gazed at Bella, as if mentally recording her features. "You're very beautiful," he squeaked.

Bella giggled, twenty-three but still easily flattered. She shook Fireman's hand and offered a proper bow. "Thank you very much, Fireman. Nice to meet you."

"And this will help her cough," I told the boy, although it was clear I'd lost my audience. "It's called horehound."

"Would you like some soup to bring home?" asked Bella.

"Yes, please."

Bella fixed a large Tupperware of soup as I wrote out the recipes for his granny's medicinal tea. "You fix her some tea when you get home. She'll sleep well tonight." We stepped onto the porch with the boy, now armed with soup and herbs. "Are you going to be okay?" I asked, "I can walk with you—"

"I'm not scared," he frowned. "I do this all the time." He eyed Bella, emphasizing his fearlessness. "I'll see y'all tomorrow."

When Bella and I exchanged looks, he explained, "At the funeral."

Once Fireman left and I was convinced no one was lurking in the woods beyond my house, I settled into my recliner, comforted first by the sounds of water running upstairs, and then silence as Bella settled into bed next to her mother.

I dimmed the lamp on the end table, soothed by the sight of my bowie double-edged, my hot tea, and my Bible. For the first time since Peony left this world, I let my thoughts drift to our lives together.

We never knew our parents. The creek community told us they'd been killed by a drunk driver. Later Peony and I wondered if they'd been the drunk drivers, or if they'd ruined their lives in some other regrettable manner. We adapted to being shuffled from family to family, always nurtured, but never really belonging. We absorbed and practiced the unique mixture of cultures, good and bad, from the Creek People. We also inherited the resentment that festered among them. And yet Peony, much like Bella, never allowed herself to be tainted or defined by the bitterness. Instead, she used her skill with herbs as a tool to help others. She exercised her faith every day with her kindness, her thoughtful way with words, and her generosity.

Four years older than me, I'd never lived a day in this world without Peony. She'd been with me as a naïve child, as an angry young teenager, and more recently, as the middle-aged man I am now, finally at peace with God's will for my life.

I opened my Bible, retrieving my most cherished pictures of my sister. I held up an old photo of us when we were young children. I must have been two, so that would have made Peony six. Her expression was a little afraid, unsure.

And then as we got older, the light in her eyes reflected confidence. She appeared poised. Happy even. Photographed beside her husband and true love, Axe, she beamed with well-being and hope. I grew sentimental as I flipped through the photos of my sister in the prime of her life, recognizing the same striking beauty in Meadow and Bella.

And then the faces in the photos changed. Missing was Axe, his kind and distinguished face now replaced with Madhawk's, the bitterest among the Creek People. Large and angry, he'd barged into our lives, altering everything. He'd stolen the fire from my sister's eyes. Replaced it with assent, submission, and ultimately, surrender. Once, when I'd been young and stupid, I'd meanly accused Peony of being afraid of Madhawk, and mocked her for giving in to him.

"No mon cher," she'd said lovingly. "What you see is grace. And wisdom. I simply choose my battles, that's all."

I picked up my favorite photo of her, and held it close to my aging eyes, desperate to remember all the details. Peony with Meadow and Bella. Meadow, who'd been fifteen and beautiful—and disgraced, shamed, and haunted.

Meadow held Bella, her newborn baby, in her arms.

I considered the way Peony rested her arm firmly around Meadow's shoulder, and her hand affectionately against Bella's tiny cheek. There was nothing scared in my sister's expression at all. I saw strength, ferocity, and defiance.

Yes, my sister most certainly picked her battles. She'd chosen the ones worth fighting for—and possibly, the ones worth dying for.

Perhaps the outrageous shirt I wore gave me the strength to get through the ceremony. My patch-shirt, as Peony had dubbed it, sported vivid greens, reds, and blue flannel squares, sewn together in hopes of creating eye-popping fashion for a special occasion. Peony had collected scraps for years, and finally, she'd said joyfully on the eve of my momentous event, "I can make you look like the prince you are."

The occasion itself had been a life altering disaster. The shirt, however, had become one of my most cherished treasures.

As I now stood in front of the enormous congregation, I was pleased to see a kaleidoscope of festive, joyous colors. It seemed a fitting way to celebrate my sister's vibrant spirit.

"I'll close this afternoon," I said to the mourners, "first with an old Cherokee saying, one that articulates how so many of us are feeling today. 'When you were born, you cried, and the world rejoiced. Now that you're gone, the world cries, and you rejoice.'"

"Amen," someone said.

"That's lovely," someone else opined. "So true."

"And next," I continued. "With a prayer from Romans, chapter eight. 'For I am convinced that neither death nor life, neither angels nor demons, neither the present nor the future, nor any powers, neither height nor depth, nor anything else in all creation, will be able to separate us from the love of God that is in Christ Jesus our Lord.'"

I resisted the pressure behind my eyes, only looking up when I was sure of my composure. My eyes landed on Desi, who stood next to Lenny and Luke. She'd become more and more like her flamboyant mother, Sunny, over the years, and wore a sparkling, red outfit that reflected her own colorful personality. She winked at me.

"And finally, a beautiful feast awaits you," I offered with a smile. "Tout le monde mange, everyone. Bon appetite!"

The mourners dispersed in various directions, the majority to tables laden with gumbo, jambalaya, and potato salad. Others approached Meadow, Bella, and me with condolences. "Merci," I thanked a tearful elder after receiving a heartfelt embrace.

As the three of us formed an impromptu receiving line, Madhawk's mother passed, offering her sympathies. "Peony was good to him," she acknowledged begrudgingly. "But who's gonna take care of me now?" The old woman held a glint in her eye. "Find him."

"I'll do my best," I replied. "I give you my word." When she moved on, I let out my breath, unnerved by the intensity in the frail old woman.

"Wolfheart," Redflyer approached tentatively. "Your sister was pure in heart, and kind." He lingered. "There was a time, not long ago, when I got in some trouble." He cut a glance toward Sheriff Rick, who chatted with Quietdove, Lenny, and Desi. "Your sister didn't judge me. Instead, she nursed me back to health." He discreetly lifted the cuff of his shirt, revealing a four-inch laceration on his arm. I recognized the stitching as my sister's. "She used rose yarrow to—"

"Staunch the bleeding," I said lightly. "I'm glad you are well now."
I leaned into him as if in thanks, and whispered into his ear, "I could
use your help."

"Anything."

"Enlist some loyal men for a search of the mounds and the black
lands. We must find Madhawk. For justice. For his mother's peace.
And for my family's safety."

He nodded, "Consider it done."

"Hello Mr. Wolfheart," interrupted a small voice. "My granny
wants to say hi." Fireman and his feisty granny waited expectantly.
When Redflyer moved on, I embraced the woman and shook the
young man's hand.

"My name is Lacey," she said. "And I slept well last night. Thanks
to you."

"I'm glad. I think you have a good and loyal servant in young
Fireman here." When Granny Lacey appeared puzzled, the boy
looked mortified.

To exacerbate his embarrassment, a few young sprouts behind
him snickered.

"Hurry up, Littlefry. You're holding up the line," one boy nudged
his accomplice.

"Who is this Littlefry you speak of?" Bella strolled over and
wrapped Fireman in a warm embrace. "I only see my boyfriend,
Fireman, here. How was the soup I sent you home with?"

"It was delicious," Granny Lacey said while the young jokesters
watched in astonishment.

"Will you come and see me again?" Bella asked Fireman. "Promise?"

He nodded, his face alight with a goofy, dazed smile.

Once he and his granny wandered off, I was at last able to embrace
my dearest friend. "Desi," I hugged her tightly. "You and your red
gave me courage today. Thank you for coming." Micah dashed over to
embrace Bella while I shook Lenny's hand. "Good to see you, Lenny."

"How're you holding up, Brad?" Lenny wrapped me in a firm hug.

I squeezed his shoulder. "Okay, my friend." When I turned to
Luke, I followed his gaze, which led straight to Bella. "And Luke,
how are you?"

"Good," Luke reluctantly turned toward me, shaking my hand. "I'm sorry for your loss." But Desi's son was distracted, reading back and forth between Bella and young Fireman.

"Robin sends her love," Desi stroked my arm. "She wanted to be here, as well as Petey and the twins."

"Come this weekend," encouraged Lenny. "They'll all be here and we're going to have food, drink, and music."

"Music?" Bella piped up. "How nice it would be to sing and dance and be happy again."

Desi enfolded Bella and then Meadow in a warm hug. "Please come. All of you."

I glanced at Sheriff Rick, who stood behind Lenny, and listened to the whole conversation with a contrary expression. "I don't know," I wavered. "We'll see."

"I'll come," Bella grinned.

"Yes! And you'll sing," pronounced Micah as she put her arm into Bella's. The two of them wandered toward the food table, with Luke heavy on their heels.

Desi squeezed my hand, "You did well today. Please come for the party. Robin will want to see you."

As she and Lenny headed to partake in the feast, I was left with Sheriff Rick, who popped a piece of candy into his mustached mouth. "Desi's right," he said. "You did your sister proud." He shook my hand, studying the crowd. "These people look up to you. You're their leader."

"Thanks, Sheriff. I get the feeling there's a *but* in there somewhere."

"I've given you a lot of leeway, Wolfheart. More than I would give most. Despite the fact you stood me up and lied about a lawyer."

"I didn't lie—"

"I know that was Desi's doing," he remarked with a snarl. "But my point is, I've had enough of this dilly-dallying. I don't wanna have to come out here, in front of all your folks, and haul you in for questioning."

An extended moment passed as we measured one another up, giving me the chance to home in on the flavor of his candy. Citrus, I determined, or maybe banana with a touch of grapefruit.

"Are you hearing me?"

"I'll come in, Sheriff. And I appreciate your patience."

Satisfied, he tipped his head, and then moseyed over to the food table. I watched as he heaped a big spoonful of potato salad onto a plate and struck up a conversation with a woman from the creek. Whether because of his respect for Peony, or his fear of Desi, Sheriff Rick was on his best behavior.

As the sun faded, and dusk befell Shady Gully, the homage to my sister passed easily. The buoyant chatter of fellowship soon replaced the somber tones of grief, as Creek People and town people mingled happily.

As if in answer to such remarkable harmony, a distinctive yowl rose from beyond the creek as the moon lit up the night. My heart leapt at the sound, and a hush came over the gathering. I sought out Meadow's face. And Bella's. There were tears in their eyes.

As another plaintive howl cried out to the moon and the heavens above, I could no longer contain my emotion.

Madhawk's hand shook as he cut, and then removed, another strip from his clothing.

He wrapped the material first around his shoulder, and then his neck. And finally, his face. While he hadn't seen a mirror, he knew his face had been ravaged along with the rest of his body. The skin around his jaw and his cheeks felt hot to the touch, and the rags he used to blot his ears came away streaked with blood and pus.

Pretty soon, he feared, he'd run out of clothes. Or he'd run out of blood.

He leaned against a river birch tree. Hot. He was burning hot, and his shoulder throbbed. And he felt nauseated.

He'd been a fool to think he'd escaped so quickly. He'd ignored his injuries, and now the pain burrowed inside him. Swirling, rising, swirling, rising.

Madhawk jerked his head to the side, and vomited all over the clay-like dirt around the tree. And then he heaved. Over and over, violent, dry convulsions racked his body. He thought they would never stop. Until at last, they subsided.

Mindful of the noise he'd made, Madhawk calmed himself, as Peony's funeral continued on the levee high above him. Although he was safely hidden in an excavated swatch of brush below the burial levee, sometimes the echoes in the swamp carried farther than the hawk flew, and he hadn't the strength for another battle.

Ricochets of the disgraceful spectacle wafted down to his position deep inside the bowels of the swamp. The thought of being cast away gnawed at him. What he would give for a feast. For drink. And yet, he was here. Bleeding, on fire, his own heart beating weakly beneath his soiled shirt, while the pretenders from town caroused with the Creek People.

No. He refused to die in the woods like an animal.

Suddenly motivated to finish what he'd started, Madhawk dragged himself to his feet. He needed food. Water. And healing medicine. And he knew exactly where to get them.

And he knew for a fact he'd have the place to himself.

He stumbled at first, and then lifted himself off the ground. Guided by the light from the moon, he took one step, and then another.

Madhawk stopped in his tracks when an insistent, mournful howl resonated across the swamp. The moon was visible, but it was much too early for the wolves to be...so active.

He shivered as a chill racked his body.

Madhawk hated wolves.

He moved with purpose.

I walked home alone, as Meadow and Bella stayed to enjoy the fellowship. I took comfort in the glorious celebration of Peony's life, and knew the time had finally come for me to rest and mourn in my own way.

Despite the overwhelming success and tranquility of the evening, I felt a heaviness come over me the closer I got to home. My hand reflexively skimmed my back pocket, to my bowie, as foreboding spread in the pit of my stomach.

I stopped. Made myself still. But I heard nothing except the clucks of Peony's homeless chickens. Not the usual clucks of contentment, but rather sharp, uneasy clucks. I quickened my steps, positioning my bowie defensively.

As I approached my home, the light on the porch illuminated the ghastly scene. Several of Peony's chickens padded and fussed about the yard in alarm, while one of their brethren hung from a string on the awning of my porch.

Bloodied. Butchered.

My hand lingered close to my knife, as I soothed the chickens and removed the heinous carcass.

After a moment I moved to the door, and almost stumbled over the blue wolf I'd put on the lost one's grave.

The stuffing overflowed from the seams—as if it had been cut from ear to ear.

PART II

Chapter Seven

BEAMING LIKE A MUSIC AFICIONADO
Luke

Apparently, upon meeting Bella, I'd lost my pride, misplaced my dignity, and tossed my sense of caution to the wind. Like now, for example. Although my hands remained precisely at nine and three on the steering wheel, I repeatedly, and rather recklessly, stole glance after glance at Bella via the rear-view mirror.

Oblivious to my shamefully impaired driving skills, she and Micah sat in the back seat and chatted about their jobs. Micah still hated hers, while Bella hoped her temporary gig at the post office would turn into something more permanent.

"Yeah, I get it," Micah said. "But you'd have to work with Claire every day, and that would totally suck."

"Only in the morning. The rest of the day I'd be delivering mail across the creek. And I'd have health insurance and all kinds of benefits."

I clicked my blinker, heading toward the airport in Alexandria. Micah had invited Bella to join the increasing number of revelers to welcome Aunt Robin. She insisted meeting her way cool cousins would take Bella's mind off things.

"Just be careful what you wish for..." Micah trailed off with a warning. "Claire is a gossip who thrives on strife." I recognized the mantra, word for word, as if it were coming straight from my mom's mouth.

"Bella is simply being optimistic, Micah," I interjected. "If only some of her positivity would rub off on you."

While my remark earned me a nasty eye roll from Micah, Bella grinned. This time, our eyes met through the rear-view mirror, and my navigational skills faltered.

"Watch out, you're gonna miss the turn!" Micah screeched.

Fortunately, I recovered my senses long enough to turn before Dad rear-ended me. He and Mom followed in their luxury van, which was big enough to accommodate all the luggage and most of the company.

"What is that music you're listening to?" Micah reached for the tuner dial. "Is it from the dinosaur age or something?"

"Hey, wait, that's Bob Seger and the Silver Bullet Band," Bella said enthusiastically.

"Yeah," I grinned, beaming like a music aficionado. "I'm a big fan—"

"'Night Moves' is my favorite." Bella bobbed her head, and her lips moved seductively as she hummed along. Or maybe that was just my perception.

"There's their plane. It's coming in now." Micah urged me to hurry as we entered the airport parking lot. "I hate to admit it," she said. "But I'm excited to see Petey."

"Me too," I answered, distracted by Bella's musical performance in the back seat.

Dad pulled into the spot next to us, and as we climbed out of our respective vehicles, Mom waved cheerily. "Isn't this exciting?" she gushed, as if she hadn't seen us forty minutes ago.

She directed Dad as he unloaded bouquets of flowers and *Welcome Home* signs. He passed some of them to me, as if he weren't quite sure what to do with them.

When I handed Bella a particularly beautiful spread of spring flowers, she smiled at me through dark eyelashes.

"I'm excited too," she said, taking the flowers. "Is Sterling bringing his guitar?"

"Of course," Mom put her arm around Bella. "He never leaves home without it. And I know he'll be happy to help you prepare for your audition with James." Unsurprisingly, Mom had finagled a tryout for Bella at James's church. The fact that it would infuriate

Jesse, James's evil twin brother, was lagniappe. "You know," she told Bella. "Sterling plays at North Lake, the big church in Kentucky."

"Yep, Uncle Wolf and I listen online every Sunday."

Dad nudged me as we followed Mom into the airport lobby. "Isn't that Tammy Jo?"

Tammy Jo stood alone, dressed in jeans and a peasant blouse. She seemed uncomfortable, clutching her purse tightly to her chest. I'd barely had time to register Petey's ex-girlfriend's presence when Mom moved toward her with a robust embrace. "Tammy Jo, Petey will be so happy to see you!"

I wasn't so sure about that, but Tammy Jo was obviously thrilled to see Mom. As the two chatted, Dad mumbled into my ear. "Are they back together?"

"I didn't think so," I replied. "Guess we're about to find out though."

Our crew from the hills of Kentucky rode down the airport escalator to a spectacle of balloons, flowers, and whoops and hollers. Aunt Robin looked classy, as always. She sported designer glasses and a short, straight bob. She was thin, but not frail like in days past. She and Mom simultaneously burst into tears and flew into each other's arms.

"So that's the legendary Aunt Robin." Bella whispered.

"And look at Petey's hair!" Micah skidded as she leapt into Petey's embrace. Dad and I chuckled as Micah ran her hands through Petey's unruly, light brown hair. "Told y'all he'd turned into a hillbilly."

"How's your shoulder, son?" Dad got a little teary eyed as he enveloped Petey in a rambunctious man-hug.

"Awesome," Petey's tone shifted as he placed his hands on either side of Dad's face. "Nice to lay eyes on you, old man." He turned to me. "Luke."

"PeePee," I joked as we did the man hug thing. I'd teased him with the nickname for *Peter* since we were kids. Although it hadn't stuck, *Petey* had, which seemed a perfect compromise to me—although I didn't think he appreciated it. "You remember Bella, Micah's friend?"

"Yeah," Petey gave Bella the once over. "You grew up." He wrapped her in a hug. "I'm sorry about your mamaw." As my brother held Bella's gaze, his sincerity, as always, was palpable. "How's your mama coping? And your uncle?"

"They're okay," Bella answered in a soft voice. "I'll tell them you asked."

I cut my eyes toward Tammy Jo, who stood to the side of the lively reunion. Petey took his cue, and hurried to her with a gigantic smile.

Micah tugged Bella over to meet Sterling and Violet. "This is my best friend, Bella."

Although they were fraternal twins, Sterling and Violet hardly looked alike. Sterling was tall, dark-haired, and muscular, while Violet was lanky, pale, and blond. For the longest time, Violet was a head taller than Sterling, although it seemed he'd finally caught up. Almost.

"I heard you got some pipes," Sterling said to Bella.

"I heard you've got a guitar," she responded with a grin.

"Perfect!" Micah clapped. "A match made in heaven."

Although Sterling was clearly taken with Bella's beauty, he remained composed. When the two of them drifted into a language that was foreign to me, something to do with chords, turn arounds, and vamps, Violet and I exchanged greetings. "How's school? You cure cancer yet?"

In a rare, impulsive gesture, Violet ducked her head into my chest. "One day," she whispered into my ear. Like me, Violet had taken her dad's death hard. Also like me, she was shy and socially awkward, which is why we'd always gravitated toward one another.

While she lacked her twin's confidence and self-assuredness, she was intensely driven. And wicked smart. "Who's she?" She peered over my head toward Petey, who was engaged in an intense conversation with Tammy Jo.

"Oh, that's Tammy Jo. Petey's..." I shrugged. "Honestly, I don't know what she is to Petey."

Violet raised her eyebrow in question.

Before I could elaborate, everyone's attention swung to an unpleasant, mournful, yowl. "That's mama's cat," explained Violet. "Buford."

Aunt Robin lowered her face to a bedazzled pet carrier and cooed, "It's okay, Buford. We're about to get our luggage and head to Shady Gully."

"God's country." Dad grabbed a couple of suitcases. "Let's hit the road."

Sterling grabbed a guitar case plastered with blue University of Kentucky stickers as it rolled around the conveyor belt. I watched as he, Micah, and Bella headed toward the exit.

"There's my best boy." Aunt Robin stood on her tiptoes and wrapped me in a tight hug. As her tiny body shuddered, I thought about what Mama had said about it hurting to look at me.

"I've missed you, Aunt Robin."

"I've missed you more," she said thickly. "You're so handsome, Luke. The girls must be falling all over themselves to get to you."

"You'd think, wouldn't you?" I teased. "But not so much." I glanced over my shoulder, hoping that Bella had heard Aunt Robin's compliment. But she was long gone. No doubt talking music with Sterling and Micah.

"I've been doing some research," she said. "I've got some statistics on incorporation. We're going to rally the troops while I'm here."

That was music to my ears.

On the way home, Sterling rode shotgun, while Micah and Bella sat in the backseat. Everything was great until Bob Seger came up. "Play some of that old guy," Micah suggested. "You know, the one we were listening to on the way."

"Yeah," Bella leaned into the front seat, eye-balling Sterling. "Bob Seger."

"Yeah, he's the master." Sterling snapped open the clasps on his guitar case. "Off the chart riffs."

"Turn it on, Luke," Bella's blue eyes pleaded.

I did what she asked, and then Bob Seger betrayed me. That whimsical notion of "Real Love" fell away as Sterling began to strum his guitar.

My handsome cousin grinned as he twisted in his seat, no doubt mastering off the chart riffs. I watched as he and Bella bonded, crooning into one another's eyes, enjoying a harmonious, musical affair all the way back to Shady Gully.

Even Micah lost her appetite for random chit chat, snapping her fingers in time.

Mary Ann and Ginger were crazy about Buford. He, however, was not at all impressed with them. A black, short-haired cat with bright green eyes, Buford frantically searched the living room for a place of refuge.

Even Aunt Robin couldn't calm him. Ginger, Mom's yappy Papillion, chased Buford behind Dad's recliner, and he, being a cat, flattened himself into a pancake and crawled into the guts of the chair. Ginger whined incessantly, positioning herself next to the chair, determined to wait him out. "I guess I can't sit in my chair now, huh?" Dad asked.

"Lenny!" fussed Aunt Robin.

Dad handed her a glass of wine, and she and Mom toasted one another. Again.

I moved toward the kitchen, sipping a cold beer and trying to keep track of Bella, who held court with Petey and Sterling. Her head swiveled back and forth, obviously dazzled by whatever brilliant, insightful, or otherwise scintillating utterances came out of their mouths.

"I guess I'm going to go."

I turned toward the female voice behind me, surprised to find Tammy Jo balancing a plate and a glass of wine. She had dark hair and an easy smile. When Dad had back surgery years ago, she'd been his nurse, and the first time she walked into his hospital room, Petey and I had taken notice. Not only because of her eye-popping curves, but we found her sunny disposition infectious. In true Petey fashion, however, he'd managed to come away with her phone number while I'd been out fetching the car.

Story of my life. Always one step behind. Always the runner up. Especially to PeePee.

"Why?" I picked up her napkin as it fell to the floor. "Stay. I know Petey wants—"

"No, he doesn't." She took her napkin. "And that's okay. We'd sort of drifted apart even before he went to Lexington. But he seems happy, and I'm good with that."

I felt a stab of anger toward my jovial sibling, and yet I also felt the need to defend him. "I think he's just trying to catch up with everyone. You know how he is."

"I do. And I know in my heart he's moved on." Our gazes naturally flashed across the room as floppy-eared Mary Ann followed Violet as she joined Petey and his circle of fans on the patio. We watched as he did a little dance, and everyone tossed their heads back in laughter. Even Mary Ann pranced with delight. Tammy Jo chuckled. "I can't get mad at him, Luke. Look at him. He's special."

"He is," I fought a grin as Petey coaxed Bubba and Daryl into his joyous orb, and again, evoked another round of laughter. Simply by being himself.

"He's a free spirit," Tammy Jo said. "And he's going to do something special. I can't wait to see what it is."

I was dumbfounded by the level of devotion my brother aroused in people, even those he disappointed. I finally muttered, "Well, I hope you'll stay in touch. Mama loves you."

"I feel the same about your family." She finished her wine and dropped her plate in the garbage can as she moved to the door. "Tell everyone bye for me. Would you?"

I'd no sooner watched Tammy Jo close the door behind her when a familiar voice sounded behind me. "Are you having fun, my sweet Luke?

I grinned. "I am, Aunt Robin. How are you holding up?"

"I'm tired." She took a sip of red wine, no doubt from a rare, expensive grape. "But it's lovely to see the gang back together. The kids are so happy here."

A comfortable silence lay between us as we considered the room. Sterling and Bella, side by side on the couch, their heads bent together as he pointed out a guitar string. Bubba and Violet against the tiki lights on the patio, watching Petey as he tinkered with burgers on the grill. Daryl having a serious conversation with Mom and Dad. And Micah greeting Quietdove as he arrived with a bottle of wine and a grocery bag. I noted the familiarity between them as they unpacked chips and dip onto the kitchen bar.

"You could move back," I told Aunt Robin.

"No, Kentucky is my home now. And besides, I can come visit anytime I want and enjoy the view on the lake." Aunt Robin owned a beautiful house along Osprey Lake, which was about thirty minutes past the creek, where Bella and her family lived. Sometimes Dad and I would stay a weekend and fish, making sure the house was secure and in working order.

"Y'all aren't going to try to drive out there tonight, are you?"

"Oh no," she held up her wine. "Your mama and I will be talking way into the night, trying to see who can hold out the longest." She looked suddenly wistful, and I wondered, not for the first time, about the deep history she shared with my mom and dad. "I love my visits here, although I'm not so sure Buford is feeling the love for Louisiana."

"Still hiding?" I sipped my beer, which had turned warm.

"I think he's nested inside your Dad's chair." She chuckled, turning her attention to Micah and Quietdove, who lingered together at the bar. "Who is that handsome fellow talking to Micah?"

"That's Quietdove. He works with Ricky. Uh, Sheriff Rick. And Max."

"My little monkey of a brother. I can't wait to see him. And Ernie too."

Aunt Robin had lost her parents in a car accident when I was a kid, and Ernie and Max were her only living relatives. Not counting us, of course.

"So," she said. "Our mission while I'm here is to get twenty-five percent of Shady Gully to sign our petition for incorporation."

"Okay." My pulse quickened. "That will take a grassroot effort, but I can get a volunteer movement going, and I believe once people understand the benefits of incorporation, we can get popular support."

"Excellent. I have total faith in you," she sipped her wine, her attitude fiery. "Once that's done, we have to provide evidence to the state legislature of financial feasibility."

"Absolutely. I've already got statistics, and a power point on the ready."

"Good. And we'll need a professional study done."

I let out a bemused whistle. According to my research, successful studies came with a steep price tag, upwards of $30,000. "Is that necessary? They're expensive."

"I've got it," she said. "We're going to get this done, Luke."

Encouraged, my heart pounded. Finally, I had someone that took me, and my causes, seriously. Sometimes it seemed that Aunt Robin was the only one who understood me and saw my dreams as worthwhile.

"I'm game," I grinned. "Although I'm afraid our good sheriff is going to be an obstacle."

"Ricky?" Her hearty chuckle got Bubba's attention from outside the patio window. He beamed as he entered the house, making quick steps toward her. "Ricky won't be a problem. Leave him to me."

Bubba enveloped Robin in a hug so massive she disappeared into the bulk of his heft. "I just can't get enough hugs, Robin. Lordy, but I missed you. Why don't you move back? I betcha' Desi can talk ya into it."

As Bubba led Aunt Robin toward mom and dad, she glanced over her shoulder, winking at me.

I meandered into the kitchen, reaching into the ice chest for a cold beer. Micah and Quietdove were so deep into a random conversation about dental hygiene they never even noticed me.

"Hey, I brought you some cake." Bella appeared, her blue eyes turning up in mischief. "It's called hummingbird cake. Isn't that funny?"

I set the beer down, smiling as I took the plate. "Mom makes it for special occasions." I took a bite, willing to eat the whole piece in one sitting to show my appreciation. "Thanks."

She said nothing. Just stood there watching me eat. "Are you having fun?" I asked conversationally, but my mouth was so full the words came out garbled.

"Yes."

"Good," I forked in another bite. She laughed, which gave me time to chew, although I needed a swig of beer to help me swallow.

"I feel normal here." She glanced around the living room, through the sliding glass doors, and onto the patio where Petey flipped burgers. "I wish mama could see how nice everybody is."

"Well, maybe she should come the next time we have a party." I ran my tongue along my teeth, tasting the sweetness of cream cheese icing. I ventured, "But you're not normal, Bella." When she squinted at me, I explained, "I mean, you're way too special to be normal."

"Oh," the way she dragged the word out embarrassed me, as if I'd said the wrong thing. Too soon. Too cheesy. Just—too much. And then she said, "Thanks. I hope I feel special when I audition for James. If I get the position on the creative team, they'll see that I fit in."

"Who? You mean people in the community? At church?"

"No. I mean mama. And Uncle Wolf."

The doorbell chimed, followed by the clicks of Mary Ann and Ginger's toenails as they rushed to the door to screen the guests.

"Come in," everyone shouted, followed by a round of merry laughter.

"Who would ring the doorbell?" wondered Dad.

"Anybody home?" Sheriff Rick peeked through the crack in the front door.

"Oh crap," whooped Bubba. "Quick everybody, hide your drinks!"

More laughter as Rick padded through the foyer, his arms loaded with cupcakes and flowers. I noted his new haircut, and his nifty khakis.

Max followed, along with his wife, Danielle, and they made a quick beeline to Aunt Robin. As the siblings reunited, and the family embrace turned boisterous, and prolonged, Rick awkwardly meandered into the kitchen.

"Evening, Luke."

"Sheriff," I relieved him of most of his party favors.

"I'll keep those—" Although he maintained a firm hand hold on the flowers.

I backed off, amused. "Would you like something to—"

"No," he answered quickly. And then, as if he realized his abruptness, he added, "No thanks. Howdy Bella, how are you?"

"Fine, Sheriff. I like your haircut."

He seemed uncomfortable by the praise, so I resisted a compliment on his sharp looking khakis. His demeanor changed when Aunt Robin approached.

"Hey Ricky." As she stood on her tippy toes, he lowered himself into her hug.

"He likes to be called Sheriff Rick." Whether the sugar in the hummingbird cake or Bella's attention prompted my teasing remark, I thoroughly enjoyed the incensed look on the Sheriff's mustached face.

"That's right," Aunt Robin looked at him. "Lenny told me you were elected in a landslide. Congratulations. You're the perfect man for the job."

My eyes practically bugged out as he blushed, and then awkwardly handed her the flowers.

"Thank you," she said. "How thoughtful."

His eyes followed Aunt Robin as she opened cabinets, searching for a vase. "You know what I would love, if you have the time?" She fiddled with the flowers, arranging them to perfection.

"What's that?" Sheriff Rick admired the flowers. Admired *her*.

"Well, Luke and I have been brainstorming about what we need to do to get everybody excited about incorporation. Don't you think it would be a good thing for Shady Gully?"

"Oh, yeah." He didn't even blink. "Absolutely."

"Well, we could really use your guidance, your help navigating some of the hiccups. You know?"

"Sure. Yeah. Anything I can do."

Stunned, I had to literally place my hand on the bar to balance myself.

"Well, for example," Aunt Robin posed. "In your mind, how would incorporation better help you do your job?"

"Well…uh…I think a government closer to the people would be more responsive to their needs. Like say, more deputies. And a fire department."

"That's a great idea," Aunt Robin pivoted. "Don't you think, Luke?"

"Yeah. I never considered that. That's smart." I forced some introspection into my voice. "That would mean more local jobs as well."

"Right, and if I'm not mistaken," the Sheriff went on, "that would give local folks more control over things like zoning."

"Sure," I agreed. "And if everyone felt like they had a voice, that would improve the community's identity."

Aunt Robin smiled sweetly at both of us. "Brilliant. And I'd love to help any way I can."

"Yeah, me too," the sheriff beamed. "Just tell me what to do."

Aunt Robin placed her hands on my shoulders. "I think we're lucky to have this energetic and idealistic young generation leading the way, and I have no doubt that Luke will be the perfect person to spearhead this project. Along with your help, of course, Ricky."

Bella, who up until then had been quiet, spoke up. "I agree. And anything that gets the Creek People involved is a positive. That goes to Luke's point about community identity." She nudged me, "I think he's totally up for the job. He's the smartest person I know."

"Yeah," the sheriff eyed me slowly. "The kid's just great."

"Perfect," Aunt Robin said. "It's all settled then." She turned to Sheriff Rick, "Now, why don't you pour me some wine, and let's go join the other old folks?"

Bella and I watched as they headed onto the patio. "Nicely done," she said.

"Team effort," I grinned.

Chapter Eight

TURNIP TRUCK
Sheriff Rick

Seeing as how I didn't get off the turnip truck yesterday, I knew full well I'd been hoodwinked. But the sight of Robin all doe-eyed, gazing up at me, asking for my opinion, for my *assistance*—

Dang straight, I'd help the kid. Incorporation had its good points, after all.

Of course, it wouldn't be easy with some of the hardliners around town, not to mention the Creek People's mistrust of authority, and their paranoia about signing anything. It would be an uphill battle, but for Robin, I'd tout the benefits from here to Osprey Lake.

When Robin and I joined everyone on Lenny's fancy patio, he, Bubba, and Daryl looked sheepish. "Nice haircut," Daryl chuckled. "Reminds me, I need to go see Dolly and get my ears lowered."

I ignored him, focusing instead on the crazy, twinkling lights Desi had strung along the wooden beams, rather than the number of eyeballs bouncing off me like BBs. Especially from Robin's kids, who could be a little intimidating with their college education and culture and such.

"Hi Sheriff." Young Sterling offered a handshake. "Nice to see you." Polite kid. Although he looked nothing like his twin sister, Violet, who was taller than him by a couple inches. She reminded me a lot of her Daddy, which meant she was tall, unassuming, and by all accounts, smart as a whip. You could just tell there were things going on inside her head that were way above your paygrade, despite the humble way she carried herself, like she didn't want to be noticed.

Truth be told, I missed Dean. He was the nicest millionaire I ever met. Only one I ever met, come to think on it.

Out of the corner of my eye I felt an energetic force close in on me, dead set on tagging me in some nonsensical behavior.

"Sheriff Rick," Petey enveloped me in an over-the-top bear hug. "Man, you look more and more like Sam Elliott every time I see you. That mustache, man. It's legendary."

Max disagreed. "No way. I see Magnum, P.I."

While I scoffed at the both of them, Robin seemed to perk up. Was it my imagination, or did she just size me up? Give me a second look? Just in case, I took the opportunity to smooth my fingers along my newly trimmed mustache. "How was Kentucky?" I asked Petey.

"It was the best. The horses were noble. The bluegrass was—"

"Green," quipped Violet.

"Oh come on, Jade, give me a break," teased Petey, making fun of her colorful name.

"How was the bourbon?" asked Bubba. "That's the most important thing."

"Now y'all know," Petey said with one of his slow, deliberate grins—the kind that made you grin back whether you wanted to or not— "I spent most of my time in church. Right, Aunt Robin?"

"That's true. Petey is Timothy's new buddy."

Thoroughly impressed, everyone drifted into a conversation about the current online series. "Aw yeah, man," Bubba bobbed his head. "Did y'all see last Sunday's service? Couldn't get it out of my head all week."

"A shame it didn't do you any good," Quietdove teased.

Timothy was the pastor at North Lake, a mega church in Lexington, and everybody and their brother talked about him like they knew him personally. I reckon in a way they did since half of Shady Gully watched him preach online. Another reason Jesse's and James's congregation numbers were dwindling.

After an overflowing buffet of hamburgers, hot dogs, dirty rice, and boudin, the younger ones gravitated inside, so they could be closer to the TV, their devices, and Sterling's music equipment.

The rest of us huddled around Lenny's firepit.

"It's so hot and humid," Desi rubbed her hands over the fire.

"And yet," Robin said contemplatively, "we always seem drawn to a bonfire, don't we?"

"That's 'cause it reminds us of Cicada Stadium." Bubba scraped his fork along the bottom of his cake plate, licking it. "Back when we were young." He tossed it onto the flame. "You know, the good old days?"

"Not so good," Desi said, glancing at Lenny. "Not always, anyway."

We grew quiet, undoubtedly lost in our own personal recollections and experiences at the old, abandoned ballpark. Located off the beaten path of a dirt road, for years Cicada Stadium had served as a venue for young people to express their independence.

"A whole new generation of rebels now," Max poked the fire.

"A whole new slew of regrets as well." Robin's tone, pensive in nature, evoked a long, awkward pause in the conversation. Desi and Lenny looked particularly uncomfortable.

I knew why. I'd been a part, albeit a small part, of the ill-fated reunion party that resulted in a five-year hiatus in Desi and Robin's friendship. Hard to imagine now that anything could come between them, but at the time, they were younger, and more susceptible to suspicion and jealousy.

Fortunately, the chinwag had faded over the years, mostly because Desi and Robin made it clear that they were, and always would be, a force to be reckoned with, but also because Dean's death discouraged any stray threads of malicious gossip.

These days, the only scandal in Shady Gully that raised hackles and heated opinions centered around Dolly and her disgraced husband, Mitch. Probably because of the sordid nature, but also because justice had never been done.

"We still round up kids at Cicada every now and again." Max finally broke the silence. "Just to let 'em know we're aware of what's going on." He put his arm around his wife, Danielle. "Most of it's harmless anyway. Isn't that where we got together, babe?"

Everyone chuckled, breaking the chill in the air.

"Dang, y'all talk like we're eligible for AARP or something," Bubba complained. "Ain't none of us fifty yet. I still got time to find me a woman."

"You better lay off Charlie Wayne's burgers then," Daryl said. "And Desi's cake."

"Come on, Rick," Bubba begged. "Don't let 'em rag on me like that. You're in the same boat as me. You know exactly what I'm talking about."

I glinted at him in a way that discouraged any further gum slapping. "Just saying." He put his hands in his pockets.

Actually, I didn't know what he was talking about. While I'd had my share of doomed relationships, I'd never walked down the aisle, nor had my name been recorded multiple times in divorce court. Bubba's history with women was so bad that the wedding planner at the Shady Gully Sacred Heart Catholic Church, as well as both Jesse's and James's churches, knew Bubba's flower of choice, and his tuxedo size. Furthermore, the family court judge in Belle Maison knew Bubba's real first name, which was still a mystery to all of us.

My situation was nothing like that.

"We got the blood results back today," Max, thankfully, redirected the conversation to an area I was more comfortable. "I left them on your desk."

"From Peony's case?" asked Desi. "What's the deal?"

My eyes flitted among the old friends around the fire, landing on Desi. "Probably not something we should discuss here."

"Oh, that's nonsense. Tell us." She was a bossy thing. How did Lenny live with her? But when I gave him a look he smiled. Very happily, obviously.

Max said, "The blood all over the rear exit of the house was Madhawk's, but it's wonky."

"Wonky?" I squinted at him. "Did CODIS find a match or not?"

"Yeah," Max nodded. "He's in the system, so sure, but there was other blood. A few droplets, a little splatter, and it doesn't match Madhawk's."

"Was it Wolfheart's? He's in the system too."

"Nope. Not his either. The lab had to send it off for more testing."

"Terrific," I muttered.

"At least we know Madhawk is involved." Lenny brought a couple of lawn chairs over to the firepit, and passed them around. "The question is, where is he?"

I opened a chair for Robin. "I don't see how he could be alive." Placed mine next to hers. "Not after losing that much blood."

Max agreed. "Quietdove thinks he wandered off to one of those revered sites and died."

"Well, good riddance then." Robin pushed her glasses higher up her nose. "He was a horrible person. And Peony never hurt a fly. I don't know why she put up with him so long."

"I agree," Desi chimed. "Everybody knows he killed her—"

"Desi, you don't know that for sure," Max argued.

"I know it. Trust me."

I frowned. "How? Did Wolfheart tell you something?" When she didn't answer, I brooded. "That's the problem, nobody is talking. Meadow's too traumatized." I raised my chin toward the sliding glass doors where the young ones lounged on the living room furniture. "And Bella, well, I hate to press her too hard. She's so young."

"She's twenty-three," Max said.

"The same age as Micah." Lenny eye-balled him. "What's your point?"

"I just think Bella is tougher than y'all think. And Micah," Max grinned. "If this had been her, you couldn't get her to stop talking."

Everyone chuckled, glancing toward the lights inside.

"For what it's worth," Daryl said. "I think Madhawk did it."

I sighed. "I'm inclined to agree, Daryl, but you can't, or I can't, ignore the fact that somebody killed—or may have killed—Madhawk. And my job, like it or not, is to find out who did, and what happened that night. And I'd rather get the story from Wolfheart than have to hound Meadow and Bella."

"So, what happens to Wolfheart if he beat up—or killed—Madhawk?" asked Bubba. "I mean, considering Madhawk just killed his sister and all? It doesn't seem fair—"

"We're getting way ahead of ourselves. We don't know…what we don't know. And we shouldn't be talking about all this anyway." I berated myself, wondering if I'd expounded for Robin's benefit.

After a lengthy lull, I said conclusively, "Anyway, we're going to expand the search this week. I've got a state team coming in with dogs and Quietdove is gonna lead us to some of those special places along the creek. So hopefully, we can get this resolved soon."

"I hope y'all find him dead," Desi said.

"Desi—" Lenny placed his hand on her knee.

"If you see Wolfheart, Desi, you should encourage him to come in Monday like he promised. And to bring something of Madhawk's for the dogs to get a scent. If he doesn't, and you can relay this message to him, I will arrest him."

"Would you really do that?" asked Robin, who had been quiet for a while. "Arrest him?"

I faltered for a moment, as her soulful eyes landed on me. But on this I was firm. "I would. I won't have those state guys thinking my judgment is skewed because it's my hometown. And it just wouldn't be right, for anybody. Can you understand?"

Finally, she nodded. "I do."

"Well," Daryl yawned, folding his chair. "I'm gonna head to the house. If you need help solving the crime, Sheriff, holler at me. I'm sure my boss would let me off for a few days."

Bubba followed suit. "Yep, me too. I gotta get up early and watch Timothy online."

Max made a face. "Please stop. I don't want nightmares of you in your bathrobe, eating Cheerios and taking communion."

"It's Cap'n Crunch, just so you know."

Max gave Robin a long, heartfelt hug. "When y'all get settled at Osprey Lake, Ernie's gonna load the family up, and come down for a big cook out."

"That sounds wonderful," she said. "I can't wait to see him."

Ernie, the middle sibling between Robin and Max, lived and worked in Belle Maison, and from what I could glean, made a good living selling real estate in the area. However, I got the feeling Robin's relationship with Ernie wasn't as relaxed as it was with Max.

Robin remained in her lawn chair when Desi and Lenny rose to walk everyone out, so I kept myself planted as well. "When do y'all plan to head out to Osprey?" I asked, offering her a taffy, which she declined.

"Maybe in a few days."

"Well, let me know. I could take a ride, have a look around. I don't want to sound like an alarmist, but we've got a fugitive out there somewhere."

She rubbed her hands over the dying embers of the fire. "It doesn't sound like Madhawk could make it that far, if he's as bad off as you think."

"You never know. Anger, fear, and adrenaline are big motivators."

The lights on the porch flickered, and then went dark, which illuminated the glow in the living room. It looked like Lenny and Desi were saying goodnight to the kids. Robin and I turned our attention to the fire, enjoying a comfortable silence. Until we didn't.

"How ya doing, Robin? Really?"

"I'm good, Ricky. "She smiled a little. "Oh wait, you don't like being called that anymore."

"Naw, it doesn't bother me. I just like to give everybody a hard time." She kept her gaze on the fire. "And the kids? They doing okay?"

"I think so. Sterling graduated from the University of Kentucky and seems happy on the creative team at North Lake. Maybe he's got bigger ambitions, but I don't know."

"And Violet?" I caught myself before adding how much she looked like Dean.

"Working on her masters. Loves animals. Loves science. My brilliant child. I never really know if she's okay though. It's been five years since Dean died, and she won't talk to me."

She seemed to drift off into her own thoughts then. She picked up the poker, tried to jab the fire back to life. When I reached for it to help, my hand brushed against hers, and she quickly relinquished the poker.

"I think she's fine. I think…I think Dean would be real proud of the way you've raised them. At how well adjusted they are." It had to be said. It was the truth, and maybe she needed to hear it.

"Do you remember that night?" she asked suddenly. "The night of the reunion at Cicada Stadium?"

"Yeah." I turned my attention to the fire. Gave it a few rousing pokes.

"I was home with the twins. They were toddlers and Violet had an ear infection." She looked at me. I focused on the fire. I didn't like where this was going. "Desi told me you took them back to her place. Remember? Lenny was offshore?"

"Yeah. Of course."

"I know you didn't go in with them, but—"

"Robin."

"What? I've always wanted to ask you about it, but it seemed awkward. Unseemly."

I let out a long, beleaguered sigh.

"It's okay," she shrugged. "It doesn't matter anymore."

"Robin, they weren't their best selves that night. Heck, Wolfheart gave Dean pot. Think about it. Dean couldn't even drink a beer without getting tipsy."

She tried a grin, but it fell flat on her sad face. A wave of panic swept through me as she swatted at a tear. *How had this conversation gone so wrong?*

"Desi was drunk, and Dean was—just all over the place." I scrambled, desperate to say the right thing. "It was late, and I made sure they got home okay."

"He was supposed to be staying at his parents' house."

"Yeah well, I wasn't dropping him off like that. I don't care how old you are or how much money you make, you don't walk into your mom's house stoned." I nudged her a little, hoping to get a laugh.

She softened. "I know. It's okay."

"He talked about you all the way home. How much he loved you. How much he loved his life. The twins."

"Stop it, Ricky. Rick." She gave me a hard look. I could tell she didn't believe me.

"You should ask Wolfheart. Dean said all the same stuff to him that night. Showed him pictures of the kids and everything. What does that tell you?" She said nothing. "It tells me you and the kids were on his mind." I poked some more at the fire, but I feared the flames wouldn't last much longer. "Besides, they were both too wasted to be romantic. Trust me."

She looked contemplative. "Does Claire still work at the post office?"

"Yep. And she's still a gossip. A pot stirrer. Speculating. Making up lies. It burns me up every time I see her. The way she took five years away from you and Desi."

"Five years." Robin bobbed her head, and I sensed another random turn in the discussion. "I can't believe Dean's been gone five years. It doesn't seem like it."

"It seems longer than that?" I asked, "Or shorter?"

"Both, I suppose. He's everywhere. In everything I do. I never really feel alone because he's always with me."

I tried one last stab with the poker, but nothing but smoke rose from the pit. "I'm sorry, Robin. He was a great guy. And I hate that your life together was cut short."

"Me too." She stood up. "I guess I'm going to head in, Rick. It's been a long day."

I gathered our lawn chairs and led Robin to the patio. Although it was dark, the lights from inside guided me as I leaned the chairs next to the ones Lenny had picked up.

One glimpse into the living room told me the young ones remained energetic and engaged. Micah and Quietdove sat side by side on the loveseat, while Sterling perched on the hearth of the fireplace. Bella hummed along as he lightly plucked his guitar. Luke watched them quietly from the couch, no doubt pondering incorporation.

Violet eyed her phone, looking solemn as she stroked Mary Ann, the black and white dog. For a moment I worried that Robin had been right about her emotional state. But then she lifted her head, laughed, and shoved her phone under Petey's nose.

"Wait," I squinted. "Is that a cat on Petey's lap?"

Petey sat in Lenny's recliner, with a big black cat curled in his lap. He lazily rubbed the cat's head, and it wasn't clear who appeared more content, the cat or Petey.

"Yes," Robin beamed. "That's my Buford! He's finally settled in!"

"You have a cat?"

I wanted to tell her about Gerty. About how spoiled she was and the way she liked to drink out of the faucet and lounge in her afternoon patch of sun. But I didn't. It was too late.

As we quietly passed through the living room, I raised my hand in goodbye. Everyone, except the cat, waved back. "Good seeing you, Robin." I managed a dignified, somewhat awkward hug. "Welcome home."

The melodic chords of Sterling's guitar faded as I let myself out, and grudgingly faced the realization that there would be no future with Robin. And then I got in my turnip truck and headed home to Gerty.

Chapter Nine

COMMUNION GOLDFISH
Wolfheart

I leisurely carried a cup of coffee to the porch, taking a moment to embrace the orange glow of the morning sun as it rose along the creek. And then I inspected the grounds for the hundredth time for remnants of the butchering and lynching that ensued during my sister's memorial. While I'd been able to hose off most of the mess before Bella and Meadow had returned that night, it had been dark, and they'd been tired and distracted.

I made my way to the shed at my property line, which was nothing more than a ragged building that served as a catch-all for animal feed, garden supplies, and an old chicken coop. The chickens greeted me with carefree clucks, their temperament much improved since the massacre. I bent to pet a stray cat that meowed at my feet, and then a dog of questionable pedigree that trailed the cat. I poured kibble into the bowls scattered under the covered tin roof of the shed, and watched as a few more dogs loped over, followed by a few of the cat's buddies.

All, it seemed, was well this morning. After I tossed the chickens some feed from a bucket, I ambled back in the direction of the house, pausing to have a looksee at my garden. I weeded around my peppers and tomatoes, moved the dirt closer to my basil, and loosened it around the hibiscus. Peony used to say that plants were our brothers and sisters, and if we listened, they talked to us.

I moved to tend to my cassava plant, a healthy shrub with an edible root called yuca. Often mistaken for cannabis because of the leaflets that radiated from a single point and the bright green color, cassava was a good source of protein, minerals, and B vitamins.

Whether from gawking at the vivid spectacle of the cassava, or because my skin still itched from the patch-shirt I wore in honor of Peony, I couldn't fight the onslaught of memories of Megan. Like a landslide, they swept through me, tugging me deeper into despondency. Determined to shake off the uninvited thoughts, I vigorously seized on the disorderly soil around the cassava plant.

Finally, drenched in sweat, I sat in the dirt, and surrendered to my reminiscences. After all this time, I could still clearly see her face. The dimples under her smooth cheeks. The shine and the wave of her long blonde hair. Her blue eyes, innocent, then sassy, and finally... mean and condescending.

We'd met in junior high. She'd been the hot, new girl from Belle Maison, while I'd been trying to solidify my image as the roughneck from across the creek. The teacher had positioned her in the desk behind me, and I could still feel the heat of her glare against the back of my shirt. She'd been so proper with her bookbag and pencils, and me, I'd simply been biding my time until I could legally quit school like the rest of the Creek People.

The other girls were jealous of her because she was beautiful. They alienated her, or worse, made sure she saw them whispering about her. She had no one to talk to, and I ignored her like the rest of the class. I waited, biding my time, as I'd perfected the art of patience, appreciating the strategy after successfully hunting deer in the swamp.

By the second or third week of school, I'd taken to sitting sideways in my desk, just enough so she'd catch my dirty looks. Soon she feared me. Like everyone else. And yet I could tell she was curious about me, astonished by my insouciance and brooding manner.

She'd been a good girl, answering promptly when the teacher called on her, while I could barely manage a grunt when he called on me. Most of the time I rested my head on my desk, and slept through class. Occasionally the teacher flicked a pen against my ear, demanding my attention. When I knew Megan was watching, I'd open one bloodshot eye, and offer the teacher an exaggerated, defiant yawn.

When she finally got up the nerve to speak to me, I stabbed her with a wicked glare and then delighted in the way she cowered. But later, when I told Peony what I'd done, she'd scolded me. Told me I should be nice, that the girl was probably lonely.

"How could she be lonely? She lives in a big house with a swimming pool and a swing set. Her family is rich. She'll never be lonely."

"Swings sets and pools aren't friends, Brad. They're just things. Be nice to her. That's not who you are." Peony always liked to say that: *That's not who you are.* She really believed I was somebody. But I knew better.

At school the next day I turned around in my seat. Handed Megan an envelope. I watched closely as she opened it, and looked inside. When she gasped out loud, I laughed. I still remember her blue eyes growing wide with panic when the teacher walked into the classroom.

She'd turned pale with fright, not knowing what to do with the envelope of weed. At the time, she probably didn't even know what it was.

That would come later.

A rustle from the direction of the shed startled me, and I quickly jumped into a crouch, reaching for my bowie knife at my back hip.

"Wolfheart," hissed Redflyer.

I eyed him angrily. Not only had he alarmed me, but he'd also disturbed my memories of Megan. I berated myself, at once ashamed. "I'm here." I answered. "Are you ready?" Dwelling on Megan was pointless.

"Yes." Redflyer glanced at his friends, Moonpipe and Youngdeer. "We're prepared. Will you be joining us?"

"No," I nodded toward the house. "I need to stay here with Meadow and Bella. I have reason to fear for their safety. Be extra cautious out there."

"We will." Redflyer raised his phone. "We'll keep you updated."

"Good. You know where to look?"

"All around the Indian mounds, yes. And the sacred places around the burial grounds."

I followed Redflyer and his friends toward the other men he'd gathered. They all exuded intensity, focus and purpose. "Excellent. And if necessary," I added, "and willing, the marshes surrounding the black lands."

"We're willing. And if we find nothing, we'll move toward Osprey Lake. If Madhawk's out there, we'll find him."

I acknowledged Redflyer and his men gratefully. "Thank you all."

Redflyer started to walk away, then stopped and turned to me. "If only the Spirit Warrior were here to help us. He'd find Madhawk."

I reacted with a sudden wave of grief. "Yes, I know. But he is lost to us now, so we are on our own."

Understanding flashed across Redflyer's face. And then resolve.

After I folded and stacked my bedding to one side of the couch, I cued up Bella's iPad. When the familiar countdown logo appeared, I climbed the steps to the bedroom. Tapped lightly at the door, and opened it a crack. Meadow and Bella were fast asleep.

"Bella. Time for church." She lifted her head, meeting my gaze. Her hair was full and untamed, and her eyes were cloudy with sleep, but she nodded her acknowledgment.

By the time she stumbled downstairs, I'd put on another pot of coffee. She walked right past the pot, however, and reached into the cabinet for two wine glasses. She then rummaged through the pantry, shaking two goldfish from a bag. "Cheesy today."

Finally, she poured us each a splash of grape juice, carried the crackers over, and settled beside me on the couch. When she rested her head lightly on my shoulder, my heart felt full. What more could any man want? Especially a man like me, who'd done shameful things and contributed to the ruin of many.

"Turn it up," she said as the music began. "I love this song." Bella hummed along as the North Lake musicians delighted the audience with worship music. "Sterling played this on his guitar last night at Micah's house."

"It went well?"

"It did. And everyone asked about you."

I raised my eyebrows in question as she sipped grape juice. "Is that so?"

"It's true. Even Sheriff Rick was nice." She set the wine glass down, absently fiddling with one of the communion goldfish. "And I'm going to help Luke get Shady Gully incorporated."

"You're what?"

She shushed me as North Lake's campus coordinator took the stage. I regarded my great niece as she released the goldfish, and leaned in for the service. While I wanted to tell her it would be better to keep a low profile now, I knew my unwarranted advice would only encourage her to do the opposite.

So I bit back my concerns, held my tongue, and determined to rest my fears and worries at Jesus's feet.

Once the campus coordinator ran through the church's business, Timothy took the stage. As usual, his warm smile belied his unruly hair and tattoo lined arms. He wasn't your typical preacher, dressed in a three-piece suit, standing behind a podium with slicked back hair, tossing out fancy words with rehearsed affectation.

Timothy was a sinner.

Like me. And he humbled himself every Sunday. He was relatable, so I believed him when he said Jesus knew all about me, and loved me anyway. When Timothy from Lexington, Kentucky, spoke of his own failures and shortcomings, and the pain he'd caused others, I felt like he could be talking directly to me in Shady Gully, Louisiana. Surely, Timothy's story was like mine, and that's why I trusted him.

When the music picked up again, Bella joined in the singing. Her voice often brought me to tears, but especially today, amid so much uncertainty.

A tap on the door made me jump. For the second time today, I'd drifted off into melancholy like some silly old man.

"Uncle Wolf, it's Desi," Bella said. "And Robin."

As I opened the door to let my friends in, Bella fetched more wine glasses and communion goldfish.

"Oh dang," muttered Desi as she set Tupperware and bags of food on the bar. "I'd hoped we'd make it before Timothy started."

Robin beamed up at me, tucking her head into my chest. "You

really live out in the sticks, don't you?" She wrapped her arm around my waist, squeezing tightly. "It's good to see you."

As she studied me, I explained. "I got old."

"Me too," she answered.

Bella handed Desi and Robin wine glasses while I moved my bedding to the floor. The four of us sat thigh to thigh, listening to Timothy's message about hope and courage.

We took communion, and then Bella sang the closing songs with the North Lake musicians. So moved by this unexpected chance to worship with friends from my youth, with whom I shared a significant history, I found it hard to control the swell in my chest. Nevertheless, I refused to get sappy. After all, I had a reputation to uphold.

"Alright, let's have lunch," Desi said. "We brought leftovers from last night."

I joined Desi in the small kitchen, helping her transfer the food to serving bowls. My mouth watered as I put barbecue short ribs into the microwave to warm. "This looks great."

"We missed you last night. All of Petey's burgers were wiped out, but Lenny saved you some of his barbeque."

"Good man, that Lenny. Sorry I missed it. How's Petey?"

"He's the same." Desi couldn't hide the joy that suffused her face as she rinsed Tupperware in the sink. "The life of the party."

"I hope to catch up with him soon."

"Where's Meadow?" Desi asked Bella as she scooted past her to get glasses from the cabinet.

"She's still asleep. She doesn't get into church like Uncle Wolf and me." Bella delivered the glasses to the table for Robin, who poured from a pitcher of sweet tea.

"Well, she's been through a rough week," Robin said. "I'm so sorry about Peony."

"Me too," I said as I moved to the table.

Robin asked me point blank, "What happened, Brad? Did Madhawk kill her?"

Desi froze at the kitchen sink, while Bella sat down, and looked at me expectantly.

Robin, undaunted, patted the chair next to her. "Come on, Brad. Tell us what happened. You know we're on your side."

"It's complicated." I sat down. But when Desi took the chair on the other side of me, I blurted, "Yes." I looked at Bella, who had tears in her eyes. "We…I…didn't get there in time to stop him."

Desi ran her hand through Bella's hair, while Robin squeezed my hand. "Peony was such a kind person, and there was so much tragedy in her life. She deserved better."

"I agree," I nodded. "If her real love, her husband Axe, had lived, I think she would have had a gentler life." When I caught Desi and Robin exchange a quick glance, I motioned toward Bella. "It's okay. Bella knows about her true papaw. What a good man he was, and how much Peony loved him."

"I had my hands full with toddlers at the time," Desi said. "But I remember he was a plumber, right?"

"Yes, he was a plumber," I answered. "A really good one."

"He was," Robin said. "My Daddy thought a lot of him. Every time he'd come to our house, he'd bring suckers for Ernie, Max, and me, and he always remembered our names."

"That sounds like him. He had a great reputation. Not only for his skill, but for the easy way about him. I guess you would say," I looked at Robin, "he assimilated well."

Bella grinned. "Maybe that's where I got it. From my Papaw Axe."

"That's probably what got him killed." We all turned when Meadow padded down the stairs. "He'd go all over for jobs. Deep into Shady Gully, Azalealand, and Belle Maison. That's what happened. He went missing after some job in Belle Maison, and they found him in his truck a few days later. With his throat cut."

"Mama," Bella breathed. "You're up."

"Yes, and it looks like I missed the party." Meadow's sarcasm didn't mix well with the bruises on her face and chin, which had now turned a ghastly yellow-green. Because her pain saddened me, I swallowed back my impatience with her rudeness.

"Well, I guess it is a little bit of a party." Bella went to Meadow, kissed her gently on the cheek. "Because we have party food. Sit down, Mama. I'll fix you a plate."

"I think I'll just have coffee." Meadow moved into the kitchen without another word. Desi's wink assured me that she and Robin weren't offended by Meadow's aloofness.

"Plus, we're celebrating my try out tomorrow. Win or lose, I'm going for it."

I held my breath. Watched Meadow's back stiffen as she poured coffee. Grateful when she didn't take the bait.

"Good for you, Bella," Desi clapped her hands. "We're going to be there to cheer you on."

"Mama?" Bella looked over at Meadow. "Are you going to come? Uncle Wolf is."

Meadow glared at me. Our disagreements about this were known to Bella, which is probably why she challenged her mother in front of an audience.

"Mama's not such a big fan of assimilation," Bella said in a cheeky tone. "But I'm not going to live out here on the creek all my life. I want more."

The silence was awkward, and God help me, I didn't know how to diffuse it. Finally, Meadow said, "I just think you need to be realistic, Bella. I'm afraid you're being set up for failure. And disappointment." She looked directly at Desi. "Who was that guy in Shady Gully who told everybody he was gonna be a country music star? I can't remember his name—"

Just before I closed my eyes, I saw Desi's face pale. *Meadow, don't do this. It's not who you are—*

"Adam," Robin spoke up defiantly.

"That's him," Meadow remained cool as she sipped her coffee. "He's washed up now. Mad at the world. The last I heard he's wrecking marriages all over some Podunk town in Texas." Her words sliced through the air, landing hard on Desi.

"Enough," I stood up. "If you don't want to eat, Meadow, we're going to pick up the food."

"All I'm saying, is not everybody's dreams come true. Look at that guy."

Robin gathered a few plates, responded in a measured tone. "The difference between Adam and Bella is that Bella has real talent."

"I know," Meadow agreed. "But sometimes the good guys don't win. Take my mama, for instance."

I walked Desi and Robin onto the patio, while Bella stormed upstairs to have it out with Meadow. "I'm sorry. Meadow is out of sorts."

"It's okay," Robin said. "We understand."

"This try out thing with Bella pushes all of Meadow's buttons. She's afraid for her."

"That's why I pray it goes well." Desi hugged me.

After we loaded their car, Robin said, "You need to tell Ricky what happened. He's not going to let up until you do."

"You know how he is," Desi added.

"Yeah, I know."

"I'm serious. You need to show up tomorrow."

"I'll show up," I eyed her. "But your stunt with the lawyer is what set him off. You know that, don't you?"

"What did you do?" Robin asked Desi, a smile forming.

Desi shrugged. "Nothing. I just told him I hired Brad a lawyer and he'd better leave him alone or I…" she gave Robin a jaunty look.

"Or you what?" Robin pressed.

"Or I wouldn't let him see you the next time you came to visit." I watched the two of them break into a hearty chuckle, and when they bent their foreheads together affectionately, they looked exactly the way they did in high school.

"Seriously Brad," Desi said when she recovered. "Ricky told us he's got state people coming in this week with dogs to look for Madhawk. Just go and talk to him tomorrow and get it over with." My heart dropped as I thought of Redflyer and his search team.

"Who's that?" Robin scanned the clearing in the woods by the shed.

My hand was on my knife when I saw Fireman walk up to the house. "Hello," he said in greeting. Stray dogs, cats, and chickens trailed behind him as he carried a handful of fresh flowers.

"Well, aren't you a handsome young man," Robin grinned at him.

He blushed. Then turned to me and offered in a formal tone, "I've come to call on Bella."

"Is that so?"

"Yes," he nodded. "And I want to be clear about my intentions."

I didn't dare look at Desi and Robin, who were clearly amused. "And what exactly are your intentions, young man?"

"I plan to marry her."

"She's pretty feisty." I raised my eyebrows. "And I'm quite fond of her. How old are you?"

"I'm ten. But I'm an old soul."

I swallowed back a chuckle. "Okay. Well, you'll have to prove yourself."

"I will," he said. "Over time, you'll see."

I stepped aside, watched as his small frame padded up the stairs.

"I just love a traditional man." Robin said as she situated herself next to Desi in the car.

I waved, watching as they drove off, and the dust settled beneath their tires. Since I didn't want to ruin Fireman's pitch to Bella, I remained on the porch. Pulled out my phone to text Redflyer.

Time was running out.

Wolfheart had allowed the mongrels to grow soft. He fed them and catered to them like babies, instead of the vicious beasts they were.

Madhawk hated dogs.

He'd come close to sticking a knife in the belly of the Heinz 57 when it had wandered over, sniffing him with curiosity. But then Wolfheart had stumbled onto the porch with his coffee, and the pesky mutt had lost interest. Off he went, to beg for his morning kibble, never giving Madhawk another thought.

Madhawk choked back a laugh. Relieved now that he knew the hounds wouldn't give him away. Nor the cats. The chickens, however, maintained an angry look in their beady eyes. Maybe they remembered him from the other night? He laughed again, but this time the sound that dragged from his throat came out raspy like a rattle.

He chugged from the bottle of whiskey he'd stolen from Stormrunner's shack. Then chased it with one of the lovely pills he'd found in his chest of drawers. It's not like he'd need them anymore. The old coot had gone down with barely a fight. The whiskey burned nicely as it slid down Madhawk's throat.

Unfortunately, while the whiskey and Stormrunner's pills had eased his pain, Madhawk had grown drunk and sluggish. Now, even with his trusty knife, and his targets within his grasp, he feared he didn't have the stamina to make his move on Peony's family.

First, he'd need some things from Wolfheart's place. And a few select plants from his precious garden.

But the day's traffic had frustrated his plans. Starting with the traitor Redflyer, and his fellow stooges, Moonpipe and Youngdeer, who had shown up with their so-called posse.

They'd been so full of chitter chatter they'd woken him from his chemically induced slumber. He'd crawled on his hands and knees past the raggedy shed, and hidden behind a pile of logs. He'd heard parts of their conversation.

All set to search for him…beyond the creek…around the black lands…

Once Redflyer left, the women came. City women, with their fancy clothes, makeup, and laughter. Rich people laughter. The kind that came effortlessly because their lives were so easy. They were soft just like the dogs.

Madhawk would have enjoyed putting them down too. Just like the Heinz 57.

Finally, the boy came. Trussed up like a Christmas turkey. His hair slicked back and his shirt tucked in. Stinking of perfume and carrying flowers like a little pansy.

The squirt got Madhawk to thinking, why not use him like a tool? Since he was so friendly with Wolfheart and the women, he could get the supplies he needed.

After that, he'd lay low. Maybe take a trip to Osprey Lake to avoid the searchers entirely.

A searing pain ripped through Madhawk's shoulder, reverberated through his neck, and ended with a pounding to his head.

Madhawk focused on his breathing. One. Two. Three.

He thought about what Redflyer had said about the Spirit Warrior. About the Spirit Warrior being able to find him.

Four. Five. Six.

There. Better now.

Madhawk had defeated the Spirit Warrior…and the memory of putting him down was like a salve to his pain.

90

Chapter Ten

IT'S ON THE HOUSE
Luke

Wthen Claire became the head of the Shady Gully Post Office two years ago, she'd developed a whole new skillset. Instead of simply being the town's leading rumor monger, she'd promoted herself to the Chief of the News Division.

Claire was like the web server that powered the local network. She processed requests and delivered data, all through the skewed lens of her agenda. The post office was the nucleus of Shady Gully, a necessary and well trafficked zone, and Claire considered the front counter her throne, and her mouth the definitive source of all information. Archived or current. Fact or fiction.

Which is why, quite honestly, I needed her on my side. I pulled another twenty flyers from the copy machine. Lifted the top, switched flyers, and hit copy again. "How are you enjoying the strudel?"

"Luke, you shouldn't have. Really." She popped the last of the pastry into her mouth.

"My pleasure. I was in Belle Maison anyway this morning. You wouldn't believe all the pastry shops there. Also, I noticed a grand opening at a new nail salon. I thought of you." I patted my pockets. "Here. This is a coupon for a free manicure."

"Oh, that's wonderful. I do love for my nails to look nice." She frowned at her chipped ruby red polish. "They say your hands are the first thing people notice, you know? No matter how many face lifts, boob jobs, or liposuction you've had, your hands give you away every time."

Claire propped up her cat-eye glasses like a headband, gathering her thick dark hair—which typically varied in color according to the latest trend—behind her ears. She had a sturdy, solid frame, and sported an array of rings. Nose, ear, and the traditional kind. A large, green ornament that stretched the length of her pointer finger nearly blinded me as she reached for another strudel. "What is that you're copying anyway?"

"Flyers explaining the benefits of incorporation. One of which is local control of development. Like say, if you wanted to zone for a new subdivision—"

"Oh, I wouldn't want that."

"Or a strip mall. Like for a pastry shop or a nail salon."

"Ooh, that would be nice. I wouldn't have to drive all the way to Belle Maison."

I nodded enthusiastically, pressed copy. "And you could hire more mail carriers if you needed them. That would leave you more time here at the front counter. After all, this is where it's at, right?"

She laughed. "You are right about that. I hardly have time to catch my breath." She scratched the chipped paint on her nails. "With Meadow out, I had to hire her daughter as a sub."

"Bella?"

"I usually don't hire anyone without experience, but like you said, I'm shorthanded. It's not like I can do everything, you know?"

"Absolutely. And if you had a decent budget, you could upgrade to actual mail trucks, rather than the carriers using their own cars. That's bound to be more efficient, right?"

"It would. And sharper looking too."

"No doubt. Incorporation would certainly give you more funding for things like that. All at your discretion, of course."

She hopped off her stool, and strolled around the counter. "Let's see one of those." She squinted as she read, but her expression cast favorably.

"Maybe you could leave some on your counter for customers to peruse—"

"Oh no, Luke. You're a darling, but I couldn't do that."

I looked appropriately contrite.

"But," she carried the flyer to the giant bulletin board that was front and center in the lobby. "I could do this." She yanked off several post-its and yellowed flyers regarding lost dogs and free kittens, and tossed them into the trash. Then she removed the thumbtacks from church bulletins, garage sales, and shower announcements, wadding them up as well.

"This is important." She tacked my flyer at eye level, nothing surrounding it but pristine bulletin board. "People need to know."

"I think so too, Miss Claire."

She blushed. "Don't *Miss* me, Luke. How're your mama and them? I understand Robin's visiting from Kentucky."

This was tricky territory. I could undo all the progress I'd made with the wrong answer. Fortunately, a car pulling into the back of the post office toward the mail room distracted her, and when Bella waved, Claire glowered. "Speaking of the devil."

"Excuse me?" I pulled another twenty flyers from the copier.

"She couldn't possibly be done already." Claire returned to her post behind the counter, and whispered conspiratorially, "Quite honestly, I'm not sure I trust her. But all my other carriers won't go across the creek. Can't say I blame 'em. Those Creek Freaks are a little sketchy. And after that killing, I just don't know what this world is coming to."

I put the last of the flyers in my box. Opened my wallet and dug out a twenty.

"Oh, that's too much, Luke. It's on the house."

Bella, her high ponytail bouncing along her shoulders, entered from the mail room in the back. Her cheeks were flushed as she greeted us. "All done, Miss Claire. Hi, Luke."

"Hey," I said thickly, distracted by the thin line of skin along her exposed neck.

"I can't imagine you finished your route already, Bella." Claire scrutinized her. "What about Prairie Road? Where the storm washed away the gravel? And Big Island Loop? That alone takes two hours."

"Yes ma'am. I got it all. I started early, remember? My try out at Shady Gully Baptist Church is this afternoon."

"Oh yes. Of course." Claire side-eyed me, flashing skeptical. "That's right. Well. Good luck then."

I avoided Claire's eyes, tempering my irritation.

Fortunately, old man Chester, Claire's buddy and the town curmudgeon, lumbered into the post office, no doubt salty over one grievance or another. He and Claire assembled daily, wallowing in the day's gripes and grumbles.

I managed a quick goodbye, and then headed to my car in the parking lot, while Bella disappeared through the mail room exit.

I drove around to the back of the post office, stopping Bella as she got into Meadow's car. "How about a bite to eat? You've still got a few hours before try outs."

"How do you know? Are you coming too?"

"I wouldn't miss it," I answered. "Mama's got the whole town lined up."

"Oh…" Bella's face fell into her hands. "No pressure." After a moment she raised her head, and smiled crookedly. Part petrified, and part exuberant. "Thanks, but I brought a bologna sandwich from home."

"What? That's not a lunch of champions." I grinned. "Follow me to the Cozy Corner."

"What'll you have?" Charlie Wayne demanded from the order window.

"How about a chicken sandwich on whole grain bread?" Bella asked, "And do you have any fruit plates?"

Charlie Wayne regarded Bella for several seconds. "I got double cheeseburgers and fries." He flicked his eyes at me. "Two for a dollar today."

"Charlie Wayne," I implored. "You don't have a banana or an apple back there somewhere? And who doesn't have chicken?" I handed him a flyer. "You know, if we can get this incorporation petition passed, you could add on here, and maybe expand your menu."

"I got cheeseburgers and fries. Two for a dollar."

"It's okay," Bella said. "That sounds great. And maybe some sweet tea?"

Charlie Wayne's eyes darted between us so long I was afraid he didn't have sweet tea. Finally, he slammed the window and disappeared into the kitchen.

As Bella and I sat at a picnic table, I watched, mesmerized, as she freed her hair from the ponytail. She ran her fingers back and forth along her scalp, and within seconds her hair fanned out along her shoulders. The act of fluffing her hair seemed remarkably intimate, and I felt obliged to look away. But I didn't.

"Gosh, that feels better," she said. "Did you get your copies made?"

"Yeah. A few different versions." I reached into my pocket for a flyer. "Aunt Robin helped me write them. And Sterling came up with the color and artwork. Catchy, huh?"

Bella pored over the flyer. "I love it. How about I put them in mailboxes across the creek tomorrow?"

"I don't know, Bella. I don't want to get you in trouble." I thought of the way Claire was itching to find fault with her.

"Here you go," Charlie Wayne said in a gruff tone as he set a bag of food before us. When I pulled out my wallet, he waved me off. "It's on the house." He grumpily stalked back to the kitchen. "Good luck today," he eyed Bella over his shoulder.

Bella and I exchanged looks. "That was unexpected," she said. "And look!" She scrounged through the contents of the bag, beaming at the sight of a plump, juicy pear.

"Your fruit plate," I said.

She narrowed her eyes as she peeked between the buns. "And this is chicken! What a sweet guy."

I guffawed. "Today anyway."

I sat back as Bella gave her lunch her full attention. In a world full of women who picked at salads, I found her voracious appetite appealing. Finally, as she bit into her pear, she seemed to remember me. "Have you met James?"

"He's the nicer of the two. A softer version of Jesse."

Bella arched her brow.

"He's reasonable. And fair minded."

"I hope so." She sipped her tea through the straw. "I wish my Mamaw Peony were here to see me today. She was my biggest fan."

"I understand how you feel," I said with empathy. "I miss my nana too. It's probably stupid, but sometimes I imagine—"

"What?"

"I imagine us having conversations. My nana was cool, and forward thinking, and I imagine her encouraging me on my mission. But then other times—" I paused on the precipice of my confession. "Other times I think she might hate it."

Bella set her sweet tea down with a plunk. "She'd love it and she'd be supportive because she loved you."

"Maybe so. It's just she never knew the grown up me, you know? And she might think I'm crazy like a lot of folks around here do."

"I don't think you're crazy. And I highly doubt she would."

I shrugged. "She was the neatest person I knew when I was a kid. I always wanted to be creative and interesting like her, but I'm afraid those genes went to Petey instead."

"I think you're interesting."

"Well, I think you're creative."

She laughed. I laughed. We clinked sweet teas.

As much as I wanted to remember the approval I saw reflected in her eyes, I resisted the urge to pull out my phone and snap a picture.

"I'm pretty lucky, I guess," she said. "I know my Mamaw Peony wanted this for me. She wanted the whole world for me. Definitely more than life on the creek."

Not unlike the moment with Claire, I knew how I responded was crucial. I didn't want to disparage Bella's culture, but I wanted to be supportive of the kind of life she sought. "It's not so bad, is it? Across the creek?"

"No. It's not bad. But it could be better." She pointed at the flyer that glimmered in the wind. "Like your incorporation, for example. I think that would make things better. I also think assimilation would make things better. But our culture is distrustful, and resistant."

I thought of Claire and her nasty remarks. Maybe the people on the creek had a reason to be distrustful.

"My papaw, now he was a line crosser. He was a barrier breaker. He mixed with people from all over, and they loved him. His name was Axe."

"Axe? I like that."

"Do you know what his name means?"

"What?"

"It means Father of Peace. And even though I never met him, I imagine him that way. Peaceful. Easy. Kind. I imagine him just like you do your nana."

"I bet he'd be happy to know you think of him that way." I stopped, hesitating.

"What?"

"Nothing. Never mind."

"Luke, come on. I thought we were being honest." She pressed. "Come on. Tell me."

"It's just the way everyone talks about Peony, your mamaw, and your Papaw Axe, I guess I just wonder how somebody like Madhawk came into your lives."

Bella fiddled with her straw. Uncomfortable, she looked off toward the four way stop sign as a big red truck passed. I'd pushed too far. And on the cusp of her big try out. Why hadn't I kept my mouth shut? I berated myself.

"Well, Papaw Axe died," she said eventually. "And for a long time Mamaw Peony made it fine raising mama on her own. You know, Uncle Wolf was always there. Watching over everything and protecting the family."

"So, what happened?"

"I did. Unexpectedly. Another mouth to feed. More responsibility." She sighed. "I don't really know all the whys and whens, just that Madhawk was always there."

"I'm sorry, Bella. I shouldn't have brought it up." I brushed her hand with the tips of my fingers. "You shouldn't blame yourself. Nothing that happened was your fault."

She snorted. "That's debatable. Madhawk didn't like me much, and he didn't like Mama. I guess he resented us for taking up space in Mamaw's life. But you know who he really hated?"

"Your uncle."

She nodded, vague suddenly as she looked at her watch.

"Is it time?" I asked. "Are you ready to go light up the church?" I teased, hoping to ease the heaviness of the conversation.

"You bet I am." She rose, collecting the food wrappers from the table. When I took the bag to the trash, Bella closed her eyes, and

97

moved her lips in silence. When I realized she was praying, I dawdled at the trash can.

An old, beat-up, black truck slowed at the stop sign. I recognized the familiar racket that trailed the ancient clunker. A hole in the muffler made the back-end sound like a bag of rattling rocks. Mama said he'd had that truck since she was in school.

"It's Uncle Wolf," Bella said cheerily. Wolfheart honked, stuck his slender, olive skinned arm out the window. He gave a thumbs up, then took a right toward the Shady Gully Baptist Church. I caught a glimpse of a small head riding shotgun.

"That didn't look like your mama," I said, confused.

"No, she won't be coming." After a beat, Bella smiled. "But my fan club has arrived."

I loved walking into church with Bella. The way everyone's eyes were drawn to us, to *her*, and I loved the sound of her name as it swelled to a crescendo among the crowd.

"Bella…"

"She's here…"

The atmosphere was thick with anticipation, and I suddenly felt anxious as I followed Bella up the center aisle. Like a wedding, it seemed that the onlookers had formed sides, and divided themselves accordingly. The pews on the left were filled with the likes of Thaddeus, Big Al, Dolly, and a few scattered ladies from her salon, while the pews on the right overflowed with my family and their large circle of friends.

My parents and Aunt Robin sat on the front row, along with Wolfheart and the young boy, who I now recognized from Peony's funeral. Behind them were Petey, Violet, Sterling, and Micah. My sister waved when she saw me.

Max's wife, Danielle, had also joined the group, as had Bubba and Daryl. I'm sure there were no questions asked when Mama suggested my employees take the afternoon off to attend the Shady Gully Baptist Church's musical try outs.

Bubba winked at me.

"Good luck," I said to Bella as I moved toward my family. Just as we each took a step in our respective directions, a loud crash echoed from the vestry and church offices. Horrified, we listened as angry shouting reverberated throughout the sanctuary.

"You broke that! You've lost your mind!"

"Allowing this to take place is a slap in my face!"

Because it was clear the angry voices belonged to Jesse and James, my gaze naturally drifted toward their younger sister, Dolly. She, however, seemed unfazed by her brothers' disagreement. Instead, she appeared stricken, and extremely troubled by the sight of Bella. She studied her with an eerie intensity that unsettled me.

"You're undermining my authority," Jesse hissed.

"What authority?" James countered. "This is my church, and I'll run it as I see fit. Why don't you go run yours?"

As the muffled argument intensified, the gathering perched awkwardly on the tip of their pews, while Bella, obviously the subject of the heated argument, remained frozen in place at the head of the nave. I was struck by her composure, the way she held her back tall and straight, and faced the pulpit with dignity.

"Just leave, Jesse. Go out the back." The sound of James's footsteps grew louder as he trudged down the hall toward the congregation. When he turned the corner, and entered the sanctuary, his eyes widened as he took in the stunned onlookers.

"I'm sorry," he said. "Everyone, I apologize." Physically, the main difference between the twins was that James wasn't completely bald, and his choice of spectacles was slightly more fashionable than his brother's. And he wasn't as hauntingly thin as Jesse.

"My. I hadn't expected such an…audience," he said clumsily. "Uh, Bella, will you be needing the piano today?"

She nodded politely, and took one small step toward the stage when Jesse burst through the hallway doors.

Highly agitated, and encouraged by the presence of his buddies, Thaddeus and Big Al, Jesse seemed intent upon continuing the fight with his brother. "This is an outrage." He confronted James at the podium.

"Jesse, please go." James, equally agitated, met his brother nose to nose.

As Jesse backed away, he considered the faces in the pews. For a moment, it seemed he'd settled down, but then his eyes landed on his sister, Dolly, who looked pale and distraught as she continued to gawk at Bella.

With renewed fury he turned once again to James. "You're disgracing our family. Stop this now." Although Jesse lowered his voice, a few words, like *sister* and *humiliation,* were discernible in his rant.

James, unhappy with being challenged in front of his flock, grumbled. "You need to drop this. Go home. You're causing a scene."

Jesse moved toward Bella. Gritted his teeth. "I've already told you no, young lady. We will not be needing your services." Utterly enthralled by the disturbing drama at the pulpit, no one noticed how quickly Wolfheart jumped from his seat, and planted himself in front of Bella.

Wolfheart clutched Jesse by the shirt, snarled into his ear.

"That's enough," James, attempting to calm everyone down, reached for his brother's arm. "We can't have this here. Not at—"

Jesse wheeled. And threw a punch so severe James's glasses flew across the stage.

Pandemonium broke out as Big Al and Thaddeus hoofed it onto the platform. Women gasped as more men eagerly rambled into the mix, further heightening the level of mayhem.

Daryl and Petey tried to pull Jesse off his brother, but Jesse was so enraged the struggle only escalated. I was horrified when my dad, who'd long since passed his fighting days, lumbered into the jumble.

Once I made sure that Bella had been safely extricated from the chaos, I latched on to my dad's arm. "Dad." At first, he looked at me with surprise, and then reason swept over him.

Relieved when he joined the rest of the family to tend to Bella, I turned my attention to the thrashing bodies on the stage. Out of the corner of my eye, I caught a glimpse of Bubba as he headed into the confusion with a purposeful look.

"Bubba!"

He turned at the sound of my voice. "It's the kid!" He pointed toward the mayhem and sure enough, the boy had slipped away from Wolfheart, and launched himself into the pile up.

Essentially flailing arms and legs, it took Bubba, Daryl, and me to extricate his tiny body from the madness. When I finally scooped him up, he continued his energetic floundering to such an extent I nearly teetered over before delivering him to Wolfheart.

As I caught my breath, I took in the appalling state of bedlam transpiring before my eyes. The sanctuary resounded with shrieks, tears, and disbelief.

And then, all at once, the noise came to a halt.

The double doors of the building slammed against the walls as they flew open. The Sheriff of Shady Gully had arrived.

And he did not look amused.

Chapter Eleven

FRESH BOX OF HANDCUFFS
Sheriff Rick

I forced myself to pause in the foyer of the church. Figured it wouldn't hurt to send up a little prayer seeing as how I was fixin' to knock some heads together.

Getting called to a brawl was one thing, but getting called to a brawl in a place of worship was another thing altogether. I cringed imagining the variety of creative memes the state boys would dream up by day's end.

Lord Jesus, help me not throw away the key after I lock all these knuckleheads up.

A quick reconnaissance of the place told me two things. Number one, nobody was in immediate danger, and number two, the usual suspects were all present and accounted for. Swell.

I noted blood on the altar, the sanctuary, and the stage, but mostly, on James's shirt. He appeared shellshocked, as his glasses dangled along his swollen nose.

His evil twin, Jesse, glared at me from the podium. As usual, he had that sanctimonious look on his miserable face, and I had to remind myself that I was in the Lord's house. "Quiet," I warned him, as I could see him revving up for a speech.

"Max," I hollered. "Let's break out that fresh box of handcuffs we got in from FedEx this morning."

Max cleared his throat. Leaned into me, all quiet like. "I believe I see my wife. On the second row. She's wearing the peach shirt—"

"Max," I turned to him. "I see your whole dang family. Starting

102

with your sister. Ain't it interesting how she finds herself in trouble whenever she's around Desi?"

"Lenny's here too."

"Yeah well, Desi corrupted him a long time ago."

"And the kids—"

"All right. All right." I walked up the center aisle, making sure my boots clomped loud enough to discourage the young ones from a life of crime. "While my deputies fetch the handcuffs, I'm gonna take statements."

In unison, they all began prattling. When I held up my hand, the racket stopped. "One from each…team." Good gracious, what a disgrace. Before they could start in again, I said, "Lenny." I then assessed the opposition, eventually settling on the lesser of three evils. "And Dolly."

I didn't bother flipping a coin. "Lenny, you start." A best friend trumps a hair stylist all day long. "What happened here?"

"Well, *Sheriff.*" I had to give him points for resisting the eye roll. "We all gathered here today for Bella's singing try out."

"A singing try out she was invited to," Desi couldn't help herself.

"By Brother James." Robin put in, feisty today.

"James had no right to invite her," Jesse reared his ugly head. "After I passed on her."

Quietdove walked in with a FedEx box of staplers and paper clips. He did a great job setting them down with a clunk, then leering at the crowd in a way that highlighted his dark and menacing side.

Lenny continued. "Everything was fine until right before Bella went on stage. We, meaning everyone sitting in the pews, could hear Jesse and James having a knock-down-drag-out."

DUH—Dum—Dum.

I never saw Robin's kid, Sterling, slide on stage behind the electric keyboard, but the low, ominous, base notes he laid down got the young ones to giggling.

I cleared my throat. Turned to Dolly. "What say you?" In spite of her heavily mascaraed eyes and her perfectly coiffed yellow hair, I sensed something off with Dolly's usually high and mighty demeanor. "What were they arguing about?"

"About…this girl trying out. She doesn't attend church here. Or anywhere as far as we know, so it's not allowed."

I glanced at Bella, who exhibited great restraint. Probably because Wolfheart maintained a firm grip on her elbow. At first, I was surprised to see him so calm, but then I realized he was playing the long game, which I admired. Wolfheart understood that the more Jesse and Dolly talked, the more their prejudices would show.

"You and Jesse don't make the rules at my church." James stuck his chin out.

Because I knew the sordid history, I had a good idea what this was all about, but it pained me that my generation was dragging the next into their wretched affairs. While I begrudgingly appreciated James for trying to do the right thing, I suspected his motivation was more about riling up his siblings.

"You know, I'm just a Shady Gully Catholic from yonder down the road past the post office," I ventured. "But at Sacred Heart Catholic Church, it's pretty clear whose church it is. And all these rules you speak of, Dolly, well, that just don't sit right with me."

Everyone pivoted at the sound of footsteps as Patty and her team of paramedics arrived to look over the injured. James, who was beginning to look a little pale, raised his hand. Patty glanced at me in disbelief as she directed her people onto the scene.

Petey, who normally commanded an audience with his outgoing and gregarious personality, had stayed silent. Until now. "I agree with Sheriff Rick. Think about Jesus, for instance. He didn't turn people away. He didn't make rules to exclude people. He associated with lepers, tax collectors and prostitutes—"

"Oh, for heaven's sake." One of Dolly's Diva Dome ladies grew aflutter.

James winced his agreement as Patty placed medical tape across his nose. "The young man with the hair is right."

Jesse grumbled. "This is ridiculous." He and Dolly grew more and more agitated.

"I'd like to be a part of the church," Bella said softly. "If you'll let me."

"That settles it then," I said. "After Patty and her crew take a gander at everybody, I say we get this place cleaned up, and listen to this young lady sing."

"No, I won't." Dolly, pale and unsteady, reached for her purse. "May I go? Or am I under arrest, Sheriff?"

"You can go, Dolly."

"Me too. I want no part of this," Jesse fumed. "I'm going home." Thaddeus and Big Al bobbed their heads, seething along with their friend.

"That's what you should have done to begin with," muttered James. After he and Jesse engaged in one last stare down, Jesse and Dolly walked out of the church.

DUH—Dum—Dum.

Sterling, with a hint of flamboyance, offered a musical perspective to their dramatic exit. A splattering of laughter erupted amongst the young ones, and then they took matters into their own hands. Violet and Petey began to right some of the upended stage equipment, while Luke helped Micah and Quietdove wipe blood off the stage.

"I really want to hear Bella sing." A small boy with an earnest expression tugged on my arm. His clothes were rumpled, but he appeared uninjured. "What can I do to help, Sheriff?" He craned his neck to peer up at me.

I dug a taffy out of my pocket, and handed it to him. "Find us a good seat."

It looked to me like Robin's son, Sterling, knew his way around music. After a chat with Bella, he fondled the headphones around his neck and moved with confidence to the electric keyboard. Or the digital piano. Or whatever they called this millennial child of the ivories. Sterling remained focused as he pressed keys, monitored speakers, and stared at a screen.

He hit a few notes, traded a few meaningful glances with Bella, and then looked at James, whose nose had grown the size of a small banana.

"Whenever y'all are ready," said James, who seemed fine taking direction from Sterling, despite his non-church-member status. "You can begin."

"Here we go," said the boy beside me. His legs dangled from the pew, and his teeth were purple from the grape taffy. "She's going to be great."

But she wasn't. Bella's timing was off, and Sterling had to start her over again. And again. "Sorry," she stumbled. "I…" Bella glanced at Wolfheart, and then Desi and her family. "May I have a minute?"

"Sure," James, Mr. Agreeable, squeaked, likely because his nose was swelling.

Bella lowered her head and silently moved her lips. And then, after she looked at Sterling, she began to sing.

Her opening altered the atmosphere in the church.

Even the kid's legs stopped twitching. Bella's melodious voice enchanted us, reminded us where we were. She mesmerized us to such an extent that the earlier anger and strife inside these walls dissipated.

The song was slow, the lyrics gut wrenching, and as Bella fell deeper into a melody about loneliness, despair, and salvation, she began to sway. Soon it was apparent she forgot the rest of us were there.

I wasn't a very deep man. I liked the purity of old country music like Waylon and Willie. None of this new-fangled cross-over mess. But this little slip of a girl with her controlled, inspired song had me thinking about things I didn't feel comfortable with, things about my own life. About the mistakes I'd made. About growing old alone. And about how much time I'd lost.

I found it impossible to watch Bella sing, and not consider her own, sad story. She sang from a place of deep pain and took us with her on her anguished journey. By the chorus, Desi and Robin reached for Kleenex, and Lenny cleared his throat. And dang it, but I had an uncomfortable itch building around my eyes.

To avoid the scrutiny of the boy with purple teeth, I turned my gaze toward the foyer. And that's when I saw Dolly. Hidden in the shadows of the foyer, she watched as Bella captivated everyone in the sanctuary. By the look on Dolly's haunted face, Bella's performance had impacted her as well, although probably for different reasons.

As the song ended, the audience appeared transformed. Desi,

naturally, led the standing ovation. And one by one, everyone came to their feet, including Luke, who looked a little unsteady.

The boy, Fireman, nudged me as we rose. "She's my girlfriend."

"Well, I'll be—"

"I'm going to marry her one day. When I'm big enough."

I patted his shoulder. "I like ambition, kid. Shoot for the stars." He turned his toothy purple smile to center stage and brought his hands together.

The only one still seated was Wolfheart. He looked straight ahead at his niece, tears streaming down his cheeks. He must have felt my gaze because he turned, met my eyes.

I'll see you shortly, my nod said.

He acknowledged me with a tilt of his chin. And then he stood with the rest of the church.

My rosy glow dissipated by the time I walked back to the substation. Not because I wasn't affected by the significance of the emotional performance, but because Jesse's spiteful face met me at the door.

"Sheriff."

"Jesse. Twice in one day. I must be living right."

"I can't believe you allowed that shameful spectacle to take place."

I took a deep breath, forced some civility into my voice. "What can I do for you?"

"I'm here to report a crime." He followed me to my office. Sat in the chair across from my desk. "And I brought evidence this time, so you'll have to do your job."

It was wrong to think such sinful thoughts straight outta church, but danged if this numbskull didn't yank my chain. Jesse reached into his pocket and presented me with a Ziplock bag of what appeared to be pot.

"Are you turning yourself in?" I asked him. "Cause that's illegal."

"It's not mine."

"Could've fooled me."

The station door chimed, and in walked Max and Quietdove, deep into a discussion of the day's events. When I waved them over, their own glows dissolved upon seeing Jesse. The man was a total buzz kill.

Jesse considered my deputies from the comfort of my chair. "Do you people ever work?"

Quietdove didn't answer. Just lowered the FedEx box into its spot by the office supplies. "You need one of these, Sheriff?"

"I'm not sure. Come take a gander at this and tell me what it is."

Both Max and Quietdove slipped gloves on, and inspected the bag. Max opened it, took a whiff.

"Jesse claims it's evidence," I said.

"It *is* evidence," Jesse argued. "I've been telling you for months that Wolfheart is growing marijuana, but you've done nothing."

"How'd you get this?" Quietdove squinted. "Did you actually go to Wolfheart's place across the creek?"

Jesse, belligerent, refused to answer.

"And he didn't kill you?" Max shook his head. "Dude."

"Jesse, let me get this straight." I rested my elbows on my desk. "Are you telling me that you dug this out of the man's garden? 'Cause I know you weren't stupid enough to go into his house."

Max closed the bag, setting it on my desk. "He didn't go into his house. He wouldn't be alive if he broke into Wolfheart's house."

"And breaking into Wolfheart's house wouldn't be legal." I eye-balled Jesse. "Are you confessing to breaking and entering?"

"Of course not. The bias around here is unbelievable. I bring you evidence of criminal activity, and you turn it around on me. Do you want them out here, Sheriff? Living among us?"

I sat back in my chair. Let his comment sit for a moment.

"I got it from his garden," Jesse said eventually. "He's sells it out there on the creek. And at the high school."

"I don't think Wolfheart's selling pot to kids anymore. He stays to himself mostly. He's religious now—"

"Come on. You don't really believe that act, do you? It's all part of their plan. Like with his niece, the bastard child. They want to infiltrate our society and—"

I placed—maybe slammed—my hands onto my desk.

"Get mad if you want, but you know what I'm saying is true," Jesse scoffed. "Look at my brother. He's buying it. I won't let it happen. I won't—" Jesse finally closed his mouth.

"Fine. Leave your *evidence* then. I'll look into it."

Quietdove looked at me funny, until his gaze shifted as mine had, to the parking lot, where Wolfheart's ancient, black jalopy had just pulled in with a rumble.

"That's what you always say." Jesse complained. "But I think you should—no, as a citizen, I demand—you search that place. Till up that garden and find out the truth for yourself."

"All right. I'll look into it," I repeated. "But Jesse, and you need to hear me loud and clear on this, stay away from Wolfheart's place. Do you understand me?"

When Jesse shrugged, Quietdove added, "Probably a good idea to stay away from the creek altogether. For your own safety."

Jesse radiated pettiness. "Is that a threat, Deputy?"

"All right." I stood. "Time for you to go, Jesse. I'm sure Thaddeus and Big Al are waiting for you." Max caught my eye, urging Jesse out of his seat.

As I feared, he and Wolfheart intersected in the lobby. Jesse sneered over his shoulder, "Time is running out, heathen."

Wolfheart stopped dead in his tracks, skewering Jesse with a potent glare.

Quietdove caught ahold of Wolheart's arm, while Max herded Jesse out the door, keeping me from having to record my second brawl of the day. First a church, then a substation, good times indeed.

"Brad," I said.

The man looked drained. There were shadows under his eyes, and his manner oozed lethargy. Resignation. "Can I offer you a coffee? Some taffy?"

"No thanks." He followed me to my office. Sat where Jesse had less than a minute ago. "But some hot tea would be nice. Maybe a little Chai, if you have it."

"Chai?"

Once Max scrounged up some fancy tea for Wolfheart, and a hot cup of java for me, we faced one another across my desk. "Bella did a great job today."

"I'm proud of her. She's a good kid. Woman, I mean."

"Yeah, I met her future husband. Good lookin' kid, about fifty inches tall."

"Purple teeth?" Wolfheart nearly smiled. "Yeah. He rode back to the creek with Bella."

Encouraged by the easy-going banter between us, I started to relax. And then Wolfheart sighed. "Let's get down to it, Ricky. I'm tired."

"Fair enough," I swigged my coffee, and considered my strategy. "When you said I was one of those kids that dabbled in some of your…offerings, I admit that straight up. But that was a long time ago, and we've both changed. For the better, I think." I watched as he sipped his tea. "I think you're a good man, Wolfheart. And that Bella is a wonder. And," I frowned. "Where was Meadow today?"

"She has problems with Bella's desire to assimilate. She thinks she's naïve. I suspect I'll get a great big *I told you so* when I get home."

"But overall, things went well. Don't you think?" Once he nodded in the affirmative, I added, "Truth is, tangling with people who think like Jesse is never gonna be easy, but in the long run, it'll be worth it."

"You almost sound like Desi's son, Luke."

I wasn't sure that was a compliment seeing as how the kid drove everybody crazy with his progressive vision. As Wolfheart grew increasingly pensive, I said, "I need to know what happened the night Peony died. I need to know if a threat is still out there. I want to protect the community, both here and on the creek."

"The threat is still out there." Wolfheart's shocking candor disrupted our rhythm, so we each took a moment, respectively, to sip and swig our beverages.

"Tell me about it," I said.

"It was Madhawk, as you suspected," he finally said. "He was into meth lately, which only exacerbated his many other bad habits. And the night Peony died, his nastiness was on full display. When he started in on Peony and Meadow, Bella ran as fast as she could to get us. We were in my garden."

"We?"

"I mean, me." Wolfheart wouldn't look at me. Rubbed his thighs in agitation. "By the time we made it back to Peony's, it was too late. He'd cracked my sister's head on the mantel of the fireplace."

"I'm sorry." The thought of the last moments of that sweet lady's life filled me with rage.

"Meadow had done her best to fend off Madhawk, but she needed... she needed..." He dropped his head into his hands, clearly consumed with guilt for not getting there in time to save Peony.

"Any clue who else's blood, besides Madhawk's, 'coulda been at the back door?"

Wolfheart shrugged, vague again.

"What happened when you got there?" I continued to push. "I imagine you confronted Madhawk, and probably, justifiably, exercised some of your anger."

"No, I didn't. Madhawk ran out the back. And he collapsed."

"Collapsed? Did he have help collapsing? Brad, if you or Meadow—accidentally killed or injured him—"

"No." His green eyes sliced into me. "It's as I said. He died on the back steps."

I shook my head in frustration, as the excessive caffeine pulsed through my veins. "So, you're telling me he died, but then he got up and walked away? Come on, Brad. You need to be straight with me."

"I would never have left my niece and her daughter in danger."

I believed this to be true. But I scoffed. "Okay then. Let's talk about that. Where'd you go? Your loved ones are traumatized, devastated, and you run off to the swamp? To do what?"

"I needed...to collect myself. So that I could come back and be strong for them."

"I get that, I do. But it still doesn't add up. There's something you're not telling me."

Wolfheart calmly sipped his tea, which irked me. Partly because my cup was dry. "You said the threat is still out there. Are you telling me Madhawk was resurrected, like Jesus? And he's—"

"No. Madhawk is the opposite of Jesus." Wolfheart fiddled with the tea bag in his mug. Cagey, suddenly. "There's an old Indian saying. I don't remember how it goes exactly, but the gist of it is that a brave man dies but once, and a coward dies many times."

Second time today I'd been reminded how simple I am. "Okay. That's lovely. But can you help an old country boy out and explain—"

"You have to find him, Ricky. Because Madhawk is a dangerous, evil coward, and he deserves to die. Again, and again, and again." Wolfheart set his mug down with finality. "He's still out there, and he means us harm."

"How do you know this?"

"Because he paid me a visit during Peony's memorial service."

A jolt ran through me. Now we were getting somewhere.

Chapter Twelve

BIG SCARY WIDE EYES
Wolfheart

"*B*ecause he paid me a visit during Peony's memorial service."

Sheriff Rick's eyes widened as he rested his jittery elbows on his desk. I let the moment pass, waiting until his expectation was palpable, and then I gently led him where I wanted him.

"You saw Madhawk?"

"No. But he left me a message." I drank the last dregs of my Chai. "He slaughtered a chicken and left the carnage hanging from my front porch."

"What?" He frowned. "What makes you think it was him?"

"Who else would it be?"

"Well, excuse my honesty, Wolfheart, but you've got a lot of enemies."

"Not on the creek. And the chicken was Peony's. It was him. I'm sure of it." I wasn't going to tell him about the decapitated Blue Wolf at my doorstep. That would only distract him, and I needed to keep him focused on one thing and one thing only. I pulled a plastic bag from my pocket.

"What's that?"

"Desi said you had people coming in with dogs. That's Madhawk's sock and a cotton shirt. It's dirty, full of his scent."

"Good, thanks." Sheriff Rick seemed disturbed. "Since we're playing show and tell, I've got something for you." He pulled a Ziplock bag out of his drawer, and tossed it next to the sock. "You ever see this before?"

"Are you being facetious, Sheriff?" I didn't pick it up. "You know I have. That's weed. And it looks top shelf to me."

"Okay, there you go talking in tongues again." He stood abruptly, snatching a paper cup from the dispenser on the water cooler. "Is that from your garden? Are you up to your old ways, Brad?" He gulped the water down, and immediately refilled the cup.

"No, of course not. I wouldn't have that around my family. I think you know that." I met his eye. "Where'd you get that?"

He shook his head in irritation. "Never mind."

We seemed to be at an impasse. I stood, "If that's all, I'm going to head across the creek."

Obviously, something nagged him, making him salty because he wanted to detain me—and couldn't.

"Let me know how the search goes, Sheriff," I told him. "I believe the dogs will help you find Madhawk."

The sheriff studied me curiously.

I explained. "Madhawk hates dogs."

After a beat, he nodded. "Will do, Wolfheart."

But the friendly banter upon my arrival had been replaced with something I was much more familiar with...

Distrust.

I couldn't get the palmate leaf with serrated leaflets out of my head. The plant was, in fact, quite beautiful, and when well cared for, the green so vivid it looked as if it sprung from a flush rain forest.

The sight of the weed in the sheriff's office brought me back to another time. A time I struggled to find my identity, my place. Fourteen, a freshman in high school, I'd counted down the days until I could drift unnoticed out of the parish school system.

Megan's hair had grown longer and blonder since junior high, and she'd started wearing makeup. A black dusting around the eyes, a red frost on her lips. Since her last name began with a W, in most classes I had the opportunity to scowl at her from a mere foot away. While I doubted I frightened her anymore, I relished the shocked expression and husky gasp that followed my scathing reconnaissance.

So, I scowled at her often.

The girls still hated her. But the boys didn't. When she tried out for cheerleader, and made it, there'd been quite a scandal. The popular girls demanded a recount because they couldn't understand how she'd received so many votes.

But the boys knew why, of course.

Megan didn't care that she had no girlfriends. Controlling all the boys was entertainment enough. She tried to pull my strings the way she did with the other boys, but I refused to play along. Occasionally, I'd respond when she spoke to me. But only occasionally.

"My parents aren't home this afternoon," she said one day after school. "You wanna get drunk with me?"

"Drunk?" I scoffed, openly mocking her. "That's adorable."

At first, she regarded me with confusion, and then embarrassment. Excellent, I thought, pleased with the way I'd manipulated her emotions. I figured it was better to keep her guessing. And anyway, I usually helped Peony tend to her herbs after school.

Axe and I had tilled a garden, and helped my sister plant a variety of vegetables and herbs. Over the years, Peony had become well-studied on the subject of growing and harvesting herbs, and her aim was to create medicinal tonics for those on the creek. She was enthusiastic about becoming a creek healer, and now that Axe was by her side, she was excited about the future. Hopeful even.

Axe made a decent living as a plumber, and had managed to save enough money to build us an upscale shanty house. He cut down trees in the swamp on weekends, and finagled one of his clients into using his planer to flatten and smooth the surfaces into wood for building. Always resourceful, he'd collected discarded tin from job sites to use for a roof. And because he was such a friendly man, Axe had easily rounded up free labor at every opportunity.

Peony was aglow with love for the noble Axe, and for a long spell our lives were rife with optimism.

Encouraged by Peony's success with her herb business, I decided to branch out and start one of my own. I cultivated my own stretch of land way beyond our shanty, a place my sister and Axe knew nothing about, and soon I had a thriving enterprise of my own.

My place, and my identity, followed soon after.

Madhawk awoke with a startle, and immediately pawed the dirt around him. He closed his eyes with relief when he found the bottle. But when he tilted it to his lips, it was dry. He cursed himself for once again indulging in the sweet oblivion of the fancy pills and whiskey. Especially after he'd vowed to get serious. To rebuild his strength. To finish what he'd started.

Earlier he'd been so desperate, he thought he'd drop in on the old biddy. He knew his mother would welcome him and happily tend to his wounds, if only she didn't croak from the shock of seeing him. But as he suspected, the sheriff had positioned one of his clowns along the familiar gravel path leading to her shanty. Forced to back off, he'd returned once again to the place he felt most camouflaged.

Wolfheart's. The big shot's property was large and dense, with a variety of hiding places, and of course…a legendary garden.

He'd almost made it to the garden when the screen door creaked open, and Meadow plodded onto the porch. Madhawk quickly retreated to his hiding place behind the firewood, and watched as she lit a cigarette. She smoked steadily, pausing only to tip ashes into a plastic water bottle. No doubt to hide the evidence afterwards. He'd wanted to take her down then, as she indulged in her nasty, secret habit.

The idea of killing her, and leaving her body with the cigarette positioned just so, had excited him, tempted him. Especially the image of Wolfheart and Bella's faces, contorted in shock when they discovered her.

But the way his shoulder throbbed kept him from making his move. He had to be smart. He'd lost time…time he didn't have. Not anymore.

Madhawk surveilled the house from his position behind the firewood, scanning the area to see what noise had caused Meadow's hasty retreat into the house.

Bella, behind the wheel of Meadow's mail carrying clunker, had the boy with her. She smiled at him, joked with him. Such a tease. Once they disappeared into the house, Madhawk prepared himself. It was now or never.

He grabbed the ragged backpack he'd taken from Stormrunner's place, and quietly slipped into the woods. His body ached as he gingerly made his way along the dirt path that led to the kid's granny's house.

He waited until almost dusk when the rat-tat-tat of Wolfheart's screen-door startled him. Within minutes of their muffled goodbyes the kid was upon him, completely oblivious, merrily humming a jaunty tune as he skipped home to Granny.

Madhawk latched onto a tree, using it to pull himself upright. He flicked his switchblade open, and sprung—

"Hey buddy!" He grabbed Fireman from behind, clutching him tightly against his chest. He covered his mouth with his left hand and used his right to edge the knife along his throat. "Where ya headed?"

The kid squirmed, and kicked his feet back and forth. The jerky movements shot needles through Madhawk's injured shoulder, and when the pain traveled down his arm, beads of sweat bubbled along his forehead.

"Stopppppp—" Fireman squealed.

Surprised by the boy's stamina, Madhawk knocked him onto the ground, covering him with his own body. As he caught his breath, he used his weight to subdue him. Eventually, when the squirt lost heart, Madhawk snarled, "How's your granny doing? Lacey is her name, right? She wears that red and yellow dress. Must be her favorite, huh?"

Fireman crumpled in fear. "How do you know...?

Pleased with his ability to instill fear, Madhawk lifted himself off the boy, keeping the knife close on his neck. "There now. I'm gonna let you up all the way, but if you scream, or try to run, I'll slice your throat. And then I'll go slice your granny's. You understand me?"

Fireman nodded. "What do you want?"

"I'll do the talking, squirt. I need you to do something for me. Kind of a secret mission. How does that sound?" Madhawk playfully waved the knife in front of Fireman's face. "Move your head up and down like you got sense."

Fireman bobbed his head.

Madhawk rested against a tree. Glared. "I need you to turn around and go back to Wolfheart's house."

"Why?"

"I've got a list. I need bandages, antiseptic, food, water." Madhawk shoved the backpack at him. "Load this up, you hear me?"

"But I don't understand."

"You don't need to, wise guy. Just think about your granny. And picture what she'd look like with her throat cut."

Fireman gulped. Tried to make himself big. "You better not hurt her."

Madhawk grabbed him by the collar. "Fill that bag up, just like I said, and maybe I'll go easy on her. You understand? And I need something from Wolfheart's garden."

"I don't know anything about plants."

"Here." Madhawk rummaged through the backpack, came up with a tatty piece of paper and a pencil. His hands shook as he tried to draw. He cursed. Thrust the paper at Fireman. "That's close enough."

Fireman looked at the sketchy drawing. Back at Madhawk. "But what do I say to them? They won't understand why I came back. I just left—"

Madhawk gripped Fireman's arm, and in one swipe, drew the switch-blade across his bicep. "They will now. Go on, hurry. Or you'll bleed to death." He chuckled.

Fireman whimpered as blood seeped from his arm.

"If you say anything about me, I'll know. You got to make it look real. Convince them. You hear me? Or I'll kill your granny, and then I'll hunt you down. Got it?"

"Yes," Fireman sobbed. "Please don't hurt her."

"Go on, then. Get!"

"I don't understand how you consume so much tea." Meadow viewed the tea bag I dunked in hot water with distaste, even as she slurped iced coke through a straw. "It can't be good for you."

"The only caffeine I get is in my morning cup of coffee. After that, I stick to herbal tea, which has no caffeine." I didn't think it necessary to mention the Chai I'd had at the substation. "You seem to be feeling better. Your bruises are fading. Your sarcasm has returned."

She frowned. Glanced upstairs toward the sounds of Bella showering. I prepared myself for the tirade to come. "I heard it was a disaster."

"Not really—"

"You know where I heard it?" Meadow narrowed her eyes.

"It wasn't a disaster."

"Claire. Of all people. I could practically hear the gloating through her text."

"Claire wasn't even there. If she said it was a disaster, her source was wrong."

Meadow read from her phone. *"After the bloody scene at church today, feel free to take another day off. You should be there for Bella."* My niece tucked her dark hair behind her ear. "Followed by three emojis. Sad teary eyes, monkey covering his eyes, and big, scary wide eyes."

Sometimes I thought Claire was worse than Dolly. "That's horrible."

"You think? And you didn't answer your phone, so I had to text Daryl. He and Bubba like me."

"Everybody likes you, Meadow. It's you who keeps people at a distance—"

"Daryl assured me Bella was fine, but that Jesse had shown up, and there'd been a scuffle." She squinted at her phone. "Daryl ended the text with a thumbs up and a party hat."

"Would you like to hear my version?" When she didn't protest, I said, "Your daughter blew everyone away. There wasn't a dry eye in church. Even the sheriff shed a tear. And James as well. And just so you know, Luke has a thing for her."

"I know. She told me."

"How do women know these things?" I shook my head, forever amazed by the accuracy of women's intuition. "Does she like him back?"

Meadow shrugged, but her expression indicated she wasn't in favor. "He's four years older than her. And where would that leave poor Fireman?"

I chuckled, turning toward the stairs as Bella bounded down. When I saw the big, self-satisfied smile on her face, my lips tugged upward in response. "There she is."

"I'm starving." She crashed into me with an exuberant hug. "I guess I worked up an appetite."

"Well, it is late." I gave Meadow a look. "Did you cook?"

"Actually, I did." She carried her coke to the kitchen. "Roast beef, potatoes, and rice and gravy."

There was a sharp, persistent knock at the door. My hand automatically fell to my hip, and remained there until I saw who was on the other side. "It's Fireman."

Bella rushed over, opening the door wide. She squealed. "Oh no, what happened?" She yanked him into the house. "Uncle Wolf, he's got blood all over him!"

I scooped the boy up, and sat him on the counter next to the sink. I shushed him in a calm voice as I gave him the once-over. He struggled for breath, and his face was caked with tears and mucous. And blood. "It's okay, big man. It's okay." The blood came from a gash on his arm.

"I fell," he gasped through sobs. "In some thicket. I wasn't looking where I was going and the branches—" He dissolved into tears.

"It's okay. You'll live." I inspected the wound, reaching into the cabinet for my medical supplies. "Let's get it cleaned up. Okay?"

Meadow handed Bella a warm rag, and she gently wiped Fireman's face. He leaned his face deeply into the rag, almost resting it there as if he were ashamed and wanted to hide. His small shoulders shook, as he was overcome with another burst of tears.

I swabbed his arm with antiseptic.

"Ouch!" he squealed. "That burns! You didn't tell me you were going to do that!"

"I always catch my patients by surprise when I do that part." I winked, trying to tease his tension away. "It's to keep it from getting infected."

"Oh." He studied the bottle.

"Sit still and let me wrap it." I carefully covered the wound with gauze. "Does it hurt?"

Fireman bobbed his head. When his mouth trembled, Bella said sweetly, "I think you're very brave."

He heeded the flattery with a blush, then produced a suddenly stoic front. "It doesn't hurt that much anymore. But I should probably take some of that stuff in the bottle home. And the bandages. In case it starts to bleed tonight."

"That's not a bad idea." I eyed him curiously.

"And if it starts to hurt? What do I do? Do you have something for that?"

"Sure. I've got some pain-relieving herbs. Some oils."

Meadow opened the cabinet. "Some Turmeric?" she asked. "And maybe some clove and bromelain?"

"Yeah, and I'll mix up some cloves and chamomile as well." I peered at Fireman. "How about a hot cup of tea now? Would that help?"

He made a face. "Can you put lots of sugar in it?"

As I began mixing herbs, Meadow asked, "Are you hungry? I've got some hot roast beef ready."

"Starving." He hopped off the counter on his own. "And could I take some home for Granny?" He pushed his backpack across the counter. "You can put it in this."

While he and Bella set the table, I watched him for any residual effects from the fall, but he seemed fine. Still, I detected an uncharacteristic neediness in his demeanor.

Meadow served the plates, as Bella filled the water glasses. Fireman surveyed the water with a peculiar focus. "Do you have any bottled water?" When he dragged his eyes away from the water, he realized I'd been studying him. "Granny hasn't been to the store lately, and—"

"Of course." Meadow put a few bottles into his backpack.

As we ate our meal, we shared light conversation, and joshed about Fireman's clumsiness, but his anxiousness continued to unsettle me. I placed my hand lightly on his leg, trying to steady his frenetic twitching. "Are you okay?"

"Yes," he whispered. "I just need to get home. Granny will be worried."

After we cleared the table, and generously filled his backpack with each and every one of his oddball requests, I walked him onto the porch. The way he scanned the woods made him look much older than his ten years. Indeed, he resembled a grown man contemplating his ability to pay rent, and feed his family.

"Fireman," I ventured. "Are you sure you're all right?" I put my hand on his head, and scratched above his temples. "You seem out of sorts."

"I'm fine. I'm just embarrassed."

"Why? Because you fell or…something else?" I pried, "Does your granny need some money?"

His eyes widened, as if the idea itself eased his mind. "Yes, that's what it is." But he didn't seem embarrassed. "Yes."

I reached down into my pocket. Handed him a few twenties. "You can always come to me, you know? No matter what's going on."

He wouldn't meet my eyes. Instead, he headed down the porch steps in a clip. "Thanks."

"Fireman." He turned to me in the dark. "How about I walk you home? Or drive you?"

"No," he answered firmly. "I'm okay." He quickened his steps, and offered a backwards hand wave.

I lingered on the porch, wondering suddenly about the backpack. Had he always had it? Why hadn't I ever noticed him carrying one before? I tried to shake off my worry. It had been a long, trying day, I reasoned, and I was probably overthinking. I rose, heading for the door, when a rustling sound stopped me.

I scanned the yard and beyond, until a tiny light caught my eye. It was coming from the direction of my garden. I crept off the porch, and approached slowly. I saw a small but familiar head dipping back and forth. The body attached to the head appeared to be tending to the leaves around my cassava plants.

I watched as Fireman gathered, and then plucked what he needed.

Perhaps I'd send Granny Lacey a tub of produce next time I harvested my vegetables.

Madhawk heard the squirt coming. He wasn't singing his merry tune this time though. He seemed much more observant, even slowing as he neared. "Here." He tossed the backpack on the ground in a way that reminded Madhawk of a cranky kid.

"What's with the attitude?"

Fireman's glare infuriated Madhawk. If not for the smell of food, he'd have beaten the tar out of the ungrateful brat. Instead, he tore into the backpack and lifted the top on the Tupperware, quickly shoveling food into his mouth.

Madhawk had always enjoyed Meadow's roast beef and gravy. And he was ravenous.

"Everything is in there. Can I go home now?"

"Hold on." Madhawk guzzled a bottle of water. Unscrewed the top on another one. "I got one more job for you."

"No. I won't do it." Fireman blinked several times. "I want to go home."

"What? Are you crying? What a big baby you are." The food had given Madhawk a sudden burst of energy. He wanted to have a little fun with the kid. "I bet you won't even be able to protect your granny when I break into your house tonight."

"A deal is a deal." Fireman gawked at Madhawk. "I got what you wanted. Now I'm going home."

Madhawk laughed heartily, exposing a mouth full of food. He pulled out his switchblade and stood with renewed vigor. He grabbed Fireman's ear, plucking it roughly. "You're right. A deal is a deal. And you can head home, but first, I've got one more job for you. Let's call it a secret mission."

Madhawk chuckled as he twisted Fireman's ear harder.

"What? Okay, stop." Fireman cried out.

"I need you to make a call tomorrow. An anonymous call. You know what that is?"

Fireman nodded, furiously swiping the tears off his face.

"Good. I want you to call the Sheriff. And give him a message for me."

PART III

Chapter Thirteen

Tofu Burger And Carrot Sticks
Luke

Perfect blue skies. A shimmering ball of sun. And a car overflowing with flyers touting the advantages of incorporation. Ever since Bella's inspirational performance at church, my humble little town of Shady Gully, Louisiana exuded optimism. The openness to change was as real as the clear skies and the twinkling sun, and folks were finally ready to move forward and embrace the 21st century.

My plan was to personally deliver flyers to everyone I encountered, and if I couldn't strike up a conversation with an actual human being, I'd place leaflets under windshields.

If only I could get my brother, Petey, to focus.

"It looks like Sprite might have actually grown an inch or two." When I looked at Petey quizzically, he asked. "Or is he just sitting on that big stool in the window again?"

I placed a flyer under the wiper of a Ford Bronco. "He's sitting on the stool." Sprite was the owner of Sprite's Quick Stop, the lone gas station in Shady Gully, which was ideally located on one of the four corners of the four way stop.

He monitored the pumps from a big window in his convenience store, where he sold everything from snacks and thread and needle to household staples like milk and coffee. Sprite was well liked, not only because his five-foot two stature made him adorable to women, but because his passion for soda—or addiction to caffeine—made him energetic and chatty. Folks also appreciated not having to drive all the way to Belle Maison when they had a late-night craving for ice cream.

125

"Let's go say hi," I suggested.

Distracted again, Petey's head bent in concentration as he drew an intricate smiley face on one of the flyers. The face featured dramatic lightning bolts for hair, and a disturbing unibrow resting above horn-rimmed glasses.

"What are you doing? A self-portrait? Come on, we have a lot of flyers to pass out—"

"What?" He stared at me, oblivious. "You are really wound tight. This is Mrs. Shanna May's car. Remember she worked in the office at school? I used to love to give her a hard time." Mischievous, he stuck the now defaced flyer under the windshield wiper of an old Buick. "Come on," he said. "Let's go say hi."

"Good idea," I muttered sarcastically, following him up the steps. I held back as we entered the store, allowing Petey his moment to dazzle and charm everyone in his path.

Sprite, surprised, hopped down from his high stool to shake my brother's hand. "Well, lo and behold," Sprite teased. "The prodigal son has returned."

Petey held his finger to his lips as he sneaked up on Mrs. Shanna May, who mulled over cake mix options for her grandson's birthday.

"Yellow goes so well with chocolate icing," she mused. "But if I went with white, I could do strawberry icing. Or even lemon—"

"No right minded, respectable kid wants lemon icing," grumbled Petey. "And if he tells you otherwise, he's fibbing. And what is the point of white cake anyway?"

"Oh, my word!" Mrs. Shanna May, now in her mid-sixties, fell into Petey's arms. She blushed like a teenager. "You gave me a fright, Peter!"

"Finally," glinted Petey. "Someone who knows how to say my name right. Look at you," he swooned. "Did you go and get Bo-Tox? Dang woman, you're drop-dead gorgeous."

"Stop that, I'm way too old to be flattered." But she looked flattered. She ruffled Petey's hair. "What's with this shaggy look? You haven't gone and become a hippie on us, have you?"

"Never. Besides, there aren't hippies in Kentucky. Just hillbillies."

Mrs. Shanna May brought the yellow cake mix to the register. "What's that you've got there, Luke?"

I handed her a flyer. "I'm trying to get signatures for the petition, Mrs. Shanna May." She appeared puzzled. "If we get enough, we can file it with the registrar of voters."

"And why would we want to do that?" She counted out her change, emptied a handful of pennies into Sprite's cupped fingers.

"Because then they'll forward the certificate to the governor."

Sprite, high up on his perch, swiveled my way. "Good luck with that."

"What do you mean?"

"I'm just saying, Luke," he lifted his shoulders. "We got a good thing out here. Why do we wanna go and get on the government's radar?" He tipped his head back, his throat bobbing as he drained the last of his soda.

"That's true. My husband likes his privacy," Mrs. Shanna May quipped. "And he's no fan of regulations."

Petey shot me a look. "That's a legitimate concern," he told Mrs. Shanna May. "But imagine if, God forbid, y'all had an emergency. The way things are now, the emergency response time would be terrible."

"Oh nonsense. Quietdove and Max do just fine." She eyed me. "And Patty too. And what about Sheriff Rick? He's no slouch." She leaned in conspiratorially. "Isn't he just the spitting image of Tom Selleck?"

Mrs. Shanna May offered Petey one last hug before heading out the door, and the ding-dong of the door-chime seemed an exclamation on her position.

"I reckon I'll take a stack of those flyers off your hands, Luke." Sprite took pity on me. "Lay 'em over there by the fishing lures."

"Thanks Sprite."

Petey directed his charismatic smile on Sprite. "How's it going, man? I bet you've got all the ladies after you, huh?"

"Pretty much," said Sprite.

"Seriously. You've gotta be the town's most eligible bachelor now, huh?"

"Well, me and Bubba kinda neck and neck."

I headed down the steps, left the two of them debating whether Sheriff Rick qualified seeing as how he had a girlfriend most of the time.

When Petey finally joined me outside, we contemplated the number of flyers strewn across the parking lot. After my brother picked them up, he patted me on the shoulder. "Let's head to the Cozy Corner. We'll pass some out there, and then order lunch for Dad."

I looked at my watch. Suddenly glad I had his company.

"What happened with you and Tammy Jo?" I asked Petey as I shoveled fries into my mouth.

"She's something special, isn't she?" By the inflection in his tone, he could have been talking about Tammy Jo or his burger. "I ordered for Dad. Should we wait?"

"No, Mom's probably got him running errands." I arched my brow. "Don't change the subject. What's going on with you?"

"What?" He laughed, incredulous. "Are you going to share some wisdom with me now that you're in a relationship?"

In a relationship? I fought back a smile. "I'm not in a relationship."

"You're close enough. And for what it's worth, I think she likes you."

"Really?" I tried to temper my delight. "Did Micah say something to you?"

"Micah says something to everyone. All the time. But no." He eyed me. "Just a feeling. Like after she sang, the first person she glanced at was you. Like she was gaging your reaction. Like it was important to her."

As I tried to process this incredible bit of information, I realized what Petey was doing. "Nice try, but back to Tammy Jo. It was awkward at the airport. Obviously, she showed up because she thought there was a chance to work things out."

Petey studied the blue Chevy truck that stopped at the four way stop. An arm flew out the window, followed by a wave and a honk. "What do you want me to say, Luke? It just didn't work out, but we're still good friends."

"You drive me crazy." I shook my head. "The way you're so maddeningly casual about everything."

"That's your perception."

"Well, tell me what's going on in Kentucky then. You've always been such a mama's boy. Swore you never wanted to live anywhere but Shady Gully." I ruffled his hair, mimicked Mrs. Shanna May's gesture. And then I forced some seriousness into my tone. "Why did you stay so long in Lexington? I mean, besides wanting to spend time with Violet—and Aunt Robin, of course."

I enjoyed the flush that stretched over his face. He again studied the four way stop, clearly hoping for another distraction. When there wasn't one, he turned back to me. "That would be weird. Violet's our cousin, Luke."

"Not technically." I contemplated my brother's many distinctions, specifically his crooked smile, which brought me back to our childhood, when he'd light up at my approval. "Just saying."

"I don't know. I like Lexington. The folks are friendly. And—"

"What?"

"The church. North Lake."

"You mean the mega church that everyone here, there, and yonder can't get enough of?" I chuckled. "Bella watches it too. Every Sunday with her uncle."

"Yeah, it's awesome. And Timothy, the lead pastor? I've learned a lot from him. He inspires me." My brother's expression grew wistful. "Being there and getting involved in the mission was great. It's different from the strife here, which is a shame because the folks here are good people. But the spiritual leadership is—lacking."

"I'd agree, with the exception of Sacred Heart Catholic Church, of course."

"Absolutely. Father Patrick is legit." Petey sipped his soda through a straw. "But Jesse and James are hardly inspiring."

"Yeah. James tries, but he's not his dad. Brother Wyatt was a force. His fire-and-brimstone was legendary."

"How's Brother Wyatt doing? Has he been to church since his stroke last month?"

"I don't think so. Honestly, I don't think he ever recovered from the great scandal of Shady Gully." I looked at him curiously. "I'd love to know what happened back then to cause so much trouble. I know it had something to do with Dolly."

Petey turned, focusing once again on the four way stop.

"Think about how we're still feeling the repercussions today." I went on, "And I can't seem to get the elders to break their code of silence." As I studied him, he refused to meet my eye. *Did he know something?*

"It certainly wreaked havoc with their family." Petey nodded toward the matching churches beyond the Cozy Corner. "Identical twins. Identical structures. Radically different messages." He tore his gaze off the dual steeples. "'Behold, how good and pleasant it is when brothers dwell in unity!' Psalm 133:1." He scoffed. "Such hypocrisy."

"Crazy how you know that off the top of your head." I watched as he shrugged, avoiding my gaze. "Hey," I frowned. What aren't you telling me?"

"What? What do you mean?" Again, with the four way stop reconnaissance.

"Hey, wait a minute. You know, don't you? About the scandal. How the heck—"

"I don't know anything—"

"Don't lie to me, Petey. Not after you just quoted the Bible."

My brother winced as if I'd punched him in the gut. "I only just found out. And it's not my place. Not at this point."

"What does that mean? Not at this point?" I glared at him, highly annoyed. "Come on. We tell each other everything. What's the deal?" His reticence stoked my anger further. "And why would Mom and Dad tell you and not me?"

"They didn't." He side-eyed me. "Aunt Robin did. In Kentucky. And I'm serious when I tell you, it's not my place to say anything. Not anymore."

"That's about as cryptic as I've ever heard. Why *not anymore?*"

"Look. There's Dad." Petey rose, visibly relieved.

"Petey?"

He appeared wrung out when he turned to me. "You just need to ask Bella. Okay? That's all I'm going to say."

Bella?

We watched as Dad's black RAM truck slowly rolled into the Cozy Corner. Unlike Mom's minivan, it made a statement. It read, *huge, powerful tank coming to save the day.*

Unfortunately, it was too late to save mine.

Dad waved at Charlie Wayne on his way to the table. When he sat down, he eyed us curiously. "Boys. I thought the goal was to get people to read the flyers, not toss them out the window. If I saw one, I saw a hundred on the way here. They were like a trail leading straight to you."

"We ordered for you, Dad. Charlie Wayne said he'd bring it out." Petey asked, "Are you hungry?"

"You bet." Dad turned to me. "Don't be so glum, son. It's a process."

Although they were both trying to make me feel better, their upbeat support only exacerbated my frustration. Petey wasn't invested in incorporation, merely wiling the day away passing out flyers. And now, he'd dropped a big, fat bombshell all over my sunny, blue skied day. A particularly unsettling bombshell because it involved Bella—*my* Bella.

And frankly, the idea that he was privy to this information, while I wasn't, infuriated me.

"Where've you been?" Petey asked Dad.

"Well actually, I ran into Bella." Dad cast his eyes on me. "We had a nice chat. I'm sure you know James selected her for the creative team with high praise."

"Yeah, I heard. Where'd you see her?"

"On the back roads past the house. She was headed to the creek to deliver mail. She had the radio blaring, singing along with all the tunes. Not all them worship music, if you catch my drift." He grinned. "She's a fiery little thing, that one. Reminds me a lot of Desi at that age."

"Oh brother." Petey whistled. "That's a red flag to consider, Luke."

"Here you go, Lenny." Charlie Wayne delivered a bag of food to the table.

"Bacon cheeseburger and fries?" asked Dad.

"No can do," Charlie Wayne replied. "Desi called. Told me only heart healthy for you. You got a tofu burger with carrot sticks."

Attempting to make amends, Petey teased me. "Another glimpse into your future, Luke."

Still stinging with betrayal, I leveled him with a potent glare.

Dad reluctantly opened the bag of food. "Ah!" He beamed. "Look at all the grease on the wrapper. I knew you wouldn't let me down, Charlie Wayne."

Charlie Wayne glowered at all of us. "If Desi gets wind of this, my goose is cooked. Y'all hear me?"

Dad crossed his heart, chewed heartily.

"And what's with all these flyers? I'll be lucky if my customers bother walking 'em to the trash can. If I find 'em all over the lot tomorrow, I'll have your hide, Luke."

I sighed. "Charlie Wayne, come on. Would you at least keep some at the order window? Talk it up to the customers?"

"Do I look like a talker? And no thanks to incorporation. Sorry Luke."

"But Charlie Wayne," Petey came to my defense, complete with the flyer's talking points. "Think of all the business you'll get if—"

"That's just it. I got more business than I can handle now." He glanced at my dad, as if they were on the same page. "It's gonna be a hard sell, Luke. Folks don't like change around here."

Petey tapped his finger on a leaflet for emphasis. "Think of all the good things. Like better road maintenance. And insurance would be cheaper. More fire and police protection."

The humidity had caused Charlie Wayne's glasses to fog up. While I couldn't see much through the haze, I saw enough to know he wasn't convinced. "I gotta get back inside," he said. Before he walked away, he gestured toward the substation. "I'd like to know what the Sheriff thinks about it. If he thinks it's a good thing, I might consider it."

When Dad went back to his cheeseburger, I rubbed my temples in frustration. After a few minutes of quiet, I sensed Petey was on the verge of some banal cliché that reeked of forced encouragement.

I gave him a look, and he swallowed back his remarks.

"I have a thought," Dad said. "If you care to hear it." He dipped his last fry in ketchup, closing his eyes as he savored the final bite. "If you could convince the people across the creek that it would be beneficial to them, I think you'd have a chance of getting it through."

Petey and I gawked at him.

"Just think of all the ways it would improve their lives. Things like cable television and better cell towers to start. Not to mention all the public services that would be available to them."

"That's true." My mind raced.

Dad dabbed his napkin at a few stray crumbs. "The greatest impact of incorporation, and the biggest improvements, would be felt by them. They'd finally have a say in things because they'd be able to elect their own public officials. Folks who would represent their interests."

"Wouldn't Jesse just love that?" Petey quipped sarcastically.

"That's a good point, Dad." As my interest and adrenaline heightened, the unsettling thoughts of the notorious Shady Gully scandal—and how it affected Bella—faded. "People in town aren't interested because they've already got everything they want, but across the creek, it's a different story."

"Exactly. All you need to do now is help them see it, and their motivation and enthusiasm will follow. I'm sure of it."

"You've really thought about this, haven't you?"

"I have. And the beauty is, you know people they trust, who can explain how incorporation would benefit them. How it would create more funding in their community." Dad gathered his lunch wrappers, stuffing them into the bag. "Starting with a decent bridge leading to the creek itself. That piddly apparatus made from sandbags and gravel is a disgrace."

Petey nodded in agreement. "It's practically duck taped together."

"Yep. It's a safety hazard. Plain and simple," Dad went on. "And there was Bella, driving across it this morning."

"She could help you," Petey said so earnestly I almost forgot I was mad at him.

"Wolfheart as well," said Dad. "And once the cloud of Peony's murder has passed, I'm sure he'd be glad to help."

"Speaking of that—" Petey started.

I interrupted, unwilling to forgive him just yet. "—I wonder how the state search is going. Have you heard anything, Dad?"

"Not yet." Dad stood slowly. "But I suppose I could leave the truck here and we could take a stroll to the substation." He rubbed his belly. "That might help me walk off this burger."

Aside from Dad's skewed calorie logic, it sounded like a good idea.

Petey tossed our garbage in a giant trash can spray painted with an arrow, and clear instructions to: *Put Trash Here, Morons!* We also cleared the crumpled flyers peppering Charlie Wayne's parking lot.

We waved at the old curmudgeon behind the window, but as usual, Charlie Wayne dismissed us with a scoff.

Dad patted me on the back. "Cheer up, Luke. While we're at the substation, we'll see if we can get Ricky to add a few words of endorsement on the next round of flyers."

"You think he'd do that?"

"I suspect he will." Dad chuckled. "As long as Robin is in town."

Chapter Fourteen

All Part Of The Pageantry
Sheriff Rick

As if my day wasn't busy enough, or twisted on its head already, Lenny came into the substation set on lollygagging some time away. Apparently, Desi had left him to fend for himself while she and Robin darted off to Belle Maison for a girl's day, whatever that entailed.

Luke followed him in, wearing a face as long as Texas.

"What's wrong with you?" Max swung his legs off his desk. "Did your dog die? Or did your girlfriend break up with you? Oh, that's right. You don't have a girlfriend."

Petey grinned, "He doesn't have a dog either."

Luke ignored Max, while Petey gyrated around the office like an electric top. As far as I knew, Petey had no girlfriend, no dog, and not much of a job, and yet, he always seemed happy. Always. The kid just wasn't right.

"Any word on the search?" Lenny asked.

"Not a thing. Quietdove's out on the creek with the team. He should be reporting in directly. Want some coffee?"

Lenny sat across from me. "Yeah, that'd be great."

"Max," I hollered. "Get Lenny some coffee." I glinted at Luke, who shuffled his feet. "What's with all those flyers in your hand? Aren't you supposed to be passing 'em out?"

"We could use an endorsement." He plopped them on my desk. "From you, the sheriff of Shady Gully."

"Luke, I ain't got time to autograph all that mess."

Lenny threw his head back and cackled, just like he used to in

135

high school. "Come on, Ricky. Folks are hesitant to get on board. Your support would go a long way."

Petey rifled through the bowl of taffy on my desk. Pocketed a grape and strawberry for later, and then tore the wrapper off a coconut one. "All you have to do is say yes, that you, the Sheriff of Shady Gully, wholeheartedly endorse the idea of incorporation."

I narrowed my eyes. "Is that all?" I could forgive Petey his constant state of happiness, but he'd just snatched my very last coconut taffy. "Would you like me to donate a kidney too?"

Unfazed by my sarcasm, Petey grinned, flashing me a mouth full of pearly whites.

While I found his constant state of jubilance annoying, his shaggy hair and studied expression reminded me of Gerty. I frowned. "Sure. Do whatever you gotta do."

Gerty hadn't been herself this morning. Her tail hung low, and a cloudiness dulled her normally bright green eyes. Most concerning, she hadn't jumped on the counter to get her morning sink water. Nor had she shown any interest in her food. "Maybe we can get a decent veterinarian out here if this thing goes through."

"Something wrong with your cat?" Luke asked.

"You have a cat?" Lenny asked.

Petey's eyes lit up with amusement. "Aunt Robin has a cat."

Robin. Perhaps Gerty's current lethargy was a reaction to my brooding over Robin. "I've got a cat. Her name is Gertrude." I glared at the three of them. "Anybody got a problem with that?"

Lenny shrugged. "Nope. By the way, Desi, Robin, and I are going into Belle Maison for dinner tonight. Want to join?"

My good buddy, Lenny, had tossed me a rope. I grabbed it. "Sure. Might be nice."

The phone on my desk pierced the easy silence. "Want me to get it?" Petey picked it up before I could swat his hand away. "Shady Gully substation. How can I make your day better?"

I traded looks with Luke and Lenny. "Give me that."

"What?" Petey's eyes widened. "Say that again, please." He pressed a button on the phone, and a ragged voice filled the office.

"I saw him…the night of the murder." The tone was muffled, as if the caller wanted to disguise his identity. "Wolfheart was burying—a body—on the creek."

"Okay. Hold on, now. Can you tell me who you are?" I urged the caller.

"It was him. He killed her." Static. The sound of shuffling. "I have to go. Look at the sacred place for lost spirits." The phone clicked.

"Dang it!" I cursed. "Max! Get in here. I need you to trace a call!"

"Uh," Max hemmed and hawed. "I used to know how, but…I'm a little rusty." He ducked into the lobby and found a pamphlet in his desk. "And I'm pretty sure you have to trace it during the call."

"Good gracious. We're like the keystone cops around here." I shook my head in exasperation.

"Where's the sacred place for lost spirits?" asked Luke.

"Heck if I know. I'll call Quietdove." Just as I reached for my phone, it rang. "That's him now. Yeah?" I snapped.

"We got something." Quietdove spoke urgently.

"What?" I asked. "Madhawk? You found him?"

"Not exactly." The noise in the background made it hard to hear. "But there's been another murder."

I made it across the creek in record time. Twenty minutes to be exact. The siren atop the department's Ford F-150 helped, but Luke's request to tag along spurred my speedy pace more than anything.

Not only did his glum demeanor cramp my style, but the kid's angst brought me down. The less time spent in the cab of a truck with Mr. Doom and Gloom the better.

He scribbled on a flyer. "You didn't argue too much about my riding along."

"I didn't have much choice, now did I? What with your Dad suggesting it would be an opportunity for you to get involved with the Creek People."

"And you just got your date with Aunt Robin and all." He side-eyed me. "Wouldn't want to mess that up."

"Don't get sassy with me, kid. I'll drop you off right here. That'd be a sure-fire way to get involved."

He grumbled incoherently, and gazed out the window with a forlorn expression.

"Why so hangdog, Luke? I thought things were going well for you. Maybe even with Bella."

He heeded me for a moment, clearly pondering something tricky. As I drove carefully across the flimsy bridge that led to the creek, he said, "Sometimes I get sick of the sound of my own voice. It's like everybody is over here—" he lifted one hand, "—and I'm over there. Alone. On a completely different page."

Good grief.

"Take Petey, for instance. Everybody adores him. He's charismatic. Charming."

"Well, I wouldn't get carried away."

"And yet he breaks all the rules. He's casual with other people's feelings. He's unreliable. Who cares though? Folks continue to fawn over him. Trust him with their secrets."

Definitely above my paygrade.

"Maybe I'm too courteous? Too thoughtful?"

I shrugged, gazed at the upcoming turn-off with longing. "I wouldn't say that. Maybe you're a tad too serious."

"Aunt Robin says I'm like Uncle Dean."

I put on my blinker. "You're overthinking, kid."

"Really? Well tell me how Bella figures in with the Dolly scandal then?"

Oh boy.

As we turned around the bend, flashing red and blue lights lit up the potholes along Stormrunner's drive. "We're here." I tossed Luke a pair of latex gloves.

The atmosphere at the crime scene was in stark contrast to the one at Peony's. The EMT's packed up their equipment without emotion. The crime scene techs traded gossip as they jotted notes into their iPads. And the grounds were absent of concerned members of the creek community.

Stormrunner hadn't evoked all the fuzzy feels like Peony had, and the only people likely to miss him were those on the fringes. Lacking Wolfheart's green thumb, Stormrunner had chosen a different path to his life of crime. Back in the day, bartering fake IDs had been fruitful, and Stormrunner had sold IDs to kids looking to get into bars, or buy beer in Toulouse or Naryville, places where nobody knew them. Unfortunately for Stormrunner, he couldn't keep up with the times, and once the technical age introduced features like Photoshop and digital scanning, he'd been forced to set aside his limited skills in lamination.

"What happened to him?" Luke asked.

"Well, I reckon Patty here is about to tell us."

Patty meandered over, offering me her closed fist. When I gave her a quizzical look, Luke brushed his fist against hers. "It's a fist bump, Sheriff." The kid looked pleased with himself.

"If you say so." I turned to Patty. "Enlighten me."

"Sixty-five-year-old male, Stormrunner—"

"I know who he is. The question is how did he die?"

"Someone cut his throat. Probably with a double-edged blade. It didn't go well."

"Oh man." Luke blanched.

Patty shrugged. "He had a lot of oxy in his system. He probably didn't feel much."

Once Stormrunner's career ended, he drank heavily, smoked dope regularly, and generally stirred up trouble wherever he went. One fight too many cost him an eye and rewarded him with a life-long limp. It also introduced him to oxycontin.

"Gotta run." Patty waved as she hopped behind the wheel of the EMT van. "The techs are wrapping up now."

Quietdove pulled to the side on his way in, allowing Patty plenty of space to avoid the potholes on her way out. When he parked, he sauntered over in the same leisurely manner as the rest of the law enforcement team.

I pointed to the plastic bag in his hand. "What you got there? Dinner?"

He flicked his eyes at Luke. "What's the mayor doing here?"

"Acquainting himself with the good people of the creek." I peeked inside the bag he handed me. "Empty Tupperware? Water bottles? Ziplocks? Now I understand why nobody invites you to parties."

"That's the only thing we found today." Quietdove wiped sweat from his forehead. "Unless the state dogs find something in the black lands. I circled back so I could meet you here."

"Dogs get frisky over anything?"

"Just this bag of throw away in the woods."

"Where'd they find it?"

"Past Big Island Loop, a little less than a mile from Wolfheart's place." Quietdove glanced at Stormrunner's dilapidated shack. "And they got antsy here."

"Enlighten me on what you saw inside, before Luke and I go take us a gander." I winked at the kid, noting the green tint around his gills.

Quietdove tugged his notebook out of his pocket. "Stormrunner's shack appeared ransacked. Tossed. Otherwise, not much to see. There were empty bottles of oxy all over the place—"

"Food?"

"Nothing to speak of. Green cheese and a moldy sandwich in the fridge."

Luke frowned, pointing to the plastic bag. "If it was Madhawk, and he was looking for food and medicine…"

I nodded. "Maybe he packed him a neat, to-go bag. Has this been fingerprinted? I'd like to take it, and show it to someone."

"I got the techs to throw a little dusting powder on the bag and the contents. So yeah, take it, but keep your gloves on. They want to look at it again."

Luke considered the bag. "There might still be latent prints. You know, from sweat, amino acids, and organic residue from fingers."

"Whoa," teased Quietdove. "Somebody watches his NCIS."

"All right," I said. "Go see how the dogs are enjoying the black lands and I'll meet you back at the station. Luke and I have a stop to make after we're done here."

"Sounds good," Quietdove replied. Hesitated. "When you have a minute, I want to talk to you about something."

I waited. Tilted my head in Luke's direction. "Is it personal?"

"Not really." Quietdove mulled it over. "When I spoke to Max a while ago, he told me about the anonymous call."

"Yeah. I was going to ask you about this sacred place for lost spirits."

"I'd be careful, Sheriff." Quietdove's words held a foreboding note. "Traipsing through those grounds, turning 'em up…there could be repercussions."

"I'll take that into consideration."

"All due respect, you might start something you can't finish."

"I've got a job to do." I pivoted toward the house. "And so do you."

My best deputy's dark eyes held mine for a moment, and then without another word, he headed to his vehicle.

"All right, Luke." I patted his shoulder. "You ready to go see a dead body?"

He cleared his throat. "I think I'll wait in the truck."

As we drove up to Wolfheart's place, the inscrutable man's head popped out of his massive garden. For a moment, just before he recognized the department's Ford F-150, an expression of tranquility filled his face. And then, just like that, it slipped away.

By the time Luke and I padded over, Wolfheart's familiar scowl took front and center. He removed his work gloves, and wiped his forehead with the sleeve of his shirt. "Sheriff. Luke."

"Don't act so happy to see us," I said in greeting.

"Is this official business? Did the search dogs find Madhawk?"

"Not yet."

He eyed my latex gloves, and the bag in my hand, while I eyed his garden. "I have to say, this is a mighty fine patch of produce you got here." I sauntered along the edges of the well maintained 30 x 30 space, complete with a homemade irrigation system. "I tried my hand at growing tomatoes once, but dang if the rabbits didn't eat up all my plants. Never got the first tomato."

"That's too bad."

"The next year I tried those pots, you know?"

He nodded, setting his sights once again on the bag in my hand.

"Didn't go much better." I scanned the design of the garden. "Looks like you've got yours in an L shape, huh?"

"That's right," he answered. "On the northeast end I've got some corn stalks, with a two-foot walk space that leads to my bean poles, where I've got a few rows of southern peas and black eyes."

Luke put in pleasantly, "Mama made some of the black-eyed peas you gave her last week. Cooked them down with some ham."

Wolfheart came close to smiling, but caught himself in time. "Yeah, I sent her some squash too. They're over there to the east side. And I've got some cucumbers to the south. Meadow's been canning some, and she's getting good at it. I'll send some habanero pickles home with you."

The way Wolfheart chatted about his garden was downright affectionate.

"And I see you have some peppers over yonder." I casually strolled toward the herbs. "And some herbs." Wolfheart stayed on my heels, as if he thought I'd tromp on one. Or he feared I'd see something I wasn't supposed to.

"What's this here?" I asked, crouching. "It looks…familiar."

"It's a cassava plant, Ricky." He knelt next to me, tenderly replacing the soil I'd swept away, as if consoling it after my egregious offense. "It's a great source of vitamin B."

We rose at the sound of tires crunching against gravel. When Bella brought Meadow's old clunker to a stop, Meadow emerged from the house with a stern, pointed expression.

"It's Bella," said Luke. He turned to me, as if asking permission to go to her.

"Go on," I said. "See if you can sweet talk her mama into giving me a jar of those pickles."

After he hoofed it over like an adolescent teen, Wolfheart asked, "Did you find what you were looking for in my garden, Sheriff?"

"No. And that's a good thing." I analyzed his demeanor, searching for any sign of dishonesty. When I detected none, I opened the bag, let him take a peep. "You recognize any of these?" He reached for the bag, attempting a closer inspection. "Just look, don't touch."

"I can't tell. Everybody has Tupperware like that. Where'd you find it?"

"The dogs found it. And they got all twitchy when they did." I waited. When he didn't react, I changed gears. "Tell me about the sacred grounds for lost spirits?"

"Why?" Wolfheart made no attempt to hide his uneasiness. "Why do you need to know about that? Were the dogs there?"

I didn't answer, focusing instead on Bella and Luke, who were in the middle of a serious tête-à-tête on the front porch.

"It's a special place for the Creek People. For generations it's been held as a place of deep reverence. It's considered holy and consecrated ground."

"What's there?"

He shook his head. "Nothing you would understand. Trust me, it's not pertinent to your investigation. You're getting side-tracked. Maybe deliberately. Who told you about this place?"

I kept my eyes on the porch, bemused by Luke and Bella's conversation, which had turned stilted and awkward.

"Focus on the dogs, Sheriff. They will lead you to Madhawk." Wolfheart let out a weary sigh. "Madhawk hates dogs."

The tablecloth was white, the candles were lit, and I wore my best pair of khakis. The restaurant echoed with intimate whispers and clinking silverware. The waiter had some bizarre accent that Desi found *simply delightful.*

"Is that truffle butter?" Desi asked in wonder.

When the blond-haired dude with the strange accent responded in the affirmative, she and Robin dissolved in pleasure. As Robin chatted with him about the wine list, she spouted off words like legs, finish, and texture. I honestly couldn't tell if they were discussing chicken or paint.

To me, the place smelled like steak and freshly baked bread. I sat adjacent to Robin, who was all dolled up in black cashmere and white pearls. I felt like a Neanderthal from Hicksville, so to make myself feel better, I focused on Lenny, my friend and fellow Neanderthal.

The waiter presented us with a tray of mouthwatering bread and at least three kinds of fancy butter, all swirled to a perfectly pointy tip. I resisted the urge to dig in, especially as Robin smiled at the flamboyant waiter and ordered something called foie gras.

I didn't blink an eye. Robin rocked my boat, even if she was a vegetarian.

Finally, Desi said a prayer and passed the bread. Desi and Robin took their time, breaking their bread in teeny, tiny plates, followed with a careful dash of the coveted butter. Lenny, meanwhile, dove in like a koi fish going after crackers at a zoo.

"So…uh," I tried to engage Robin. "When are y'all headed to Osprey Lake?"

"Probably in a few days. I've been having so much fun at Desi's."

Lenny, who resembled a weary chaperone at a teenage girl's slumber party, asked, "How's the investigation going? Luke said he enjoyed spending the day with you."

"It's fine." I really didn't want to talk about work, so I steered the chitchat in a lighter direction. "He saw Bella at day's end, so I suspect he enjoyed it more than he's letting on."

"I just love her," Desi said. "Although Micah disapproves."

"Why?" Robin leaned in. "You'd think she'd love the idea of her big brother dating her best friend."

Lenny sipped his tea. "That's probably why she doesn't approve. She's afraid she's going to lose her status with them both." He glanced at his wife. "You two hens need to stop plotting, and let things play out naturally."

"Lenny's right," I said, recalling the awkward discussion between Luke and Bella today. "I'm not sure they're even a—thing—yet."

Both Desi and Robin frowned at me.

The waiter brought a bottle of red wine to the table, and then whisked off the white cloth like a magician, revealing it to Robin with a note of self-satisfaction. As she squinted to read the label, I thought she was as cute as a button with her sassy glasses and chic bob.

After Robin nodded her approval, the waiter put on an extravagant show of uncorking the bottle, sending the ladies into a frenzy of expectation. He poured a teensy amount into Robin's glass, which struck me as a little chintzy. I was on the verge of calling him out on it when I realized it was all part of the pageantry.

144

We watched anxiously as Robin swirled the wine, sniffing it, and then finally, sipped. Lenny, Desi, and I leaned in with anticipation. The waiter dude held his breathe.

"It's exquisite," Robin pronounced.

A wave of perspiration broke out on my forehead.

I grabbed another piece of bread. Devoured it like a hungry koi. What was the point? Things were going badly.

Lenny glanced my way. "How's Gertrude, Ricky?"

Desi and Robin whipped their heads in my direction. "Who's Gertrude?" Desi asked.

"Gertrude is my cat. I call her Gerty."

"You have a cat?" Robin asked, interested. "What color is she?"

"She's orange, with white feet. Green eyes."

"She sounds beautiful," Robin said. "Do you have a picture?"

I reached for my phone. Found a flattering picture of Gerty in her sun patch. I thought her eyes looked especially fetching. "Here she is."

Robin took my phone, beaming. "She's got ears just like Buford." She retrieved hers from her purse. "He's black. Remember you saw him at Desi and Lenny's? He's a little skittish, but so sweet."

As Robin introduced me to a digital folder of Buford's glamour shots, Lenny quipped, "The cat ate a hole clean through my recliner."

Robin defended Buford's honor. "He was only trying to hide. He's not comfortable in Shady Gully yet. And I couldn't leave my baby at home. I'd worry myself sick." I admired the delight in her wide eyes, and the easy smile on her lips. Yes, this woman definitely rocked my boat.

"I understand exactly how you feel," I told her as I swigged the bougie wine with legs, texture, and finish. "Gerty hasn't been herself today. I don't know if it's something she ate or…if she just isn't happy."

Soon Robin and I fell into a riveting discussion about Buford and Gerty—and the night was off and running.

Chapter Fifteen

Like A Roll Of Toilet Paper
Wolfheart

The sounds of discord kept me in my garden well past dark. While I welcomed the time among my treasured foliage, the antagonism between Meadow and Bella shredded my already ragged heart. As pieces of their quarrel drifted through the opened windows on this breezy night, it saddened me that the past had come to spew its venom on our present.

"Mother, you need to let it go. It's been years—" The *mother* was Bella's jab to the chin.

"Almost twenty-three, to be exact. Trust me, I know." Meadow's uppercut.

Although I could only hear their voices, I imagined them circling each other, Bella flashing her blue eyes defiantly against her mother's green ones.

I directed my gaze toward the light of the full moon, as one of Peony's beloved strays sprawled on the edge of the garden. The dog marked me with his sorrowful brown eyes, as if the hurtful words pained him as well.

While exiled from the house, I trolled the stems and leaves in my garden, inspecting them for insects threatening the fruit, and pruning around several lifeless blossoms. The sheriff had been impressed with my abundant harvest, but he couldn't conceive of the amount of watchfulness, and the never-ending fostering it took to maintain.

Like a child, I thought, a garden was to be nurtured and cultivated.

"I'm tired of hiding. Hanging my head. Being ashamed." The breeze carried Bella's unsteady voice, thick with tears. "I'm fine with who I am, even if you aren't."

"I'm fine with who you are, Bella, and I *love* who you are." Meadow sounded weary. "None of this is your fault."

"It's not yours either. You should hold your head high."

"I'll never be able to do that. I'm defined by what happened."

And there it was, I thought. The impasse. Young people were so bold, everything clear cut, black and white, while adults held too tightly to the angst of their pasts, clinging to their sorrow like a favorite blanket, instead of casting it away.

As a plaintive howl resonated along the creek, my heart skipped. I scanned the tree line, hoping to catch a glimpse of the broken-hearted beast, but the wolf's lament was only to be heard tonight. His lyrical cry just a reminder that he was there, and we weren't alone.

The mosquito screen clacked against the door frame, indicating that either Bella or Meadow had retreated to the front porch. Meadow held a mug of tea, spying the night sky. When she flicked her gaze in my direction, I meandered to the house.

"Thanks." I took the mug into my hands.

"It's vanilla and lemon grass."

I lowered my aching body into a rocking chair I'd broken in like an old friend. "I'd ask who won, but it seems it was a draw. As usual."

"Doesn't she realize what it will do to me? I can't relive it again. All the shame, the talk, the looks—"

"Most of the town already knows. It was a long time ago."

"Yes, I know, and I don't want to go back."

"Would you call what you're doing now moving forward? Meadow, love, you've been at a standstill for years. Maybe holding your head up, like Bella says, would help."

"I blame Desi's kid. Luke. He stirred it all up, wanting Bella to talk to him."

I considered my words carefully. "That's probably true. But Bella is not one to sit back. She's passionate. She's wants to embrace life. To experience what's beyond the creek. This was inevitable."

"Why?" she demanded in frustration. "Why won't everyone just let me be?"

"It's not just about you anymore." Although her anguish pained me, I pressed on. "Meadow, do you really want Bella to hide out on the creek her whole life? Is that seriously what you want for her?"

Tears slid silently down her cheek. "Dolly is going to fight ugly. She'll lie about me. She'll make it sound like I seduced Mitch."

"You were fourteen, Meadow. He was the guidance counselor at school. Nothing Dolly says—"

"She'll lie. You know she lies all the time."

"I do. But the facts speak for themselves. I honestly think—even though it will open old wounds for you—confronting it…addressing it…after all these years, will liberate you. And maybe even Dolly."

"What? Who cares about her?"

"Put yourself in her place."

"No."

"For a woman obsessed with status and appearances, it must have been humbling to lose it all in such grand fashion. Her reputation. Her husband. Her *home*. Can you imagine trashing your own dream home because you can't stand the thought of someone else living in it?"

"You're talking about Desi's house?"

I nodded. "As soon as they signed on the dotted line, Dolly neglected the place, disrespected it, and by the time the closing came, and Desi and Lenny finally turned the key, Dolly had diminished it."

"I don't feel sorry for her. She could have reached out. She could have—"

"What? Helped you raise the baby?"

"No. Never." Meadow fidgeted, drumming her fingers along her jeans.

I sighed. "She looked like she'd seen a ghost when she saw Bella at the audition."

"Yeah well. That's too bad. Sorry our presence is inconvenient for her." Meadow added bitterly, "She can't just banish us because we're a painful reminder."

"I agree, and that's my point. Own your place in Shady Gully, Meadow. And let your daughter do the same."

"Bella," she breathed, the word heavy with affection. "She's been asking if I know where he is, where he ran off to."

I snorted. "God only knows. I wish I'd found him."

"It was probably better you hadn't."

"What are you implying?" I rocked in my chair while Meadow jiggled her fingers. "I'm sure he's long gone now."

"Yep. And even if you had filed charges, it's too late to do anything now."

I stretched my gaze in the direction of the creek, keeping my face blank.

After a beat, Meadow asked softly, "Did you hear the wolf crying to the full moon earlier?"

Her poignant question extended our melancholy, and as the silence lengthened, we nursed our memories and grief. Finally, I said, "You remember the water and food we sent home with Fireman the other night?"

"Yes. For his granny?"

"Supposedly." I sighed. "The sheriff, or the dogs, found it in the woods not far from here." I didn't want to alarm her, so I kept my suspicions to myself. "You and Bella be mindful about the gun. Just in case."

I'd held all the cards in the beginning, when Megan, the beautiful darling of wealth and privilege, couldn't get enough of me. Our pairing, for lack of a better term, developed authentically. I supplied her and her friends with weed, while she provided me with amusement.

Ours was a business arrangement that lifted her status among the popular kids, and lined my pockets with money. My growing bank account motivated me to stay in school, and with only a year left until graduation, Peony's delight was palpable.

Admittedly, I basked in Megan's blue-eyed adoration, and welcomed the murmurs of outrage among the suitable, proper folk. Supposedly, Principal Jethro had expressed his concern to her parents, telling them how their angelic daughter was cavorting with the depraved boy from across the creek. Megan and I had laughed about that as we got high one afternoon at Cicada Stadium. And then I'd shown her just how depraved I could be...

When our paths crossed during school, she embraced her part as the fearful innocent, while I refined my reputation as the no-account loser from the across the creek. The difference was it was a role for her, and for me—it was the truth.

Over time, the cards in the game shifted. Megan wanted more and more product, and paid me less and less, if at all. "No problem," I'd scowl at her, letting her drag me off to the woods, where my supply and demand worries faded with each tantalizing kiss.

The day of reckoning always came though, and I'd find myself scrambling for product, sometimes forced to drive an hour and a half into Belle Maison, where I'd troll the back lanes for whatever she wanted. And pay double for it.

One time when Megan wanted to slip the girls at her hay ride a party gift, I'd found a source in Toulouse who bagged product in tiny little gram bags. I'd been thinking about how I could pick up some colorful stickers at Walmart, and make them look festive, when one of my tires blew and I landed in a ditch along the back roads of Toulouse.

I'd stuffed my baggies into my windbreaker, trekking through the woods in blinding rain. Eventually, the moon led me to the highway, where I hitchhiked a mile before a trucker picked me up. Fortunately, rather than knife me, he dropped me at a gas station where I called Axe.

Axe and Peony were married by this time, and she was pregnant with Meadow. Axe hadn't been happy leaving his warm bed in his cozy shanty to come to my rescue. He gave me a big lecture on the way back to the creek. Encouraged me to do some soul searching and figure out what I wanted out of life. And then, toward the end of the lecture, he'd grown as stern as I'd ever seen him, and warned me that he wouldn't have *that* around when the baby came. We both knew what *that* was…and I felt properly shamed.

I got Megan her gift baggies though. And made it to Walmart for the stickers with bright colored stars.

And since I didn't want to disappoint Axe, I got creative and found a new square of land farther along the creek. Many a night, using only the light of the moon and the headlights on my truck for illumination, I tilled row after row after row. Determined to expand my harvest, and to please Megan, my enterprise bloomed.

One fall night, after a particularly naughty parking session in the cab of my truck, I reached over Megan's head and drew a heart on the foggy window.

Megan sat up, frowning as she pulled on her bra, and buttoned her blouse.

"What's the matter?" I growled. "You seem off tonight." I quickly wiped my hand through the heart.

"Nothing." She ran her fingers through her long blonde hair.

I longed to do that, but it seemed too intimate a gesture for our relationship. "Doesn't sound like nothing."

"Have you got anything? I'm kind of wound up." She slanted her blue-eyed gaze at me beneath her lashes.

"Just what I already gave you." I forced some gruffness into my tone.

"That's for after sixth hour tomorrow. I just need a little bump now."

I shrugged. Implied it was her problem. Cursed myself for not stashing extra in my truck.

"Do you know that guy, Taylor?" she asked. "Big, bulky jock. Number forty, I think."

I didn't. "What about him?"

She turned to the window, regarding the smudge. "He told me I was a tease today. In front of Judy and Lola." When she pivoted back to me, her eyes were full. "And he said the strangest thing. It was stupid. But kind of mean."

"What did he say?" My blood boiled. "Tell me, Megan."

"He said that I was like a roll of toilet paper. A little went a long way." She placed her fingers under her eyes, carefully blotting a smear of mascara. "What does that mean? I think it's mean. Don't you?"

After school the next day I found number forty. Although he was at least fifty pounds heavier than me, he was out of shape, and slow to react. "Hey Taylor," I said.

"Heyyyy," he wheeled. "Creek Freak. How ya—"

I punched him solidly on the chin. As he doubled over in pain, I said, "There's an old Apache saying that goes like this, *it's better to have less thunder in the mouth and more lightning in the hand.*"

As he tried to stand, I threw an upper cut straight to his nose. Blood spewed. "Stay away from Megan."

News traveled fast at Shady Gully High and I was suspended by the afternoon. Although I'd upset Peony, and disappointed Axe, it had been worth it. Megan smiled easily, fawning over me anew…especially when she took me into the woods each day I was banned from school.

By then Megan held all the cards, and I never even noticed the transition in the game. Only that my heart flipped at the sight of her, and she was in my thoughts even when we were apart. Even the sound of her name caused a jump in my spirit.

Somewhere along the way, while I'd been entertaining fantasies of a life together, I'd missed the change in her. While I'd softened, she'd become harder. So when she invited me to her big mansion on the hill for a party, I said yes.

Madhawk made it to Osprey just before dark.

He slowly studied the houses on the lake, determining which were occupied, and which were what the wealthy called, "summer houses." Pretty straightforward, especially when it was garbage day at Lake Osprey.

Once the old, retired folks rolled their red garbage cans to the curb at dusk, Madhawk set his sights on a hoity toity house—without a red can. Easy peasy.

When night fell over the lake, Madhawk quietly shuffled to the storage shed in the carport. He found it locked, but the bolt was flimsy, so he used the light of the moon to search for a rock big enough to do the job.

He grunted with satisfaction when he found a cluster of dried concrete crumbling along the driveway. Raising it high over his head, he swung at the deadbolt, thrilled when it gave way, revealing a shed full of goodies.

"Door prizes," Madhawk chuckled to himself.

Beyond the usual yard equipment, like a tiller and a lawn mower, he found a couple of battery-operated lanterns and a crowbar. "Yesiree. I must be living right."

He panted as he climbed the two flights of steps to the house.

While his pain had eased thanks to the squirt's fruitful trip to Wolf-heart's place, he needed good lighting to properly tend to his wounds. And he needed a bath, a soft bed, and a good night's sleep.

He winced as he pried open a window with the crowbar, and then rejoiced when no alarm rang in his ears. Rich people were so stupid, he thought. You'd think with all their money they'd have better security.

He climbed through the window, quickly shutting all the curtains and blinds in the house. He used the flashlight the squirt had swiped to set out the lanterns he'd found in the shed.

Light bloomed in the house. "Well, well."

The place was ritzy. Big, comfortable chairs. A flat screen TV. And art. Lots of art. Paintings with thick ornate frames in every room. Madhawk traipsed his muddy boots through the bedroom, straight to the master bath. "Ohhhh," he groaned at the sight of the giant tub. And a shower as well. Heck, he might take one of both.

But first, he returned to the kitchen with the sunny, yellow walls and the granite countertop. And the sub-zero fridge. Madhawk opened the double doors, groaning at the sight of the stocked fridge. Milk, beer, eggs, and hot dogs!

Madhawk opened an expensive bottle of beer, then nuked a couple of dogs in the microwave. He scarfed them down as he walked around the house, browsing the paintings like a swanky art connoisseur.

He stopped, pausing at one in particular.

Hung over the fireplace, in a place of honor, something about the portrait of a group of kids at a bonfire seemed familiar. Especially the two young girls highlighted in the festivities. "Hmmm."

Madhawk quickly lost interest in the art, tracking back into the kitchen, where he scrounged through the freezer until he found a nice steak. After he tossed it in the sink to thaw, he grabbed another beer, and headed to the master suite. This time he noted the blue walls, the soft bed, and the fluffy, over-sized pillows.

"Beautiful," he muttered, anticipating the night ahead.

But then, as he thought of the one thing that would elevate this luxury, he grew annoyed with the squirt for failing his mission.

"You cut the wrong plant, dummy." He'd cursed at what the squirt had cut from Wolfheart's garden.

"I did not. Maybe you just can't draw right."

"Lose the attitude, smarty pants. Or you'll wake up with this on your neck." Madhawk had pulled his blade so quickly, the kid had melted into a puddle of snot and blubbering tears.

Just for fun, Madhawk had added, "And it will already be slick with your granny's blood."

Sated after a good, hot meal, Madhawk twisted the hot water faucet on the tub as far as it would go. He gingerly stripped off his dirty clothes, and took in his bruised and battered body. He stank of grime, blood, and infection.

He found a big, soft towel in the cabinet, and then slowly lowered himself into the hot bath water. After another greedy pull from the beer, he rested his neck on the mounted pillow in the tub.

Despite the squirt's incompetence, it was turning out to be a nice night. And after a good night's rest, he had plans to express his disappointment in Wolfheart's product. He'd leave the kind of fiery review that would surely get Wolfheart's attention.

Chapter Sixteen

A Stroll Down Hummingbird Trail
Luke

Iused my key to let myself into my parents' house, juggling the coffee and pastries I'd picked up from the Cozy Corner. The orange-yellow sunrise burst spectacularly through the kitchen windows as I padded down the hallway toward the bedroom.

The closer I got, the louder the laughter. They were all piled on the bed like a pack of dogs, including Ginger and Mary Ann, the actual dogs. Dad, still in his pajamas, his thinning hair twirled to an unruly tip atop his head, wore his reading glasses as he perused the newspaper.

Micah tapped on her phone, leaning sleepily against Dad's shoulder, while Mama sipped coffee from her purple and gold LSU mug. Her fire-engine red glasses matched her bright flowery robe, and her spikey hair looked trendy rather than unruly.

At the foot of the bed, mesmerizing them all, was Petey. Shirtless, he spun what was surely an embellished tale from the hills of Kentucky. Despite my recent impatience with him, I couldn't help smiling at his exaggerated story.

His boyish dimples and tussled hair gave him the look of a mischievous teenager, while his muscular, sinewy build provided him the magnetism that made women swoon. My brother commanded an audience regardless of the narrative, just as women adored him even after he broke their hearts.

It would be easy to be jealous of Petey. But it was impossible to do anything but love him. Along with the rest of my family, I laughed at his slap stick antics, made funnier by his *Christmas Vacation* pajama bottoms.

"Hey big bro," he grabbed the box in my hands. "Are those bear claws?"

"I want one," Micah whined. "With a lot of icing."

I handed my sister a napkin and a pastry. "Were y'all having a party without me?"

Mama patted the edge of the bed. "Honey, you are the party. Come sit by me."

"I don't think there's room, Mom." I frowned, weighing out the benefits of shaking things up. "But since we're all here, who's going to tell me how Bella factors into the Dolly scandal?"

For once, Micah had nothing to say.

"You've got to be kidding," I said, incredulous. "*You* know?"

My sister slowly chewed the bear claw while considering her response.

"Geez," I scoffed. "Am I the only goofus in Shady Gully?"

"Of course not," Petey selected another pastry. "There are plenty of goofuses in Shady Gully. You're just the only one who hasn't put two and two together."

Dad gave Petey a stern look. "Or maybe, he's just not that interested in gossip."

Petey snorted. "Well, he seems to be interested now, doesn't he?"

Micah dabbed her mouth with her napkin. "I don't know anything for sure. Bella's never said anything to me. But…"

I gave her a pointed look.

"Luke," she rolled her eyes. "You're so dense. It obviously has something to do with Dolly's husband, who's old like mom and dad. The rumor is he high-tailed it out of town after getting a student pregnant."

"A very young student," Petey chipped in.

My mind raced, braking to a hard stop when the realization hit me. I sat next to my mother, ignoring the ominous creak in the bedsprings.

Petey said, "Why do you think Jesse and Dolly pitched such a fit when Bella sang in church?"

Mom speculated. "That would have happened regardless."

156

Dad folded his newspaper. "Mitch was a guidance counselor, which makes the whole thing even more sordid. He was a person of authority. Someone the students were supposed to be able to trust." He side-eyed Micah. "And we weren't always old."

Mom rubbed my shoulder. "Mitch was around twenty-four, twenty-five, I think. And Meadow…about fourteen. It's been so long ago."

I held my breath as Petey joined us on the bed. When it didn't collapse, I asked, "Is he in jail?"

"He took off shortly after he and Dolly sold us this house," Dad said.

Mom harrumphed, momentarily drawn to the memory of an old grievance.

"As far as I know," Dad continued. "He hasn't been seen since. The family didn't press charges. They wanted to keep it quiet."

Mom arched an eyebrow. "I don't know about that. Once DNA became a thing, Brad told me he was considering approaching Mitch's family about giving him a DNA sample."

"Really?" Dad cast his eyes on her.

"…but I don't know if he ever did, or if anything could even be done with that. And anyway, Mitch's family have all moved since, so…"

"Well, the statute of limitations ran out." Dad shrugged. "So, it's a moot point."

Micah scoffed in distaste. "What a sicko. That's just gross."

Mom regarded me. "Why don't you ask Bella about it?"

"I did. And it didn't go well."

"What? You blew it already?" Petey shook his head. "Maybe Micah can talk to her."

Annoyed, Micah stood huffily, showering Dad's newspaper with pastry crumbs. "I can't talk to her. I have a bunch to do today."

She glanced at me on her way out. "But she's cleaning at the school today if you want to beg her forgiveness."

Mom nodded enthusiastically. "That's a great idea. I'll use the leftover meatloaf to make sandwiches. I'll pack y'all a sweet lunch."

Dad stood, swiping crumbs off his pajamas and newspaper. "Don't give them all the meatloaf."

"Or," Petey presented another option. "You could come to the lake with me later. Aunt Robin and Violet are running errands today, but once they get settled in tonight, we're going to rent a boat for tomorrow." He grinned, "I promised Violet I'd get her up on skis."

I bit back a smirk. "I bet."

Mom and I traded amused looks.

I noticed a flurry of activity as I drove past the substation. If not for the igloo packed with meatloaf sandwiches, sodas, and Popsicles, I'd have stopped. Perhaps offered my assistance. Or at the very least, asked what was going on.

I tracked the sheriff's grimace as he tossed a shovel and other assorted hand tools into the back of his truck. When I waved, he ignored me as usual.

Determined to make amends with Bella, I resisted the temptation to stop, and continued straight toward Shady Gully High School. I rehearsed my apology as I drove.

Shocked to find mine the only car in the parking lot, I wondered fleetingly if Micah's disapproval of my dating Bella would merit a hoax.

After dawdling in the parking lot for several moments, I worked up the nerve to walk to the home economics building. I discovered it vacant, along with the gymnasium, which wasn't unusual since school was out for the summer.

I then padded to the faculty offices, and found Bella bathed in fluorescent light, busily mopping the floors in the lobby. She wore tennis shoes and green scrubs, and swayed gracefully along with the music spilling from her earbuds. Unaware of my presence, she seemed totally absorbed in the melody. While I didn't want to startle her, I couldn't draw my gaze away from her uninhibited movements.

The jaunty angle of her chin as the chorus picked up.

The dark, wavy strand of hair that had escaped the clip at the nape of her neck.

The moist line of perspiration along—

"Luke!" Bella ripped off the earbuds. Her chest rose and fell with a cocktail of fright and outrage. "What are you doing here? You scared me!"

"I'm sorry." Contrite, I held my hands up in apology. "I didn't mean to startle you." I stopped, reading her expression.

"Are you alone?"

"Yeah," I answered. "How'd you even get here? There wasn't a single car in the parking lot."

"Good." A slight grin tugged at her lips. "Come with me." Bella took my hand and led me down the office corridor. We passed the teacher's lounge, the principal's office, and the faculty restrooms. "This way." She used a key tied on a chain around her neck to unlock the door to the secretary's office.

"What are we doing?" My heart raced for various reasons, specifically the sense of adventure I read on Bella's face. "Are we going to get in trouble?"

When she wheeled, I nearly crashed into her. "Luke," she glinted. "I've never known anybody like you in my life."

My throat caught, and I resisted the urge to lower my lips to hers.

She giggled. "You're such a rule follower. Don't you think it would be fun to get in trouble every once in a while? Have you even been in trouble? Like, when you were a kid, did you steal a cookie or anything?"

"A couple of times." I forced some lightness into my voice, although my mind raced with with what getting-into-trouble scenarios with Bella would look like.

But she'd moved away again and rifled through a shelf behind the secretary's desk. "This is it." She hurriedly flipped through the pages in a yearbook. "You asked." She lobbed it into my hands and pointed. "Meet my dad."

I looked at the handsome face of—by all accounts—a very horrible man. Clearly Bella inherited his enchanting blue eyes, and probably his boldness. Mitch's self-assured grin suggested a cockiness built upon entitlement. His was a mug that had rarely been told no.

With rising anger, I looked up from the yearbook, and was surprised to see an eager smile on Bella's face.

"He's handsome, don't you think?"

"Well, I…" I glanced at the picture again, struggling for the right thing to say. "There's the sheriff," I pointed out. "And Mom and Dad."

"Yep. They're all there. Your Aunt Robin, too. Even Dolly." She grew impatient. "But what about him? You wanted to know about him, so what do you think?"

"I don't know, Bella. What do you want me to say?"

She looked at me in confusion.

"I just learned what happened. My family told me. And I hate what he did to your mom. But he's your dad, so I—"

"It's okay," she shrugged. "It was just cool to see all the pictures. There's one of him in his jersey. And another when he scored a touchdown." She flipped pages. "And there he is with all the girls. I think he was popular."

"Seems to be," I said. "Probably very personable. Like you." Despite the bizarre tone of the discussion, my observations brought another smile to Bella's face.

"I took a bunch of pictures with my phone so I can look at them later. Mama would kill me if she knew." Bella checked her watch. "Crap. Her mail route is almost done. She's going to pick me up soon." She put the yearbook back in its spot, and quickly scanned the office.

When we made it back to the lobby, I said hesitantly. "I'm glad you aren't mad at me."

"I was never mad at you. I was just mad."

I asked, "Do you want to go on a picnic? I know it's getting late, but—"

"A picnic?"

"I'm serious. I want to show you something. And Mom made us food."

She regarded me with bemusement.

"Come on," I pushed. "Call your mom. Tell her I'll bring you home."

Bella grinned as she handed me the mop. "Don't forget the corners. Principal Jethro inspects them."

I'd never been a fan of meat loaf sandwiches—even Mom's—but they tasted better sitting on a candlelit blanket next to Bella.

"Your mom is a great cook," Bella said as she finished her sandwich. "Now it's Popsicle time." She grinned as she removed her hair clip, and did that thing with her fingers to shake it free. "Let me guess your color."

I couldn't think straight. Between the hair and the mischievous grin and the incredible way she wore scrubs. "My color?"

"We've got a blue one, a red one, a green one, and a purple." She frowned. "Sorry, there aren't any white ones. We'll have to go with your second favorite flavor."

As we both sat Indian style, I leaned closer, bumping my knee against hers. "That didn't sound like a compliment. Am I as boring as white? Really?"

"No, you're not boring. You're clear. Transparent. Pure." Bella deliberated. "In lieu of a white, I'm going to say you're a blue."

I leaned back, considering her serious expression. I loved the way Bella brought enthusiasm to the most mundane conversations, which made me wonder about the passion she'd bring to other activities.

"Blue. Because it means loyal. Strong. And trustworthy. Yes, you're definitely a blue."

"You're very good with words." I relaxed my knee against hers. "Like the way you know what names mean. Axe, for example. Your papaw. What did you tell me it meant?"

"Father of peace." She grinned as she selected a red Popsicle. "Ask me another one."

"Uh, how about Quietdove? That's always intrigued me."

"Quiet means peace as well. And stillness. Calm. Dove means delicate and refined." Her lips stained redder with every lick of the Popsicle. "Knowing him like I do, I think that fits him perfectly."

"And Bella?" I moved closer to her.

Tickled, she tossed her head back in laughter. "Beautiful, of course."

"I concur." I tapped my blue Popsicle against her red one.

Bella leaned back, studying the half-moon as it wrestled with the clouds in the sky. "I wanted to tell you about my dad, but I had to talk to Mama first. She didn't want to have it all dredged up again. I understand that, but…"

"But what?"

"I guess I'm weird, but I'd like to meet him one day. I think about him a lot."

"I think that's normal, but that would probably devastate your mom."

Bella twiddled with the red stained Popsicle stick. "I know. And I've hurt her by wanting to go public. Wanting to tell you. Trying out at church. Gosh, speaking of that, I'm nervous about singing Sunday. I hope people aren't mean."

"I hope so too. It might be rough at first, like when you tried out, but people will get used to it. Even Dolly."

"I don't think so. I'm sure she'll go to Jesse's church to avoid seeing me. I can't believe it's caused such a ruckus. I mean, I thought most people in town knew about what happened to Mom, but she said they didn't."

I thought of myself, who'd been totally clueless, and what Dad said about gossip. "It's probably half and half."

Bella seemed to accept that. "I don't want to hurt her. She's already been victimized, but I'm tired of being ashamed. And feeling forced to hide away on the creek just to prove my loyalty to Mom, and to make life easier for Dolly and her family."

I nodded in agreement. "Shining a light on the sin might be the first step to recovery." I rolled my eyes. "Geez, now I sound like my brother."

"Yeah, that was pretty deep." Bella eyed me curiously. "What did you want to show me anyway?"

Encouraged by her interest, I blew out the candles and gathered the trash from the picnic. "Let's put this in the car." I grabbed my flashlight. "And then let's take a stroll down Hummingbird Trail."

While Bella and I meandered along the notorious make-out trail, I tried to work up the courage to hold her hand. As I grew increasingly frustrated by my awkwardness, Bella lightly brushed her fingers against mine.

With a clumsy desperation that caused my heart to skip, I firmly clasped her hand, marveling at how her fingers nested perfectly into mine.

"So?" She pressed, "What were you going to show me?"

I stopped, waving my free hand about like a magician. "This. All of it. One day, it's going to be the Shady Gully Recreation Center. Or," I squeezed her hand. "Maybe you could come up with a better name."

"What happens at this recreation center? And where will all the lovers go?"

The way she said *lover* sent a flutter through me. "Well, I don't know. But people can fall in love here, and even get married." I pointed. "You see over there? On top of that hill? I'm picturing floor-to-ceiling glass windows overlooking the woods. It would make a great place for weddings and receptions. And then over there—" I drew her attention to the large, flat pad of ground that was once a baseball field "—there we can build a cool building with pool tables, and ping-pong tables—"

"I like ping-pong!"

"And we can set up badminton and tennis courts over there." I scanned the land next to a long-forgotten pond. "We can clean up around that pond, and make it beautiful again. Heck, we could stock it, and rent fishing poles for kids to fish."

"You've thought a lot about this, haven't you?" She leaned into me, tugging her arm around my waist.

I tried to focus on sharing my vision, but it was impossible to concentrate with her soft curves pressed against my body. "This place has ruined so many lives over the years, and I'd like to change its image. Turn it around and make it a fun place for families to gather, and yet, cool enough for teenagers to congregate. Anyway, if we can get the funding—"

"—and get incorporated," she finished with a laugh. "Yes! Let's do it!"

Driven by a rush of affection, I impulsively lowered my head, and kissed her lips. To my surprise, she kissed me back. What started out as a soft brushing of the lips quickly turned into something more urgent.

Distracted, I nearly missed the sound of leaves snapping, and the undeniable feeling of another's presence. We quickly pulled apart, and I positioned myself in front of Bella.

"It's okay," I told her, facing the intruder. Muscular, with vivid blue eyes, he stared at us with chilling intensity.

"He won't hurt us." To my horror, Bella moved closer to the animal.

163

"Bella, don't."

The wolf twitched his tail, and turned away from us as casually as he'd approached. "Hey," Bella said in a soothing tone. "Hey, wait. Are—are you hurt? Hania?"

The animal locked eyes with her, studying her closely. And then, with his ears pointed straight up, he let out a long, plaintive cry.

I'd never been so close to a wolf. And I'd certainly never heard one howl so sorrowfully. The striking creature gazed upon the half moon, and again wailed with what sounded like grief.

"Bella," I whispered. "We should move back."

"They don't really howl to the moon, you know." She calmly explained. "Sometimes they howl to their pack-mates out of affection. Or sometimes they're lost and trying to find their way home."

Bella and the exquisite animal continued to gaze upon one another, as if they were deep in a language too profound for words. And then, suddenly satisfied, the wolf turned and disappeared into the woods behind Cicada Stadium.

As I slowly regained my breath, I cast my eyes on Bella…whose eyes were bright with tears.

Chapter Seventeen

THE LONG, NASTY EVENING
Sheriff Rick

My deputies and I, along with a few dedicated volunteers, prodded through the swamp for hours. We sweated like pigs, fought off mosquitoes the size of hummingbirds, and painstakingly waded through the presumed sacred grounds.

I didn't see much sacred about it, frankly. But what did I know? The overgrown spot of swamp held no markers, had no boundaries, and if Quietdove hadn't begrudgingly muttered, "Here," I'd have slogged past the area, missing it entirely.

Littered with haphazard rocks, weeds, and ragged feathers, the mysterious section of land seemed completely untamed. And yet, Quietdove cautioned a volunteer when his hoe ventured too far in one direction. "Careful there."

"You see something I don't?" I asked.

"Yes," he responded flatly. "I do."

Excellent. An unpleasant evening all around. My disgruntled deputy and I plodded on.

It was well past dark when we finally called it quits, and the sense of relief was palpable as we loaded up and headed out of the creek. We'd made it as far as the jury-rigged bridge when Luke's gray car bounced over a few potholes ahead of us.

I flashed my headlights in irritation, as I was dog tired, hungry, and ready to get home to Gerty. Naturally, Luke stopped, eager to chat. When he emerged from his car with a big, loopy smile, I had half a mind to use my breathalyzer on him.

"Sheriff. What's up?"

"What do you mean, *what's up*? It's late. It's dark. And I ain't in the mood for your Dudley Do-Right routine." I squinted at him. "Have you been drinking? You look goofier than usual."

Despite being aggravated with me, Quietdove chuckled. But his expression hardened the moment he saw me glinting at him.

Luke meandered over to my truck, making a face when he noted my rumpled, dirty clothes. "Wow. You're—" He stopped, deciding to get to the point. "Did you learn something in Miss Peony's case?"

"No. Another dead end. Not that it's any of your business." I extended my arm to the side of my truck, pounded a few times to signal my team. "Let's go, men. One vehicle at a time." I added under my breath, "It's like a lottery, crossing this thing."

Luke and I watched as Quietdove slowly steered his deputy's truck across the bridge. The metal on the makeshift structure clanked like percussion cymbals with each rotation of the truck's tires. "Is he okay?" Luke asked of Quietdove. "He seems upset."

I didn't respond. Gestured to the next truck as Quietdove cleared the bridge.

"The connection out here is terrible," Luke frowned. "My calls have been dropping ever since I left Bella's."

While amused that the kid made a point of weaving his date with Bella into the conversation, I sparked with annoyance. "So happy you had a nice evening," I glowered. "But it's a heck of a time for all that talk about Mitch and Meadow to surface, don't you think? We've got enough division in the community as it is." I signaled the next truck forward.

"What? That's not my fault. I thought everybody knew anyway." He jabbed his phone. "Hello? Hello?"

"Not everybody knew. But I reckon they do now." I felt my phone vibrate. "Yeah? Hello?" As my call dropped, I urged Luke to the bridge. "You next. Let's go."

But as Luke finally got a connection, his expression turned serious. "What happened? Is everybody okay?" He raised his eyebrows at me, shouting into his phone. "Just sit tight. I'm with the sheriff now."

"What's wrong?"

"Someone broke into Aunt Robin's lake house." He pocketed his phone. "Follow me."

I didn't argue. As long as he led me to Robin.

As we tooled down the tree lined road toward Robin's house, my headlights illuminated the glistening night-time water of Lake Osprey. Under other circumstances, I'd enjoy gawking at the upscale, two-story mansions in the exclusive lake front subdivision. Most of the properties sported elaborate docks and boathouses bigger than my apartment. Massive party barges nuzzled along the water's edge, while expensive fishing boats nested underneath the carports. It appeared many of these folks were what they called *two boat families.*

Several of the homes had alarm systems, or at least signs advertising they did, but Robin's did not. As I parked behind Luke, bursts of red and blue lights told me the calvary had beaten me to the scene.

I threw a pair of booties and gloves at Luke. "If you're going in, dress appropriately. And for heaven's sake, don't touch anything. I had to promise my first-born child to your mom and dad to keep them from rushing out here."

He eyed me as he tugged on the gloves. "First born? Really? Not much of a gamble at your age, is there?"

I scoffed, incredulous over the sudden cockiness in the kid's manner. One date, and suddenly he was Bert Reynolds. "Careful, whippersnapper."

He gestured toward the coroner's van. "Why is he here?"

I waved at Dan, the parish coroner. "He lives around here. Probably curious." I ushered Luke up the stairs to the house with a warning. "Whatever you do, don't look him in the eyes. That man can talk a log straight into a fire."

The crime scene techs had managed to keep Robin, Sterling, Violet, and Petey contained in the living room, while they moved from room to room gathering evidence. The three youngers appeared in good condition, hardly fazed by the violation.

Robin's face, however, told a different story. Her eyes were puffy behind her chic glasses, and her demeanor suggested a weariness I hadn't seen before. "Ricky," she moved toward me.

"Sorry. I was out of cell range, or I'd have been here sooner."

Wrapping my arms around her seemed natural. It's what Luke did the second he saw her, and what Lenny would have done, if he were here.

"Thank God you're okay, Aunt Robin," Luke said. "I was across the creek, and the reception is spotty."

"I'm fine," she squeezed Luke's waist. "But this—" she indicated the house— "isn't okay."

The home smelled of badly cooked meat, and the grease splattered along the stove suggested a careless and hurried cook. A dirty plate, along with used silverware and a whiskey glass were piled in the sink. "We'll be able to get prints from that," I told Robin.

She nodded, glancing at the stripped walls. Most of her paintings, likely painted by Desi's Mom, had been removed from the sunny yellow walls, stomped on and defiled. Hateful and gratuitous, I thought angrily.

"Why?" Robin's sorrow was palpable. "Why not just steal them?" She pivoted when her brother, Max, entered from the master bedroom. "Did you solve the crime, baby brother?"

Although his face was grim, the knucklehead's focus was impressive. Perhaps Max would evolve into a fine deputy after all. "Sheriff. We found blood and other body fluids in the master. In the tub. On the bathroom floor." He hesitated. "And the bed."

"Good," I nodded. "We'll get some DNA. I saw a team scouting the perimeter of the house. Are they interviewing the neighbors?"

"Yes sir." He glanced at his watch. "As much as possible. We'll have better results in the morning."

"Good job, Max." Robin smiled approvingly.

"Good thing your shopping spree went long," Max teased her. "Y'all might have run into Goldilocks otherwise."

We all swiveled as Violet yawned. "Sorry."

"Why don't y'all head back to Shady Gully for the night?" I glanced at my watch. "Or what's left of it. The techs will finish up in a bit, and then tomorrow we'll do another sweep. Question the neighbors. See what else the light of day reveals. Y'all need a ride?"

"I can take everybody back to Mom and Dad's," offered Luke.

Robin rubbed Violet's arm affectionately. "Y'all go on ahead with Luke. I'm not ready to leave yet."

When Robin's gaze settled on me, I took my cue. "That's a good idea," I told Robin's kids. "I'll drop your mom off at Desi's later."

It didn't matter that it was close to three in the morning and I'd been awake for twenty-two hours straight. I sat in a lawn chair on the cedar deck of a two-story lake house, overlooking the moon's reflection off a beautiful lake. And Robin sat beside me, smacking adorably on a green apple taffy.

The activity surrounding the crime scene had dwindled to a low hum, as the techs packed evidence and forensic equipment into their vans. Even the curious neighbors along the lake had darkened their lights, no doubt sending up grateful prayers that their own homes had been spared.

"We're heading out, Sheriff," the lead tech said with exhaustion. "We'll touch base tomorrow with the results." After a glance at his watch, he clarified. "Or today."

I waved. "Keep your eyes peeled on the way out."

Just when I thought I'd have Robin to myself, I heard the heavy tread of boots chugging up the steps.

"Howdy Sheriff."

"Dan," I shook the hand he offered. "Awfully nice of you to come by." While I focused intensely on the glistening water of the lake, the chatty coroner sat down with a heavy huff.

Great.

"It's been a long night, eh? How've you been, Robin?" Dan raised a contented sigh as he sank farther into the lawn chair. "Aside from this business, of course." He made a show of sniffing the air. "Is that strawberry taffy I smell? Dang if I hadn't had one of those in ages."

I swallowed the exasperated grunt tickling my lips, and leaned on one haunch to dig the last taffy out of my pocket.

"Thank ya, kindly, Sheriff." After he smacked and sucked the strawberry clean off the candy, he asked Robin, "Does your son do any fishing when he's out here? I caught a nice mess of white perch last week."

Robin smiled politely, clearly running on fumes.

I decided to turn the conversation in a direction that might be useful. "Say, doc," I started. "I've been meaning to ask you a hypothetical question."

"Sure," he said eagerly. "What you got?"

"I was wondering if it's typical for someone to, well, for lack of a better term, come back from the dead?"

He squinted, reflecting on me a long moment, while Robin looked at me curiously.

"Take a person who's been injured, for example. Attacked. He's bloody, and in bad shape. You check his pulse, and you get nothing. Zip. How in the world would that rascal get up and walk away? Or drag himself off?"

"Oh, I see where you're going. Yeah. Yeah, right. Actually, Sheriff, I've heard of that. It's not uncommon. Could be a number of things. For instance, there's a thing called Lazarus syndrome, where you could mistake the living for the dead."

"That's horrible," Robin said, appalled.

"It happens," Dan leaned in. "Could be a pressure build up in the chest. Or adrenaline. Sometimes potassium levels are too high. Or it could be as simple as a faulty pulse check. Usually, even after CPR, it's prudent to wait ten minutes or so—just to make sure."

Robin gasped, just as Dan's phone buzzed.

"Well, shoot. I hate to run, but that's the Missus. She'll be worried."

"No problem, Dan," I patted his shoulder. "I appreciate the insight."

"Thank you for coming," Robin said pleasantly as the coroner trudged down the stairs.

Within minutes the echo of Dan's departing tires faded, giving the floor to the cicadas as they cheered on the darkness. Robin and I sat together, quietly, for a nice, long spell.

Eventually, a forced chuckle rattled from her throat. "I forgot how loud they were."

"They don't have cicadas in Kentucky?"

"I imagine so. I guess I don't stay up late enough to hear them."

Soft waves lapped against the retaining wall along Robin's house, the rhythm lulling us into a comfortable silence.

"I'm sorry this happened," I said eventually. "We're gonna get him."

"Or her. Goldilocks," she said lightly. "It makes me sad, is all. Everything in there, probably even Sunny's paintings, can be restored, replaced, cleaned, and fixed."

"It makes me angry. Not sad." My gaze landed on her. "And I suspect it's a he, not a she. And I have a suspicion who it is."

"Madhawk? Because of all the blood?"

"We'll know tomorrow. Or today." I studied the black waves brooding over the lake. "How's Buford?"

She chuckled, for real this time. "Better. It's a good thing I left him at Desi's until we got settled in here."

"He's probably set into another piece of Lenny's furniture by now."

"Maybe so." Robin's smile didn't quite reach her eyes.

When my phone rattled in my pocket, I reluctantly glimpsed the caller ID. "Come on," I griped aloud. "What else could go wrong tonight?" I swatted my phone with irritation. "Sheriff here."

I recognized the calm, deliberate voice on the other end. "Geez, you're kidding?" I glanced at Robin, incredulous. "Okay, I'm on my way."

"What's happened now?"

"That was Quietdove. There's a fire at Wolfheart's place."

"What? Is everybody okay?"

"Unclear. Quietdove said the EMTs and fire department are in route." I stood, offering her my hand. "I'll bring you to Desi's before I head out to the creek."

"No, that's out of your way. I'm coming with you."

"I don't think that's a good idea. You've been through enough tonight."

"I'm not going to be able to sleep no matter what," she said offhandedly, making her way down the steps.

"But what about Desi? I promised to deliver you safe and sound. She'll have my hide."

"Come on," she called over her shoulder. "I'll protect you from Desi."

We saw the flames as soon as we crossed the dilapidated bridge into the creek. Robin made a face, lifting herself to see over the rear window of my truck. "How will the fire trucks get over that thing?"

"Very carefully." I glanced behind me, assuring myself that the crossing was still in one piece. "Let's hope the Creek People are making a dent in the fire by now."

"Doesn't appear so." She raised her brows in speculation. "You do realize how important it is to incorporate now, don't you?"

"I'm beginning to see its advantages." After a flicker of satisfaction crossed her face, I added, "But things aren't normally like this, Robin. Shady Gully is a quiet town—"

"And reinforcements had to be called in from Belle Maison because of all the *noisy* goings on in your otherwise quiet town. And this all-nighter in Mayberry forced poor Max and Quietdove to alternate between scenes."

I kept my eyes on the road, feeling downright reprimanded.

"And when you have to wait for a fire truck to come from Belle Maison to put out a fire, well, that's simply unacceptable. That's living on a prayer."

"I wouldn't—" I stopped. Number one, there was no point in arguing because I wouldn't win, and number two, the smoke was thick against my window and I needed to focus.

"Slow down," she nagged.

I bit back a smile, sort of enjoying her feistiness. I reckon I wouldn't mind having a woman hounding me all the time, as long as that woman was Robin. When I clicked my blinker, she chuckled.

"What?"

"Nothing." Robin maintained her self-satisfied little grin until we reached Wolfheart's house.

When we parked, I took hold of her arm, preventing her from exiting.

"I'll be fine," she argued.

"Of course you will. You're an independent woman and all that jazz. But remember," I squeezed lightly. "I'm responsible for you. And Desi is scary."

The scene was sheer pandemonium. Half the creek had turned out, forming an old school volunteer-firefighting posse. A bucket passing line relayed water as fast as hoses filled them. Spry little tykes like young Fireman plucked the empty buckets as soon as they were discarded on the ground, running them quickly back to the hose for another round.

"His house is okay," muttered Robin. "It looks like it's—"

"His garden," I said regretfully. I felt a stab of empathy for Wolfheart, recalling the devotion and work he'd put into his passion. I searched the faces of the old school fire fighters, until I finally landed a glimpse of Wolfheart.

His face was covered in smut nearly as black as his hair, and his green eyes appeared flat and emotionless. When his line of vision intersected with mine, he looked away. Defeated. Wrung out.

"Oh Brad," Robin sprinted toward him, and he welcomed her in his arms. While I envied the easiness between them, I was glad he had an old friend to comfort him now.

A rugged young man, the one they called Redflyer, pointed in my direction. "Well, it's about time," he said sarcastically.

Before I could get my hackles raised, the scream of sirens punctuated his remark.

I quickly corralled the frenzied bucket carriers aside, especially the little ones, as the big, red fire truck slammed to an impressive stop.

We all watched as the professionals took over the scene, tossing massive hoses across their shoulders, and circling the flames with the intensity of soldiers.

"Cool, huh?" The kid appeared out of nowhere, gazing at the firefighters in awe. "I want to do that."

I squinted at Fireman. "Looks to me like you were doing just that."

Unaffected by the compliment, he dashed over to Bella, who sat on the steps of the porch next to her mother. I approached tentatively, because while Bella was quite personable, Meadow was not known for her friendliness.

Robin took a handful of blankets from the firetruck and wrapped them around Bella's and Meadow's shoulders. She offered one to Wolfheart, but he shrugged. "It's going to take more than that," he said with dead eyes.

"Wolfheart," I said in a somber voice. "I'm sorry. I mean that."

He regarded the flames in silence, watching as the firemen speared his beloved vegetables and herbs into slimy piles of roasted soot. "It could have been worse," he said hoarsely, glancing at Meadow and Bella, no doubt considering the human toll spared by the fire.

"The EMTs are here," I said as Patty's van, red and blue lights flashing, parked next to the firetruck. "I can have her take a quick look at the women."

"That's a good idea," Wolfheart nodded, aimlessly roving toward the patch of land he'd tended for years. The slush beneath his boots made a popping sound as it splattered against the legs of his pants.

Once I got Patty settled with Bella and Meadow, I asked Robin, "Will you keep an eye on them for a minute?"

"Of course." She eyed Wolfheart. "I'm worried about him though. We might have to get Desi here."

I stalked over to Wolfheart with renewed purpose. "Brad, tell me what happened? Did somebody try to break into the house? Did you hear anything? See anybody?"

He shook his head, "No. The smell of smoke woke me up. The sky was orange as soon as I opened my eyes." Our gazes drifted to the firemen as they lugged rakes over the smoldering debris. It seemed to me Wolfheart winced with each comb of the tool.

"It's a damn shame," I said, cutting a glance at Redflyer and his buddies, who lingered near Wolfheart.

After a long moment, Wolfheart speculated, "Madhawk? Maybe he hoped it would spread to the house?"

"Maybe. If so, he gets around for a dead man. Robin's place on Osprey was broken into last night. Or night before last." No sense even looking at my watch at this point.

"What? What happened?"

"Somebody enjoyed the hospitality of her lovely abode, and then showed their appreciation by trashing the place. The techs found blood, discarded bandages."

"You think it was Madhawk?"

"I don't know yet. Crazy times we're living in, for sure." I shook my head. "When I first heard about the fire in your garden, I halfway thought Jesse had been out here again."

"Again? When was Jesse out here?" Wolfheart exchanged a glance with Redflyer.

I blamed the long, nasty evening for the slip of my tongue. "Just speculating," I said vaguely, trying to backtrack. "You're not his favorite person. And he's worked up about Bella singing in church Sunday. You know what an oddball he is."

"Yeah," Brad said, his green eyes turning black as they zeroed in on mine.

Chapter Eighteen

TONY CHACHERE'S
Wolfheart

"*I* *halfway thought Jesse had been out here again.*"
The key word being *again*. The idea of that slimy worm lurking around my home, my garden, and my family, filled me with rage. While the sheriff went on, babbling about Bella singing and Jesse being an oddball, all I could think about was why the dogs hadn't barked.

I scanned the yard, half blinded by the beams of the fire department's lights. The brown mutt lay on his back, back right leg twitching as an EMT rubbed his belly. One of the other strays licked soot off his paws. I beckoned to him, and he hoofed over listlessly.

"What's wrong, boy?" I knelt, scratching him behind the ears. His breath smelled of steak, peppered with garlic, and Tony's Chachere's seasoning. "Did your paws get too hot?"

"Is he okay?" Patty asked, hobbling over with a roll of bandages in her hand. "A couple of the cats had some pad burns. This guy looks okay though." She handed me a handful of antibiotic packets. "A little dab will help. Put some socks on him."

When I laughed out loud everyone looked at me oddly. Bella walked over, looking concerned as she rested her hand on my shoulder. "Mamaw would get a kick out of socks on the dogs and cats."

My legs creaked as she pulled me to my feet. I held her close. "She'd probably want to sew special ones that accentuated their eyes."

Robin joined us, carrying a cat with bandages on its paws. "Full disclosure. Desi called, and I had to answer while I had service. I understand reception is spotty all over the creek."

"Reception is okay around most of the homes," Bella explained. "But the dead spot around the bridge has always been a problem."

Once Bella headed back to Meadow, I asked Robin, "Desi's not driving out here, is she?" I didn't bother looking at my watch. I knew the sun would rise in a few hours.

"I think I talked her down." She yawned. "You're safe for now."

"Why don't you go on back to Desi's. You must be tired."

"I'm worried about you. I know how much your garden means—meant—to you."

"I'll replant. And you'll repair." I eyed her. "The sheriff thinks it was Madhawk who tore your place up night before last."

"Someone did. They ate my food, slept in my bed, and destroyed Sunny's paintings. Or tried to. I'm hoping I can have most of them restored. Whoever did it was gone by the time we bought groceries and headed to the lake yesterday evening."

Sheriff Rick dawdled over, offering the cat in Robin's arms a friendly scratch beneath the chin. "I just got an earful from Redflyer." He appeared rueful.

"I tried to warn you, Sheriff," I shook my head. "You should have stayed away from the sacred grounds."

"This is a cluster, for sure." He peered at Robin. "Are you ready to head to Desi's? Get a little rest?"

Robin handed me the cat, and then squished it between us as she pulled me into a solid hug. "Desi and I will see you in the morning. Late morning."

"Hey Robin," I called out as Ricky opened the passenger door for her. "You use Tony's at your place?"

"Of course." She eyed me quizzically. "I may live in Kentucky now, but I know how to season food."

After Bella went upstairs to get some sleep, Meadow and I rocked side by side on the front porch. She'd made us both coffees, and generously spiked mine with extra cream and sugar.

"I needed this." I set my gaze on the upper bough of the sun as it peeped over the horizon. "Thanks."

Meadow exhaled loudly, tapping her fingernails restlessly against her cup. "I heard the sheriff tell Quietdove he thinks Jesse did this. Can you imagine? How dare he even come out here?"

"It's a free country. He can go wherever he wants."

"No, he can't. This is private property. Why are you defending him?"

"I don't think it was him."

"Oh, here we go," she fidgeted.

"Why don't you just go ahead and light one up?"

"What? I don't—"

"—smoke? Yeah, you do, and I don't even care right now. I just need you to stop squirming. I can't enjoy my coffee."

She pulled a cigarette from somewhere inside her shirt, and lit it with the practiced skill of a seasoned smoker.

"Although I don't know why you'd want to inhale any more smoke now."

When she shot me a pointed glare, I refrained from further nagging. "Jesse isn't familiar with the creek," I said finally. "He would have floundered around in the dark, alerting the dogs. I believe it was someone comfortable with life in the swamp."

"Who knows?" Meadow brooded. "It's all so muddled lately. Especially now that the cops dug up the sacred burial ground."

"They didn't dig. They sifted. That's what I heard anyway." I was incensed as well, but it would do no good to encourage Meadow's resentment.

"That's semantics, Uncle. It doesn't matter anyway. Between the grounds and this," Meadow pointed to the garden with her cigarette. "There's going to be hell to pay. I don't think Bella should sing Sunday. Everything is too volatile now."

I glimpsed the orange ball as it finally erupted through the clouds. "You have a point. But I'll be there. I'll make sure she's okay."

"Right. Just like you did with Mama."

I sucked in a ragged breath.

"I'm sorry." Meadow blew a gust of smoke in the opposite direction. "I didn't mean that." She waved her hand toward a brown dog as he rambled up the steps of the porch. She scratched the scruff of his neck with affection. And then: "I had a dream. About the Spirit Warrior."

Another jolt ripped through me. How I'd prayed to see my sister and her beloved Spirit Warrior again, but it seemed their spirits had chosen to avoid me—even in a fugue state.

I didn't respond. Only gazed wearily upon the rising sun, vowing to remain patient for that gift, trusting that it would come in due time. But the polluted haze of smog from the destruction of my garden stained the sun, denying me any peace.

Eventually Meadow withdrew inside, no doubt finding my sullen expression too much to endure. Relieved to finally be alone, I lowered my hand to the dog's ears, inhaling the dust as his tail pounded it into a small tornado.

My fingers, blackened with soot, left smudges on his fur as I stroked him. When the mutt's sad eyes settled on mine, I wondered if he too craved a quiet, profound moment with another soul.

I removed my hand, cursing the sentimental fool I'd become.

Meadow was right. Things were hopeless. And perhaps they'd always been, and foolish dreamers like Bella and me just couldn't accept it.

Peony had been delighted to hear of my invitation to the bonfire at the big house with the swimming pool. She'd immediately sat me down at the kitchen table, wrapped a towel around my shoulders, and pulled out the shears.

"No," I argued, proud of the long, unruly locks that reinforced my menacing image. "I'm not trying to impress anybody." But of course, I had been, and as Peony cut my mane, and the tufts of thick, dark hair fell to the floor, I liked the change. I looked like one of them now.

"I look ridiculous." I snarled.

"Nonsense. You look handsome. And I'm tired of that shaggy mop hiding your beautiful bone structure." She scrunched her face into a smile so tight her eyes disappeared. "And your pretty green eyes. Nobody can ever see them with all that hair."

I scoffed, watching as she slid a storage box from under her sewing table. "Let's see if we can find something to show them off." She bit her upper lip in concentration, rifling through layers and layers of ragged material until her face softened. "Oh, this is beautiful. Don't you think?" She raised a swatch of emerald green fabric.

I smirked. "I guess. If you think seaweed is beautiful."

She ignored me, scrounging deeper into the tub of castaway material. "I don't have quite enough."

Shoot. "It looks like throw up anyway."

"But how about this blue? That would blend—" She whooped in delight. "Oh, and I love this gray. I know, we can make a patch-shirt."

"A what?"

She handed me a pair of scissors. "It will be perfect, Brad. We'll do squares. And I'll sew you the loveliest patch-shirt to wear with your jeans. Let me draw you a pattern." I moved closer, squinting at the precise squares she drew. "I'll pin. You cut. Are you ready?"

We spent the afternoon that way, merrily pinning and cutting squares, Peony chatting about party etiquette, and how it would be polite to bring flowers to the host. "I'll put a fresh batch of wildflowers together. My mums are starting to bloom now that it's fall, and I can trim some from the firecracker bush to make a bouquet. Won't that be nice?"

"Yes," I answered. Although I couldn't imagine myself presenting flowers at Megan's bonfire. "That sounds great." But Peony was happy, so I went along. "Listen," I said as an outraged squeal resounded from the small bedroom. "It sounds like the little creature from the swamp is awake."

Peony looked at her watch. "Goodness. The time flew. Go see to Meadow, would you?" She hopped up to prepare a bottle, her face flushing with contentment. "And Axe will be home soon. Hasn't this been the most wonderful day?"

"I'll go take care of the monster," I griped, skulking my way to the baby's room. Although I'd never admit it to my sister, I enjoyed holding the baby, and I found Meadow's big mouth amusing. She apparently had a lot to say, and cried in frustration because she couldn't properly express herself.

I slowly opened the door a crack. My niece stood in her crib, her coal black hair plastered to her head.

"Pssst." I teased. "Hey, monkey."

The grumbling stopped. Her eyes, which had been closed tight in exasperation, flew open. A squeal of joy wracked her body. When I dawdled too long, she became indignant, squeezing her fists into tight little balls, demanding that I hurry. I couldn't help but laugh.

As she pounded the railing of Axe's hand-made mahogany crib, I worried that the dowels he'd carefully measured to safety standards would shatter under her fury.

"What?" I laughed, picking her up. "Why are you mad?" But she wasn't mad any longer, as her little fingers tightly clutched my shoulder. She cooed in a ridiculous rhythm only she could understand, giggling the whole time I changed her diaper. We babbled nonsensically all the way back into the living room.

Axe, dressed in dirty coveralls, burst with pleasure as he took his baby daughter into his arms. "Look at you, girl. Brother got you all powdered up." He smooched Meadow until she dissolved in a full-fledged round of cackles.

I always appreciated the title of *brother*. Axe's thoughtful term of endearment was meant to assure me of my importance, and place, in the family. He danced around with Meadow in his arms, arching his brows at the outline of squares on the table. "Looks like the makings of mighty fine duds there."

I nodded. "The colors compliment my eyes."

"And that haircut." He whistled.

"It accentuates my bone structure."

"I'll say," he chuckled.

Over dinner, while I fed Meadow bits of roast beef and dollops of mashed potatoes, Axe told us about the work he was doing at a big house in Belle Maison. Peony laughed at all his corny jokes, and he told her he'd weed her flower garden on his day off.

Once Meadow was down for the night, Axe sat at the table with Peony and me, and together we cut dozens of perfect squares for my patch-shirt.

I knew something was off the moment I arrived at Megan's the night of the bonfire. For one thing, Taylor, who'd recently equated

Megan to a roll of toilet paper, rested his big, beefy arm along her shoulder. And she didn't seem to mind.

As he and several of his buddies gaped at me with contempt, I swallowed back a swell of panic. Megan finally detached herself from Taylor's side, but avoided my eyes as she moved to greet me. Inspired by the sheer beauty of Peony's prized blooms, I'd brought the flowers in a moment of weakness. When I offered them to Megan, she took them with a glint of amusement.

The bonfire lit up the back yard, and the crowd from school grew louder as beer traded hands. Megan flitted around the way hostesses do, attending to everyone's needs. Everyone's except mine. She seemed unaffected by my presence, and I found myself standing alone most of the time.

"You want a beer?" Lola, one of Megan's friends, sidled up to me.

"No, I'm good." I had no taste for the stuff.

"I like your haircut," Lola giggled, startling me as she ran her fingers through my hair. I bobbed uncomfortably, taken aback by her gesture.

"What's wrong, Wolfheart?" Taylor asked. "You don't like girls?"

All his jock friends slapped their thighs in hilarity. I scanned the party for Megan, relieved as she tottered over, carrying a plastic cup. Only she strutted straight past me, and planted herself next to Taylor.

"What did I miss?" She ducked her head into Taylor's chest. He whispered something into her ear, and she tossed her head back in delight. She suddenly seemed to remember I was there, pivoting in my direction. "Did you bring any weed?"

"No." *I brought flowers.*

"What's the point of you then, Wolfheart?" asked one of the jocks. "Why are you here?"

"Get a load of that haircut?" cackled another jock. "Who cut your hair anyway?"

Megan chuckled along with all the boys, and so did Lola, and Judy, Megan's friends.

As I strategized about how to make a dignified exit, Taylor's hot breath disorientated me as he goose-stepped in my face. "I'm digging that shirt, man. Where can I get one?" His beefy hand flicked my collar.

182

"I think he swings the other way," teased one of Taylor's posse.

Taylor tugged the seam of my patch-shirt. "I mean it. I want one." Another tug. "Where can I get one?" A hard yank, pulling my shoulder down a few inches. "I know. The salvation army!"

Uproarious laughter spread among Taylor's crew, as heat flooded my face.

When Taylor tugged on my patch-shirt again, I swung. Hard. My punch was so well timed, number forty's massive body twirled in a sloppy pirouette before he dropped to the ground.

Things turned ugly then. Clearly outnumbered, all I could do was fight until I couldn't anymore. They surrounded me, pinning my arms behind my back, and took turns slugging my face into mush. Unwilling to surrender, I roused my weak legs into action and kicked at everything that came within an inch of my body.

They laughed. Taunted. And then heartily cheered the one who grabbed my legs, dragging me to the dirt with a thump that knocked the breath from me. Someone sat on my legs then, and another doubled down on his hold of my arms, rendering me defenseless. I lay on the ground, immobile, gagging on the blood in my mouth. My vision narrowed as my eyes swelled with each new punch.

My body grew wet with my own blood and vomit. And still they pummeled me.

The high-pitched squeals of females rang out as I felt my ribs cave inside of me.

Just before I lost consciousness, I turned my head to avoid the sharp heel of a boot, and saw my sister's flowers scattered on the ground beneath the picnic table—ketchup and mustard soiling the vivid colors of her prized blooms.

Saint John's Hospital became my home for what seemed an eternity. Rigged on a suspension, with my leg buoyed awkwardly, I felt like a grotesque puppet on a string. I'd lost so many teeth, my diet consisted of liquid in an IV, until the glorious day I graduated to pudding.

My ribs were wrapped tight, and my face was a mass of stitches that tickled my eyes at night. When I could hobble, my sister walked me to the bathroom, and when I cried in agony from the commode, Axe held my hand, soothing me with his deep, loving words. "It's all right, brother. Just take your time."

Eventually my vision cleared, and my breathing became less labored, but when I strolled the hospital hallway in my gown, with Axe and Peony on either side for balance, the looks of pity were indisputable.

When I was finally able to go home, I'd never been so happy to see the baby swamp creature called Meadow. She regarded me with fascination, studying me with a melancholy unusual in a toddler. Sometimes she'd giggle. Other times she'd cry.

One day as I shuffled to the living room, I saw my sister repairing my patch-shirt. "Don't do that. I don't want to remember."

"But you must," Peony said in a thick voice.

"Why?" I cried angry tears that stung my swollen, stitched eyes.

"Because," my sister said with her usual grace. "You must always remember how brave you were for trying."

Unrestricted by incessant female nagging, Madhawk roamed his old house freely. He glided from room to room, soiling the floors with dirt, and smudging the refrigerator with the soot from his hands.

As the yellow crime scene tape flapped in the breeze outside, Madhawk felt safe knowing that the cops were either combing the sacred ground for clues, or the lake house for evidence...or putting fires out at Wolheart's.

He grunted with amusement as he rifled through the pantry, proud of himself for staying one step ahead of the clowns.

The fancy lake house had been a kick, but this was home. His home. He'd taken it years ago...just as he'd always taken what he wanted. Including Peony. Especially Peony. He'd set his sights on her as a young man, and when she'd rebuffed him, preferring instead the goody-goody Axe, Madhawk had begun to strategize.

He'd played the long game.

Now, as he reflected on his patience, he scrounged through the cabinets, finding a muddy glass. As he filled it from the faucet at the sink, the spigot gurgled a few times, bringing a smile to his lips.

Peony always pestered him about fixing the spigot, and once, she'd made the mistake of bringing Axe's memory up, touting his handyman skills and his all-around dependability.

She never made that mistake again.

As Madhawk continued to wander through the house, he noted the changes.

Bella and Meadow's room appeared larger now that it was free of Bella's music equipment. And even Meadow's side of the room was free of clutter since her books and magazines had been moved to Wolfheart's place.

People thought Bella was the dreamer, but Madhawk knew better. Meadow with all her fashion magazines and her romance novels. Madhawk suspected she still had fantasies about her Prince Charming coming back to Shady Gully and whisking her away to happily ever after.

His laughter echoed off the vacant walls. Now Wolfheart had to deal with all their junk. All their drama. Served him right.

For years, Madhawk spread the word about Axe's abilities, building up his work ethic in countless communities, referencing him here, there, and everywhere. And then, when the time was right, he'd set the trap. He'd tracked him. Hunted him. And on an old country road in Belle Maison, with only the light of the moon to do the deed, he'd taken him out of the picture with one glorious swipe.

Only then to have Wolfheart threaten his plans.

Wolfheart had been an angry young man when Madhawk reintroduced himself into Peony's life. The resentful little punk had actively conspired to keep Madhawk away, and his overprotectiveness had hindered his progress with Peony. For a long time, he and Wolfheart had circled each other, both fighting and clawing for Peony's attention.

Madhawk had moved slowly at the beginning, making the most of the time Wolfheart was out carousing, breaking the law, and causing his sister nothing but grief. While Peony fretted over her troubled, spiteful brother, Madhawk played the part of the good, supportive man. When Wolfheart finally moved out, settling into his own shack nestled in the swamp, Madhawk considered it a victory.

Although Wolfheart's influence lingered, and he continued to bring Peony food, garden supplies, and literature on herbs and healing, fate was on Madhawk's side.

Especially when Meadow got knocked up.

Quite the drama, as Madhawk recalled, and the timing couldn't have been better. He'd finally won Peony over when he'd offered to take her kid—and her kid's kid—to raise. What single woman could pass that up? Madhawk thought himself quite the catch. Especially when Peony's beloved brother was a worthless troublemaker.

As soon as Madhawk moved in, Peony had become beholden to him, and he'd easily been able to keep her in line. He'd run the house with a heavy hand, and when Peony got out of line, he'd discipline her before the defiance spread to Meadow and Bella.

For a time, Madhawk had almost been happy.

But then the Spirit Warrior came into their lives—and he was never happy again.

PART IV

Chapter Nineteen

HANIA
Luke

"I can't get the smoke out of my hair," Bella complained, sniffing the end of her ponytail with distaste.

I regarded her as she sat at my kitchen table, licking flyers, and then stuffing them into envelopes. Not only did she smell wonderful, but she looked especially fetching as she'd missed the tiniest speck of soot along her left temple.

"Thanks for helping me do this," I said, my fingers lingering as I lightly stroked the soot away.

"It's fun." She grinned beneath her lashes. "And I didn't have any cleaning jobs today, and Claire hasn't invited me to sub at the post office lately." She pushed a stack of envelopes to one side. "Remember to put the ones for the Creek People in this pile."

"Yes ma'am." When she seemed unfazed by my teasing, I asked, "Your mom didn't say much when she dropped you off this morning. How are she and your Uncle Wolfheart doing? Still upset, I imagine."

"They are. Especially Uncle Wolf. Mama's more upset about church this Sunday."

"Because you're singing?"

Bella nodded. "As if I'm not nervous enough."

I reached my hand across the table, concealing my delight as she returned the squeeze. "You have nothing to be nervous about, and you can count on my entire family being there."

"Good."

"They're like the navy seals, but twice as spirited."

She hopped up, taking our glasses to the kitchen. "I like your apartment. How is it living next to the sheriff?"

"It's okay. Especially since I'm his landlord, and he breaks the rules."

"No!" Bella refilled our glasses with coke. "What does he do?"

I joined her in the kitchen, peering outside the window. "Let's take a break, and I'll show you."

We carried our cokes as we strolled along the sidewalk of the duplex. The sky was overcast, which fortunately tempered the thickness of the late morning humidity. "Tell me, what do you see in all these windows?" I asked, pointing out the newest tenant's duplex.

"Not much."

"Well, what about this one?" As we turned the corner that made up the wall of the sheriff's living room, an orange cat glared at us from the sunny windowsill.

"Oh!" Bella shrieked enthusiastically, rousing the cat. "She's beautiful. And so huge." The cat blinked, sizing us up. Unimpressed.

"She?"

"Yes. Look."

I shrugged, bending to tap on the window as the cat scrutinized us. Clearly uninspired, the ginger feline yawned before hopping off the sill and slinking into the kitchen.

Bella appeared melancholy. "I like cats. We have several strays at Uncle Wolf's who followed us from Mamaw's. Chickens and dogs too."

"I saw them." I led her to a picnic table behind the duplex, perfectly positioned under the shade of a big hardwood tree. "I like that you're an animal lover." I wiped off the seat for her.

"I am." She narrowed her eyes, "And I *don't* like that you don't allow pets in your duplex."

I grinned, amused by her banter. Until I realized she wasn't joking. "I will reconsider that rule. ASAP."

"Good." She tipped her head in a feisty manner, drawing my attention to the soft lines of her throat.

"I had a dog once." I started. "Really he was my mom's. I remember him always being old, but I was crazy about him."

"What was his name?"

"Winston." When she looked perplexed, I teased, "What? That one got you stumped?"

"No. Its origin is British—I know that."

"My nana named him after Winston Churchill, so you're correct."

"See." Bella beamed triumphant. "But I need to research it more."

"Can I ask you something?" I blurted impulsively. "About our encounter the other night?"

"The kiss?" she said coyly. "Or the wolf?"

"Well, both actually. To tell you the truth, they both kind of scared me."

"Neither scared me."

A little incredulous, and a lot thrilled, my heart fluttered. "You called the wolf by a name." I waited, noting the change in her manner.

Finally, she said, "Yes. He reminded me—"

"Of what, Bella?"

She shook her head. "Nothing. The whole thing seems surreal now." She side-eyed me. "I'm not even sure he was real. Wasn't there a dream-like quality about him? Like he—"

"He was real, Bella. Trust me. He came pretty close, and he seemed unusually tame for a wolf."

She looked thoughtful, as if she were wrestling with a significant decision.

"Tell me," I pleaded. "Please."

"The shock of it—of seeing him—it brought back a terrible loss. He reminded me so much of the wolf pup my mamaw raised."

"Wolf pup? Are you serious?"

"Of course. Do you want to hear the story?"

"More than anything."

Before Bella began, she considered me. "Okay," she leaned in, becoming animated. "It all started late one night when a pack of wolves surrounded our house."

I shot her a look. "That doesn't sound like a Disney beginning."

She shushed me, deep in story-telling mode. "The dominant, high-ranking wolf in the pack was badly injured, and her packmates lurked in the brush at the edge of the woods just beyond our house. They howled for hours."

"What was wrong?"

Bella didn't respond, completely lost in her story. In her memories. "Uncle Wolf was there, and he and Mamaw kept vigil from the window, but the plaintive cries continued."

"That's terrible."

"It was hard to listen to, because something was obviously very wrong, and it put Madhawk on edge."

I waited, allowing Bella time to process her mixed memories. "With binoculars, Uncle Wolf could see that several of them were bloody, and limping, as if something had attacked the whole pack."

"Louisiana black bears? Eastern cougars? Or a pack of coyotes?"

"I don't know. It could've even been someone with a gun." She looked blankly into the distance, her recollections taking her farther away. "Their cries were heartbreaking. Full of misery. I was only ten or eleven at the time, but I'll never forget the pain and grief in their yowls."

"Why do you think they came?"

"If you could have known my mamaw, you'd understand. Strays of all kinds naturally gravitated toward her, especially vulnerable or wounded ones." She added wistfully, "Even needy humans stopped by to sit with her at times. Of course, she'd offer them herbal remedies, but what they really appreciated was her calm, steady manner. She was a true healer, and she had a gift for easing the spirit in those who were lost." Bella turned to me. "I'm convinced those battered wolves came that night to get her help."

"Her help with what? What happened?"

"As they came closer," she explained with a sense of wonder. "The wounded mama appeared, along with her newborn pup."

"Incredible." I couldn't help but smile at the inflection in Bella's tone.

"The cries and howls got to be too much for Madhawk though, and when he loaded his gun, Mamaw stopped him. She told him she'd handle it." Bella added with a note of pride. "And he backed down."

"Good for her."

"She and Uncle Wolf finally walked into the yard. Real slow like, real quiet. As soon as the talas saw them, they began whining and actively communicating with one another.

"Talas?"

"Wolves," Bella smiled. "Oh. Did I forget to tell you that's the name for—"

"—wolves. Got it." I smiled, falling in love with her more and more with each word translation.

"It went on forever it seemed. I remember Mama and I watching from the window while Uncle Wolf and Mamaw just stood in the yard, whispering to one another. Waiting."

"What was Madhawk doing?"

"Sitting in his chair with his gun across his lap." Her expression hardened. "Eventually, when the pack felt safe, they crept out of the shadows, fully revealing themselves. The mama tala coaxed her scrawny little pup along. He had small ears and a little rounded head. He was deaf and blind." She turned to me, offering an explanation. "All talas are when they're little.

"From the window, Mama and I could see Mamaw gesture to Uncle Wolf, signaling him to lower himself to the ground. The two of them sat there forever, just waiting and watching while the wounded wolf licked her pup. Grooming him, loving him."

"Telling him goodbye?" I asked.

"Yes," she answered thickly. "Finally, the mama flashed her blue eyes at Mamaw, and slipped off into the woods, and the rest of the pack limped along behind her. We never saw her again. Uncle Wolf found fresh tracks all around the area for weeks after. He thinks that the rest of the pack, the ones who survived, came back periodically, lingering in the woods behind our house."

"Checking on the pup?"

"Yes. And mourning his mother."

I remained silent, sensing that Bella had drifted into an emotional place unknown to me.

"Mamaw named the pup Hania, and fed him from a bottle until he was big enough to eat. And Uncle Wolf killed squirrels and other small rodents for him." Bella stared into the distance. "We'd sit for hours, laughing as he learned how to howl. We were his pack, I guess." She grinned at the memory. "Uncle Wolf played videos of howling baby wolves, and even howled himself to demonstrate."

I chuckled. "I take it he learned just fine."

"Oh yeah. He became a—" She stopped, suddenly guarded.

"A what?"

Bella rested her head on my shoulder. "Something about him—that magnificent, regal wolf—made Mamaw stronger. Invincible almost."

We spent the afternoon passing out flyers across the creek, and although we encountered mostly elderly folks, young Fireman's Granny Lacey invited us in for a spell.

"Come and sit," the old woman herded us inside. "I baked some zucchini bread." She set plates out, telling Bella, "Your Uncle sent a whole basket home with my grandboy last week."

"It looks delicious," Bella said, winking at me. Because it didn't. "Where is he anyway? My little Fireman?"

The zucchini bread was as hard as stone. "This is wonderful," I lied, wheedling it down my throat with sweet tea.

Lacey's eyes narrowed into slits. "I'll send the recipe home for your mama." She turned to Bella. "How's Wolfheart doing? I guess I won't be seeing anymore squash or zucchini now that his garden blew up." She shook her head regretfully. "A shame, that."

I suspected Granny Lacey lamented the loss of produce more than the violation of Wolfheart's property.

"He's okay," Bella said. "Don't worry. He'll replant." She asked again, "Where'd you say Fireman was?"

"I don't know where that boy gets off to half the time. He carries on like he's a teenager already." When she looked at us expectantly, Bella and I choked down another bite of zucchini bread. "He mumbled something about a meeting in town when he left." She tapped the flyer. "I'd expect you'd know about that, seeing as how you have big plans for Shady Gully." Her expression was accusatory.

"Uh…I haven't heard anything about a town meeting. No."

"Anyway, a truck packed with Creeks pulled up, honked for him to hurry."

After another glass of tea, we bid Lacey goodbye. We spent the afternoon knocking on door after unanswered door. "Maybe they're not answering because they've heard how annoying I can be."

"You're not annoying." Bella arched her brow. "You're just focused. Passionate."

I shook off the way her lips moved when she said *passionate*, and pressed on, bobbing along from pothole to pothole, without a soul in sight. We settled for slipping flyers under porch rugs and sliding them into mailboxes.

As we headed back to Shady Gully, I lamented the lack of engagement across the creek.

"Well, there's everybody." Bella pointed toward the substation as we neared the four way stop. "They're lined up from the sheriff's office all the way to the Cozy Corner."

"And beyond Jesse's church." A sense of foreboding swept through me.

"They're carrying signs."

Since my auto body shop was one of the businesses occupying the corners of the four way stop, it too was swarmed with people toting signs. *You Trespassed Over our Hallowed Ground,* and *We Don't Forgive Trespassers,* among the colorful slogans.

Sprite's gas station, as well as Charlie Wayne's Cozy Corner, were equally occupied.

None compared to the fury pulsing in front of Jesse's church though, and the verbiage on those signs touted a more specific demand. *Jesse is a Liar! Send Jesse to Jail!*

If the goal was to disrupt the busiest intersection in town—the four way stop—the operation had succeeded. The Creek People's protest extended farther than my eye could see, and as their signs pounded the air in anger, their frustration was palpable.

"What the…" I slowed, regarding a fresh wave of outrage. "Does that say…?"

"*Justice for Wolfheart!*" Bella read another sign. "Uncle Wolf wouldn't want this." She reached for her phone.

I watched as Sheriff Rick tried to calm the crowd, but his actions were in vain as the protesters angrily thrust their placards in his face. I almost felt sorry for the ornery curmudgeon, but my concern for him vanished when an unruly group, including Youngdeer and Moonpipe, swarmed my car.

I shifted to park, and rolled my window down.

When they saw Bella sitting beside me, they appeared uncertain, and glanced at Redflyer for direction.

I nodded toward my auto body shop, where Daryl and Bubba munched on chips and handed out water to the protesters. "Why don't we go to my shop and talk this out?" I tried reasoning with them. "I'm sure we can—"

"Look!" Bella put her phone aside. "There's Fireman!"

Bella jumped out of the car, and stalked heatedly toward the chanting boy, who carried a sign with a flame drawn around the words, *Fight Fire with Fire!*

"Bella—"

She grabbed Fireman by the arm, tossing his sign to the ground. When she finished fussing at him, she set in on Redflyer. The big man shrunk in size as Bella waved her finger at him.

Quietdove managed to move a few folks aside, allowing me to open the door of my car. "You should probably lay low like your buddies over there." He pointed across the road toward Daryl and Bubba, as they chatted easily with those lined up around the shop. I watched as they rewarded their favorite signs with good natured thumbs-ups.

"Good gracious," I muttered. "It's like we're in a big city."

"I reckon it is," Sheriff Rick bristled as he strode toward me. "Isn't that what you wanted, kid?"

"This isn't—"

"Dang it," he cursed. "Now here comes Jesse and his bunch."

Max hurried over. "This is gonna get ugly, Sheriff. What do you want to do?"

"You go over and calm Thaddeus and Big Al down. And Quietdove, you hold the fort here." Sheriff Rick glanced about, eyeing Bella. "Your uncle is the only one they'll listen to."

"I know," Bella answered.

"See if you can get him out here."

Bella punched buttons on her phone, moving aside and plugging her ear to muffle the chaos.

"What started all this?" I asked Sheriff Rick.

"Ah," he snapped. "My fault."

I stared at him in shock.

"The sacred grounds for one thing," he bemoaned. "And I probably made it worse at Wolfheart's when I mentioned Jesse and his garden in the same sentence."

The sheriff's words were immediately drowned out as the two opposing sides collided, and pandemonium erupted.

Quietdove grunted, steeling off Redflyer and Moonpipe as they lunged toward Jesse and his group.

"Arrest him!" Youngdeer pointed at Jesse. "Or he'll face the fire!"

Vicious taunts and excited screams combined to create an exaggerated level of chaos. I locked eyes with Bella, who still had Fireman by the arm.

"There's only so much I can do," Quietdove hollered at the sheriff. "I've never seen them like this."

"This is terrible," Bella cried.

I swept Fireman into my arms. "Y'all come with me. Hurry." I quickly herded them toward the body shop where Bubba and Daryl held the door open. After we all filed in, they shut the door tightly behind us.

"Want some chips, kid?" Bubba offered the bag to Fireman.

Fireman shook his head, barely acknowledging Bubba. Instead, his gaze was fixed on the mounting rage outside.

When I turned, I saw the baseball bat in Jesse's hands.

Chapter Twenty

Doomsday Netflix Series
Sheriff Rick

It had finally gone and happened. Shady Gully, Louisiana had spun into a doomsday Netflix series. Everywhere I looked, the pleasant faces I'd normally chat up in the mornings at Sprite's gas station had morphed into angry protesters demanding justice.

Justice for who? Jesse? Wolfheart? It was impossible to tell anymore. It looked to me like everyone was just plain mad at the world. The only solace I had was knowing Robin and her kids were at Lake Osprey, safe and sound. Headstrong as ever, she'd hired a crime scene cleaner, followed by a traditional house cleaner, and then she and Desi had taken a cloth and a mop to it themselves. Once the house was rid of any trace of the unwanted houseguest, she, Lenny, and Desi had set out with the young ones, intent on a day in the sun.

Lenny had grumbled about being stuck with the hens all day, but I suspected he was sitting back with a cold brew in his hands about now, soaking up the rays, clueless as to the chaos consuming his sleepy town.

As a loud crash echoed like a shot, I instinctively brought my hand to my gun belt. Turned out it was a couple of football players from Shady Gully High, revving up their four-wheel drive as they peeled out of Sprite's gas station.

When I feasted my eyes on the danged whippersnappers, they cackled, enjoying the way the antsy crowd tensed each time their vehicle backfired. I had half a mind to arrest the little riff-raffs.

Before I could move in their direction, the spinning beam on

Meadow's dome light cut into my peripheral vision. To keep her from driving straight into the mayhem, I flagged her down.

"What's happened?" Meadow swiveled around a box of bulky packages and mail.

"Just park and leave your car. Bella's at the auto body shop with Luke. Why don't you head over there?" When she seemed reluctant, I added with more bravado than I felt, "We'll get this resolved shortly." Shortly was optimistic, but my tone sounded confident enough to get her moving.

A loud wail drew my attention to the center of the brawl, where Jesse had just clobbered Redflyer with a baseball bat. I watched as the giant man crumpled to the ground, blood dripping down his ears. His dazed condition triggered raised threats from several of his pals, including Moonpipe and Youngdeer.

Redflyer, tough enough to rally from the crippling strike, grabbed his switchblade and got in a few well-aimed flicks at Jesse's ankles.

While I only saw a little blood, Jesse hollered like an IED blew his leg off.

Naturally, this set the likes of Big Al and Thaddeus into motion, and as the two forces collided, Max rushed me in a panic. "This is bad."

"Good observation." I watched as James attempted to calm the group around his brother, but Thaddeus wasn't having it, and when he shoved Youngdeer squarely into Moonpipe, they tumbled into a heap on the ground. "Everybody's going crazy."

When a young man who normally passed the collection bucket at church whizzed past me, I latched onto his hair. "Stay where you are, son."

The kid frowned at me, clearly disappointed he'd been denied a role in the brawl.

I turned to Max. "I think it's time we make some arrests."

Max brushed his hand along his gun.

"No, knucklehead. Just go get the handcuffs."

"The Fed Ex box? There aren't really—"

"Max," I glowered. "Just go get as many as we have."

I tugged at the little tithe collector's hair once more, piercing him with my evil eye. "Go home." I sent him off with a strawberry taffy, watching until the mutt disappeared past the Cozy Corner.

I surveyed the crowd again, settling on the window of the auto body shop. Once I caught Luke's eye, I beckoned him over. As Meadow and Bella appeared to be in a heated argument, he made his way reluctantly.

Out of the corner of my eye, I noticed the little scoundrel, Fireman, full of fire and intent, slip out the side door of the auto body shop.

"Great," I muttered to no one in particular. "I got unattended kids all over the place."

"Sheriff," Max approached, handing me a bullhorn. "Quietdove and I are all set."

I switched on the horn. And whistled as loud as I could. The high-pitched shriek resounded throughout the four way stop, and for a moment, I had everyone's attention. "Salutations, one and all."

Luke plowed through the throng to stand beside me. "What do you want me to do?"

I ignored him. "Here's how this is gonna go down," I said into the bullhorn. "My crackerjack deputies over there got a box full of handcuffs with your names on 'em. They're brand spanking new, and shiny as all get out. This nonsense stops now. You will desist. Are y'all hearing me? Anybody who aggravates me for any reason whatsoever gets a free night in my jail."

"No fair," muttered someone from Jesse's tribe. "This ain't justice. You can't stop us from expressing our first amendment rights."

"Oh, cut the crap," I said, climbing atop a bench in front of the station. "This is Shady Gully. Once someone gets injured in my town, that first amendment ship don't sail anymore. Jesse, lay that bat down right now." I glanced toward Redflyer's people. "And I know y'all got some blades. Lay 'em down. Come on, now. We need to get the injured looked at."

Begrudgingly, some of the Creeks slowly emptied their pockets, while Jesse dawdled, drawing squiggly lines in the dirt with his bat." James nudged his brother, encouraging him to follow my order. But Jesse remained belligerent.

"Max," I said. "Handcuff Brother Jesse, will ya? And if he resists, pepper spray him."

A few lookee-loos on the outer perimeters of the milieu got the message and started shuffling home to their recliners and refrigerators, while Redflyer managed to sit up with the help of a few of his comrades.

"The longer I gotta wait to get my medics in here, the more aggravated I'm gonna get." I glared at Jesse. "You ever been pepper sprayed, Jesse? It's a dandy, let me tell ya. Not only do your eyes burn like the dickens, but the membranes in your nose and throat swell up. And there's this nasty nasal discharge—"

When Jesse tossed the bat to the ground, it ricocheted off Youngdeer's foot. A long, tense moment passed as the two sized each other up. Max, impressively, nicked the bat and handcuffed Jesse, preventing another confrontation.

Taking his cue, Quietdove strolled over to the Creeks, dangling his own set of cuffs in warning. I turned to Luke, who hadn't moved an inch since I'd started talking. "You can breathe now," I told him, handing him the bullhorn, urging him onto the bench. "You're turn."

"What? What do you want me to do?"

"Relax, kid. I don't want you to arrest anybody. I'm giving you your chance. Talk to 'em."

While Max and Quietdove prowled among the crowd, checking for weapons and injuries, Luke tapped awkwardly on the bullhorn. "H-h-hello? Testing. One. Two. Three. Four—"

Charlie Wayne, who'd remained on the periphery of the action, rolled his eyes. "Giddy up, Luke. We ain't got all day."

"I…uh…I'm glad nobody is seriously hurt."

"Speak for yourself," Redflyer remarked, as Quietdove handed him gauze for his head.

"I have some flyers—"

"I'm outta here," muttered an old man everyone called Chester, who stood next to Claire. "Ain't nothin' on those flyers I care about."

"Max," I asked. "You get a chance to check Chester out yet? Make sure he's not suffering any ill-effects from all the excitement?"

"Not yet," Max quipped.

I eyed the ornery old coot. "You'll stay until my deputy sets his eyes on you."

Sprite shrugged. "Luke, you're a stand-up guy. We're just not feeling incorporation. We like things the way they are."

"Of course you do, Sprite," said BlueJay, an amiable, soft-spoken old timer who lived across the creek. "That's 'cause things are workin' out pretty good for everyone on your side of the creek."

The gathering pivoted as one, shocked by the usually reserved BlueJay's remark.

Encouraged, Luke nodded. "I believe today was a result of the growing frustration in Shady Gully—"

"What about the creek?" pressed Moonpipe.

"The creek *is* Shady Gully. I want to make that clear. For too long we've treated the creek, and the residents there, as separate. You are part of Shady Gully. You, and the creek, and its citizens, all matter. You have the same rights as everybody else."

Jesse scowled aloud, prompting a wave of disapproval among his supporters.

"We all want the same things," continued Luke. "We want better cell towers. Better roads. We want a better school system. Am I right?"

A murmur of assent spread, and suddenly Bella was on top of the bench, standing by Luke's side. "Luke is right. We all deserve a say. A vote."

Redflyer cursed under his breath, obviously recovered from his head injury. "A vote? That's a waste of time. It's all rigged against us."

"If it's rigged against you," said Luke, his confidence rising, "it's only because you aren't registered to vote. That's how you unrig it."

"We passed out flyers today," said Bella. "We put them in your mailboxes. There are easy instructions on how to get registered and how to sign the petition for incorporation."

"This is your chance to be heard," said Luke. "To be counted. If we're incorporated, your district can elect people to represent you on the counsel. To champion you and your interests."

"I've heard enough," Jesse sniped. "Don't fall for this fancy talk. This is a slippery slope and this kid," he sneered at Luke, "is as slick as a shoe salesman."

Charlie Wayne cleared his throat. "Well, that might be going a little too far. Old school, yes. A nerd, yes. A—"

"Charlie Wayne," I stepped in. "You ain't helping."

"Just sayin'—slick ain't a word I'd use to describe Luke here. But honest and good intentioned, sure."

I nodded, pleased with Charlie Wayne's clarification, because it seemed the kid was finally making an impact. A car door slammed somewhere beyond the post office, and my stomach dropped when I saw Robin hurrying over with a few of the young ones.

Sterling and Violet, along with Petey and Micah, trailed behind Robin, who I couldn't help notice had acquired a pink flush on her cheeks after a few hours on the lake. When she grinned at me, my stomach dipped a notch or two. Or three.

Behind her were Lenny and Desi. As usual, Lenny lagged behind Desi's purposeful march. I inwardly cringed as I considered the likely possibility that Desi would jump on the bench beside Luke, and call out anyone who looked at him crosswise.

Thankfully, she showed restraint, planting herself at a safe distance along the steps of the substation with the rest of her family. Luke, unaware, continued his oration with remarkable aplomb. "This is our town—"

"It's not a town yet," said Jesse. "And it won't be if I have anything to do with it." He harrumphed while a slew of his sycophants nodded in unison.

Luke ignored him. "Some of us have deep roots here. Our parents were raised here, and their parents before them. It's our home, and it's what we make it. Let's make it good for everyone. Let's all have a say."

I almost choked on my taffy when there was a scattering of applause, and not all from Luke's fan club perched on the steps of the substation.

Claire squinted. "What about nail salons? I'm in if we can get one here."

"And a vet?" One of Dolly's oldest customers, Mrs. Guidry, raised her brows. "I do hate going all the way to Belle Maison to take Juliet to the vet."

"Yes," Luke smiled at one and all. "And if you've ever dreamed of opening your own business, we can help make that a reality. Wouldn't it be great to spend your dollars locally? Instead of spending all our money in Belle Maison, and helping *them* thrive?"

"Dang city slickers," mumbled Sprite. "Think they're better than us."

"What about health care?" someone asked. "Could we have a hospital here?"

"Maybe not a hospital," Luke answered honestly. "But perhaps an urgent care."

Mutters of approval spread throughout the gathering. I watched as Bella looked up at Luke, and batted her eyelashes. He blushed, but I swear the kid stood a few inches taller.

"I believe in him," Bella said, directing her gaze at the Creeks. "We can trust him. I promise."

Quietdove gave me the all-clear regarding weapons, while Max directed Patty's EMT van onto the scene. Seemed the only serious injuries were Redflyer's head and Jesse's ankles, and probably his pride.

Overall, the tense eruption had now been reduced to a simmer, and we could potentially wrap this up with Band-Aids, a few stitches, and several warnings. I glanced at Robin, finding her especially fetching with her stylish sunglasses perched atop her head.

Maybe I'd see if she'd like to meet Gerty, seeing as how the duplex was only a stroll away.

"All right, well great." Charlie Wayne's bug eyes widened behind his coke bottle glasses. "This has all been swell, but unless y'all are placing orders—" he motioned toward the folks still lined up at the Cozy Corner "—pick your trash up and scoot. See the big barrel? Come on, now. How hard can it be to throw trash in a barrel?"

A scattering of giddy laughter swept through the crowd, and I half expected someone to break into song, singing Kumbaya or something.

And then I heard a voice in the crowd. Anxious, jittery. "Wait everyone, is that smoke I smell?"

Chapter Twenty-One

BAD JUJU
Wolfheart

I took the long, scenic drive out of the creek, embracing the sunshine and the vivid hues of summer. The crepe myrtles erupted with bright pink buds and the billowing magnolia trees blossomed creamy white. All the colors seemed brighter today. Possibly because my once prized and fertile topography had been reduced to a sickly, dull gray.

Aimlessly, I'd driven by Desi and Lenny's house, hoping to catch them home, but only the dogs, Ginger and Mary Ann, yapped at me through the window. Unable to return to the gloom of my dwelling, I decided to take refuge at Sacred Heart Catholic Church. Somehow the somber atmosphere and the dignified reverence of the austere church suited my mood. And if I were lucky, I'd run into Father Patrick.

I parked in the modest gravel lot and lowered my sunglasses as I headed to the entrance. The heavy cherry wood doors squeaked as I opened them. The church was dark, except for the muted colors filtering sun through the stained glassed windows.

I sauntered down the long nave, stopping to kneel and genuflect before settling into the hard-wooden pew. I sat, staring at the crucified Jesus at the head of the church, for much longer than I intended.

I desperately missed my sister. She'd known me better than anyone. She'd intuitively understood how the layers of unrelenting disappointment weighed on me, until eventually I became comfortable with despondency. Expected it. Embraced it. Thrived on it.

After the ill-fated bonfire at Megan's, and the long journey back to health, my hopelessness grew like a tumor inside me. It evolved into defiance, and the town's scorn, along with the consequences of my insolence, only fueled my anger.

It had been during that period of boldness that I'd met Desi and Robin. Eight years my junior, they and their classmates had been terrified of me, including young Ricky, the future Magnum P.I. of Shady Gully.

While I'd been earning my reputation as the town villain, Peony had been a young mother grieving the brutal murder of her husband, Axe. And during Peony's years of profound sorrow, I'd been too self-consumed to rise above my own wallowing to recognize the depth of her anguish.

I supported her financially, sure, but she resented my *dirty* money, and she couldn't depend on me emotionally. Unknowingly, I set in motion the perfect storm that had been Madhawk. I'd driven her right into his arms, and even worse, I hadn't fought for her.

Once he came into the picture, I made myself scarce. Partly out of resentment because she'd allowed an interloper into our lives, but mostly out of guilt. Guilt because I'd been too in love with my own self-loathing to do the right thing. The guiltier I felt, the more I hated myself, and round and round it went.

Meadow was a different story. Our mutual disdain for Madhawk brought us closer than ever, and I committed to spending time with her and providing a refuge from Madhawk. But I never imagined the turmoil in her young life, much less what fate had in store for her. And yet, once again, instead of rising to the occasion when the older, perverse Mitch got her pregnant, I sat back and let Madhawk solidify his place in my family.

The next decade was a haze of drugs, jail time, and physical skirmishes, most of which were with Madhawk. While he fancied himself a savior to Peony and the girls, he couldn't manage to hold down a steady job, or pay the light bill.

Between getting friendly with the folks at the electric company, who sometimes accepted a little weed in lieu of payment, I traveled through Texas, Arkansas, and Mississippi in search of the despicable Mitch.

Bitter, and hardened by fury, I hadn't trusted the law to do what needed to be done. Had I found the scumbag, I'd have killed him. But that, I understood now, would have ultimately ended me.

Praise Jesus and his unfailing mercy, I breathed a prayer up toward the giant crucifix.

He brought me back slowly, and gently, even as I rejected him again and again. I still did what I did, sold drugs, caroused, and reveled in my rebellion—but I gradually worked my way back to my family.

And it had been on such an occasion that a courageous pack of wolves cemented my bond with my sister.

We sat on the ground together, fully accepting whatever happened next. Either the wolves would attack us and shred us alive, or the mama wolf would present us with a gift. Our bodies were electric with the dozens of wolves' eyes marking us from the darkened woods, while our backs were warmed by Bella's and Meadow's concerned gazes from the window.

"Steady now," said Peony. "They're deciding if we're worthy."

"Of dinner?"

"Shhhh." She cracked a smile.

"They're all hurt," I said lightly.

"And only one pup. Something evil got them."

"Or someone," I muttered.

Since Peony and I had always been comfortable with silence, the minutes slipped by easily. We'd grown up being shuffled from shanty to shanty, never quite knowing the genuineness of the hospitality, so we'd quickly learned the advantages of remaining meek, and showing deference to one's host.

"Here she comes," Peony glanced at me, excitement coloring her cheeks.

It was then I knew all was forgiven. In that moment, Peony, who was surely an angel herself, drew me back as her baby brother, her childhood companion, and her best friend. All my bad choices, as well as my shameful behavior, fell away.

I was forgiven.

The mama wolf regarded us as she hobbled over with her squirmy pup. Finally, she set the gray wolf pup a few feet from us. "Don't move," Peony said in a cooing tone, but I understood the words were meant for me.

We watched, respectfully, as the injured wolf licked her pup with an eye for detail, carefully spiffing him to a pristine gray. "He's magnificent," Peony told the injured mama in compliment. "You must be proud."

After a little restlessness spread to the rest of the pack, the mama wolf sat next to her pup, and exchanged a long, meaningful look with my sister. "We'll take good care of him," Peony said tenderly. "I promise."

The injured mama wolf cast her eyes on me for only a second, and then limped into the woods to join her waiting packmates.

My sister stroked the wide-eyed wolf pup, who mewed and squiggled against her thigh. "Well, what are we going to name you?"

We named him Hania. And he changed everything.

Hania became the project that brought Peony and I closer than ever.

Hania grew stronger, and his coat shone thick and gray, with a regal ring of white under his collar. We kept him full and satisfied with a healthy diet of fresh meat, and against the odds, and likely due to his attachment to Peony, we domesticated him. Hania rarely bothered the chickens or other random strays who passed through hoping for a free meal and a warm bed for the night.

He did, however, terrify Madhawk. Whenever Madhawk entered a room, Hania's hackles would rise, and he'd let out a low, guttural growl. Perhaps fearful of the formidable force Hania would grow into, Madhawk tried a few times to hurt him. But Hania was more than just strong. He was wise.

Once, Hania pretended to be asleep as Madhawk crept out to the barn with a loaded pistol dangling at his thigh. About to shout a warning, I noticed a slight shudder along Hania's lower legs. I watched, amazed, as Hania allowed Madhawk to move in closer.

Just as Madhawk lifted his pistol, Hania rushed him, and within seconds, Madhawk's trigger hand was shredded.

Their dislike for one another grew more intense over the years, especially as Madhawk became more aggressive with Peony. Hania's fierce devotion and loyalty to my sister comforted me, because his constant presence tempered Madhawk's violent tendencies.

Occasionally, when I'd catch a tentativeness in the way Madhawk held himself, a wince as he reached for something, or a drag in his walk, I understood the mistreatment of my sister continued. But also that Peony's protector made sure there were consequences.

"Ah," Father Patrick interrupted my morbid thoughts. "Is it too bright in the Lord's house for you, Mr. Wolf?" He indicated my sunglasses as he angled his pudgy frame into the pew ahead of me. "Or perhaps you're incognito for a reason?" He scratched his fingers along his red beard curiously.

I removed my shades, considering his clerical garb, which seemed in sharp contrast to his casual, jovial manner.

"Oh please, I beg of you," he said. "Spend me a yarn about some scandalous secret mission. Perhaps you're about to take off to Peru to wrestle a notorious drug lord. No?" He guffawed. "How about a jaunt to Tahiti to meet a glamorous, shapely spy, dead set on turning her into a double agent?"

I couldn't help but laugh. "Afraid not, Father. How are things with you?"

"Business is quite good actually. No doubt it will continue that way as long as Cane and Abel carry on as they do down the road."

I laughed again. Twice in one day.

"Shame on me. Gossiping is wrong. Now I'll have to go to confession."

"Are you going to confess to yourself?" I teased.

"I'll have you know, Mr. Wolf, I'm a very good listener." He considered me. "Sorry to hear about your incredible garden. Simply tragic. Especially those tomatoes. All gone up to create a heavenly marinara for our Lord, I suppose."

"I'll replant. Eventually. Maybe grapes this time." When his bright blue eyes widened in delight, I added, "I'll need a taster."

"Splendid! I'll be happy to volunteer." He frowned at me. "That's right, you don't touch the stuff, do you? Indeed. It's a horrible, nasty, habit. I'll take care of it so you don't have to, don't you worry."

I chuckled, as Father Patrick was known for his love of rich food, and fine wine.

He appeared thoughtful. "Perhaps a nice chardonnay grape to start? They're fairly easy to grow, or so I've heard. But you absolutely must have a cabernet sauvignon grape vine. They'll provide delicious medium to full bodied wines. Dry, with tannins and acid to balance." He twirled an imaginary wine glass. "Ahhh." Sipped. "Bold. With legs. Simply excellent."

"I have no idea what any of that means."

"Leave it to me." He considered me. "How are Bella and Meadow? The fire must have been frightening. Especially on the heels of what happened to that saintly sister of yours."

"It's been hard, but they're good. Bella is getting ready for her big debut Sunday."

"Exquisite! I plan to attend. After Mass, of course." He waved off my shock. "There's plenty of our Lord to go around, now isn't there?" He leaned over, adding in a conspiratorial tone, "That preacher in Kentucky is quite good, isn't he? A true man of God, and extremely charismatic. I stream online, like the cool kids do, and I must say, he's quite gifted—"

My cell phone buzzed. "Sorry, Father."

"No worries. Rules were made to be broken. That's what keeps me busy."

"Hello?" I answered. "What's wrong?" I stared at Father Patrick as I listened to Bella. "Okay. I'm coming now." I took a deep breath, trying to steady my pounding heart.

"Trouble?" asked Father Patrick.

"At the four way stop."

I rolled first past Dolly's Diva Dome, and then James's church, and finally, Jesse's Church of Christ. I regarded the small figure scrambling out the rear of the church, probably where the back vestry or hall would be.

Fireman stopped abruptly when he spotted my truck. I opened the passenger door, waiting for him to climb the hill back to the road. He hesitated. "What?" he asked defensively.

"I just thought you might need a ride."

He climbed into the cab, his demeanor unusually surly and unsettled.

I drove a little further before the scattering of people lining the four way stop came into view. "Wow. Quite a scene." I glanced at Fireman, who still reeked of soot and smoke. I sniffed my own shirt, assuming it smelled as well. "It's impossible to get that smell out of your nose, huh? Even after a shower."

His gaze remained fixed straight ahead. Finally, he remarked, "Jesse hit Redflyer with a baseball bat, but the sheriff didn't do anything. Just like he didn't do anything when Jesse set your garden on fire." He anxiously tapped his fingers along the leg of his pants.

I narrowed my eyes, catching a whiff of gasoline.

"It's not fair," he muttered. "You should just park there. You can't get through because of the crowd anyway."

Although disconcerted by his uncharacteristic bossiness, I saw Fireman's point. I pulled into Luke's auto body shop, feeling relief as I saw Bella and Meadow through the window. My relief was short lived however, when the crowd bounded our way.

"What's going on?" I mumbled, but the incited group rushed right past us. Fireman didn't bother with a response, and instead hopped out of the truck as if he had a pressing matter to attend to.

"Uncle Wolf!" Bella tackled me with a hug, followed by Meadow, and Luke, who seemed to pulse with adrenaline. "Luke talked to the crowd and got everyone settled down."

"Good," I said. "But what's going on that way?"

Desi and Lenny approached with Robin and the kids, while the sheriff peeled off, rushing in the same direction as the crowd. Sirens blared as the EMT van sped past us, along with a line of pick-up trucks topped with spinning dome lights.

"Volunteer firemen," Lenny said. "Looks like Jesse's church is on fire."

"What? I just drove past there." But when I turned, I saw a huge billow of smoke, and the first sign of flames bursting from the chapel's roof. Panic dropped low in my stomach.

Sterling, Violet, and Petey, ran toward the fire.

"Violet?" shouted Micah. "Where are you going?"

"To help put out the fire." Robin's daughter's face flooded with excitement.

"Don't worry," Micah told Robin. "Petey will watch out for her."

Lenny bounced on the balls of his feet. "I should—"

"Don't even think about it," Desi warned. "But let's get a little closer. Maybe there's something we can do."

I cautiously wandered over with them, the knot in my belly deepening with apprehension. Despite all the volunteers and the unlimited access to water, the church had quickly gone up in flames. While keeping my eyes peeled for Fireman, I handed out bottled water to the volunteers.

Unfortunately, Jesse stalked the scene like a restless panther, feverishly searching for someone to condemn. As his gaze scrutinized the onlookers, I busied myself adding ice to the chest of energy drinks.

"Praise Jesus," someone said. "At least nobody was inside."

"Amen," said Petey, who walked among the gathering, intermittently patting old women's shoulders, and delivering firm, encouraging handshakes to the men. "And thankfully we were able to contain it before it spread to James's church."

As mutterings of assent swelled, and a sense of optimism bounced between the volunteers, Charlie Wayne said, "Never understood why we needed two churches side by side anyway."

James tramped along the edges of the debris, positioning himself at the center of the crowd. "Come this Sunday, I'd like to invite everyone right next door." He pointed to his church, only yards away from the destruction. "We'll pray together, and enjoy some worship music."

Even from several feet away, I sensed Bella gasp, undoubtedly considering the added pressure of her performance Sunday.

A mumbled curse sliced through the atmosphere, and everyone pivoted as Jesse shook his head, his anger and hatred palpable. "You."

Filled with dread, I met his furious leer.

"You did this. Look at his hands, everyone."

Reflexively, I hid my hands, realizing too late it made me look guilty.

"They're black with soot." Jesse stalked over, pointing. "And your fingers. Look." He closed into my space, narrowing his eyes. "You did this."

"He came from that direction," someone confirmed. "I saw him when he drove up."

"And the fire started right after he got here," another of Jesse's mouthpieces chimed. "I think Jesse's right."

"That's ridiculous," said Lenny. "Brad's garden went up in flames last night. It takes more than one shower to get that stench out."

"Yeah," Redflyer revealed his own ash smudged hands. "And we didn't have access to fancy fire hydrants. Or trained volunteers. We put it out all by ourselves."

"Wait," said the ancient Chester, who lingered next to Claire. "Look at the kid. His hands are even worse." The ornery man latched on to Fireman, who'd slipped unwittingly into the crowd. "That's fresh grime. And he stinks like gasoline."

As the outrage intensified, Sheriff Rick stepped in. "All right. Let's everybody calm your britches." His face flashed beet red. "Is that what we're doing here? Convicting a little boy based on a smell test? On when he last showered?"

Sprite cleared his throat, spoke reluctantly. "The little guy did buy five bucks worth of gasoline this morning. And I watched him fill up a gas can." He glanced regretfully at Fireman. "Sorry kid, but burning down a church is bad juju."

As everyone shouted back and forth, Fireman ran off at a gallop, his small frame weaving in and out of bodies with the skill of a linebacker. Just before he knocked two stunned old ladies to the ground, I plucked him. "Shh. Take it easy," I whispered. "I've got this."

"Sheriff!" Jesse shouted, enraged. "Arrest that little mongrel."

Trying to maintain a sense of order, Sheriff Rick pleaded with the overexcited crowd. "Folks, relax. Let me do my job." He approached us with an exaggerated sigh. "What are we doing here?"

I held Fireman firmly behind me, meeting the sheriff's eye. "He didn't do it. I did."

As a hush swept over the scene, Jesse couldn't contain his smile.

I proclaimed loud enough so my voice could be heard by everyone: "Jesse set my garden on fire. I wanted revenge. I did it."

"I didn't set your garden on fire," Jesse said. "But Sheriff, it seems you've got a confession. Finally. Now can we get on with the arrest?"

"But he didn't do it," Bella cried. She looked helplessly at Luke. And then at me. "Why are you saying this?" Meadow held Bella on one side, while Luke braced her on the other. "It's not true," she cried.

I felt the ragged jerks of Fireman's little body as he dissolved into tears. My grip remained firm as I bent to offer him soft, comforting words. "Just be cool, little man. Be cool."

Sheriff Rick shook his head. "All right. I'll take care of this. I want everyone to go home."

"But—" Jesse interrupted.

"I'm going to arrest Wolfheart," the sheriff snapped. "But I want everybody out of here. Right now. Or you'll be next." The sheriff signaled Quietdove and Max, who started rounding everyone up, herding them toward their vehicles, or on their way on foot.

"Go home," I told Meadow. "Bring Bella. Don't worry about me."

"You're too good for your own good." Meadow eyed me knowingly and then led Bella to her car.

Luke coaxed Bella into the seat next to Meadow, and sent them off with a weary wave. I felt as forlorn as he did, watching my niece and her daughter disappear toward the creek.

Jesse snickered, clearly delighting in my moment of shame. "It's long overdue, hoodlum."

Fireman clung to me, sobbing, as the sheriff approached with a pair of handcuffs. "You're a mean sheriff. You're the worse sheriff in the whole world."

"Let's go, Wolfheart," the sheriff said. "We'll get out of the spotlight and talk in the station."

But Jesse followed us inside, and strolled gleefully toward the jail cells. "It's time to put you in a cage where you belong."

"Wait," Fireman cried. "No, wait."

"Kid," the sheriff pleaded, filling his hands with taffy. "Don't you have somewhere to go, buddy?"

"Please don't put him in there," Fireman sobbed, holding on to me tightly.

When he tugged me down to his level, he whispered, "I'm sorry. It's all my fault. I made him better. I helped him."

"What?" I crouched lower. Glanced at the sheriff, "Can we have a minute?"

"Make it quick."

"What do you mean you made him better?" I asked softly. "Who'd you help?"

"Madhawk." Fireman's tears moistened the hair around my ear. "He made me get medicine at your house. He said he was gonna kill my granny if I didn't."

"You did what you had to do. Where did you see him? Tell me slowly."

Fireman glanced at Jesse, who was holding the cell door open with a mocking smile. And then he cupped his hand around his mouth and breathed salty tears into my ear. "He's gonna hurt Bella. And her mama. He said once he got strong again, he was gonna get them on the creek," Fireman sniffled. "And I helped him get better. And you're in jail because of me, and now Bella and her mama are all alone. It's all my fault."

"That's enough," Jesse griped, running his hand along the rungs of the cell to make a clanking sound. "How long are you going to allow this, Sheriff?"

Sheriff Rick sighed, giving me the eye. "Okay. Let's get this over with."

"Wait!" Fireman cried, "No, wait!"

Before the sheriff hauled me to the cell, I leaned down, and whispered urgently. "Fireman, "Go find Luke. And tell him exactly what you just told me. Hurry."

Chapter Twenty-Two

Spirit Warrior
Luke

*M*adhawk *wandered through the swampy wetlands along the creek, marveling at the heaviness in the air. He would need to move on soon. Probably to Oklahoma where the old biddy had some family. Maybe, if he were feeling generous, he'd send for her.*

The medicinal herbs, disinfectant, and bandages from the boy had helped him recover from his injuries. And the food and bath at the fancy house on the lake, followed by the needed rest at Peony's, had energized him, and renewed his focus to complete his plan.

But he'd lingered too long in the marsh, and now he needed to get the job done and disappear.

He'd seen Wolfheart head to town earlier, which meant that Bella and Meadow would return soon after Meadow's mail route. And they'd be alone.

Madhawk had his knife, which he could handle blindfolded, and to improve his odds, he'd brought a crowbar from Peony's shed. While they were mere women, there were two of them, and capable of an array of trickery.

Madhawk positioned himself in the brush ahead of the bridge, drawing stick figures in the dirt to occupy himself. His plan was to catch them before they crossed the bridge and headed toward Wolfheart's place. There would be dogs at Wolfheart's, and although Madhawk had been successful using seasoned steak to control the mutts before, the mongrels might rear up to defend the women.

He'd fantasized about slaying the dogs as well, along with the chickens and the cats, but his wounds had humbled him, and after today, he'd be content with what he'd accomplished.

He'd killed his rival, Axe, as well as the overly glorified Spirit Warrior. He'd punished Peony for not putting him above everyone else, and for treating him as something to be tolerated, rather than celebrated. In the end, Madhawk had shown none of them mercy.

Nor would he show mercy to Meadow and Bella.

His only regret was not having time to end Wolfheart. But then, Madhawk chuckled to himself, he'd leave him to rot in his grief. He'd have nothing then, not even his precious garden.

The sounds of a car approaching the bridge drew Madhawk to the present, and the familiar clanks and rattles of Meadow's clunker sent a rush of adrenaline through him. He gripped his knife in one hand, and held the crowbar in the other, enjoying the weight of the tool against his thigh.

Madhawk walked onto the road, blocking the car from the bridge. He smirked at them, enjoying the look of fear on Bella's face as she pressed her phone to her ear. He doubted she'd get a signal in this dead zone, but it wouldn't matter anyway. He'd be long gone by the time help came.

Meadow slammed on her breaks. Stupid woman. She could have run over him if she'd wanted. Madhawk moved swiftly to the stronger of the two, planning to take her out first, before she got her bearings. He'd use the crowbar since it was efficient. And fast.

He yanked the driver's door open, his eyes locking on the nasty, mean-spirited Meadow. Both women screamed as he grabbed Meadow's arm and yanked her out of the vehicle.

Madhawk recognized the glint in the hardened woman's eyes too late, and when she lunged at him, he staggered. She used her fingernails like tiny razors, slashing viciously across his face and eyes.

As rage swept through him, he couldn't resist one last insult upon ending her life. "Your daddy cried like a baby when I slit his throat."

He lifted the crowbar. Quick. Effective.

"Noooooo!" screamed Bella, jumping out of the passenger side.

But it was too late. The crowbar had made contact, and Meadow crumbled, her legs giving way as she collapsed to the ground in a heap. Madhawk leered at Bella with a twisted grin. "Bye-bye Mommy."

Bella rushed him, striking his chest, and kicking his shins. But she was powerless. "You are a silly child," he snorted.

But like her mother, she demonstrated a flash of…something. Determination? Defiance? This time she aimed her punches for Madhawk's shoulder and neck, where his wounds were still healing. He experienced a swell of agony, and faltered as vomit rose inside of him.

Emboldened, the brat pounced again.

But Madhawk had regained his footing. "Enough!" he glared at her, his fury sparking anew.

His tone frightened her, and she turned, running toward the bridge. "I can run faster than you," she shrieked over her shoulder. "And I'll get Uncle Wolf's gun!"

As Madhawk chased her onto the bridge, his breathing became labored. He forced himself to concentrate on putting one foot in front of the other.

He was almost close enough to grab her shirt. Just one more inch and he'd be able to get a hold—

But then Bella stopped on the middle of the bridge.

Her halt was so abrupt, Madhawk grunted as he nearly crashed into her. She pivoted, and looked over his shoulder. And she did the strangest thing. She smiled.

Disconcerted by her expression of calm, Madhawk turned to see what had drawn her attention.

He gasped. "Oh…oh." He didn't recognize the plaintive sounds emerging from his chest, and as the pathetic mutterings continued to pour out of him, his legs grew wobbly. His nemesis, the Spirit Warrior, stood over Meadow, furious and set on revenge.

Madhawk trembled as Peony's great champion growled, and his blue eyes turned red with rage.

"But…I…" Madhawk swiveled to Bella, who was still smiling, her demeanor fearless and unafraid.

He turned with dread back to the Spirit Warrior. "But I killed you." As Madhawk continued to babble incoherently at the terrifying vision before him, the ground quaked and shifted beneath him. He stumbled, his legs rocking unsteadily as he desperately tried to gain footing.

But still the mighty gladiator moved closer, bold and defiant, vengeance dripping from his glistening tongue.

217

Madhawk's heart pounded as his bloodthirsty opponent closed in on him, and as the ground beneath him gave way, Madhawk's heart burst inside his chest.

The Spirit Warrior's ferocious blue-red eyes and sneering, snarling face were the last things Madhawk saw before his world went black.

I pushed my pragmatic gray car to its limit on the way to the creek, winding recklessly through unforgiving, narrow country roads, and roughly along treacherous potholes and gullies.

I also threw caution to the wind, and broke the law when I pressed the call button on my cell phone. "It's about time you picked up," I shouted at the sheriff when he answered. "What if somebody really needed help?"

"I just got Jesse outta here, and Wolfheart told me what was going on." He cursed. "We're on our way. Just stay where you are. Where are you anyway?"

"I'm about a mile from the bridge."

"Don't go any further. Wait for reinforcements, dang it!"

I hung up, punching harder on the accelerator. Not even thinking what I'd do if I encountered Madhawk. All I knew was I had to get to Bella, to see her in one piece. But when I saw Meadow's vehicle parked at an odd angle at the foot of the bridge, and a crumpled figure on the ground next to the driver's side, my fear escalated.

"Please God," I muttered, unable to verbalize a coherent request. "Please."

I threw my car into park, racing over with an increasing sense of dread. "Meadow," I shook her gently. "Meadow." I stabbed the button with the sheriff's face on my phone again, this time, praying specifically for reception.

"Ughh," Meadow groaned. "Bella…"

"Make sure you bring an ambulance," I shouted into the phone, hoping a few of my words were audible through the broken call. I inspected Meadow, who had a severe gash on the right side of her forehead. I took off my shirt, pressing it firmly against the wound.

"Ouch," she tried to sit up.

"No, no. Just stay still. Help is on the way." I asked tentatively, "Bella?"

"Bella," Meadow sobbed. "I don't know. I can't remember what happened after he hit me with the crowbar. Madhawk. It was—"

"I know. So does the Sheriff. Help is coming."

As she collapsed into tears, I again tried to temper the bleeding, but my shirt came away soaked with blood. I peered over the hood of the car, looking for signs of Bella or Madhawk. I saw nothing. "Meadow, can you hold this? And press hard? I—"

"Go. Go find her." She took my drenched shirt.

I placed my phone next to her. "Just keep pressing hard. I'll be right back."

The instant I stood up to get a better view, I spotted the abandoned crowbar several feet to the front of me. As I moved toward it, I realized with growing horror that something else was off with the landscape. But it wasn't until I got to the edge of the bluff that I grasped the enormity of the situation.

The wretched bridge to the creek had disappeared.

It lay in a pile of wreckage twenty feet below.

The terrain was arduous, consisting of haphazard rocks, dagger sharp branches, and murky water undoubtedly swimming with snakes and alligators. Not to mention the twisted metal and rotting wood that had held the shameful bridge together for years.

"Bella! Bella!" I raised my voice over the current.

I used my hands and butt to brace myself, and then scooted down a few feet, searching for either a foothold on a rock, or a reachable branch. "Bella!" I called again, spotting a limb that might or might not be able to hold my weight. I couldn't care less. It was a way to get closer to Bella.

As I gripped the limb, my weight took it down farther and faster than I'd anticipated. I ended up skidding down to the water, and bouncing off jagged impediments that ripped my naked back to tatters.

"Bella!" Once I regained my footing, I waded along with the current. "Bella!"

I hadn't gone far when I stumbled over a large, male body, floating face down in the water. I half swam and half crawled to the figure, finding Madhawk, who was dead—for sure this time.

I continued to move in the same direction as the water, and my anxiety increased with each new step. Was I going to find Bella like that? Her face pale and unseeing, her beautiful hair tangled awkwardly against the bed of the creek? No, I refused to let my mind go there.

"Bella! Bella!" I shouted, encouraged by the wailing sound of sirens in the distance. As the current roughly pushed me around a bend in the water, I spotted Bella clinging to a branch on the opposite side of the creek. "Bella!"

"Luke!" Her head bobbed perilously in and out of the water.

Even though I didn't know what kind of shape she was in, she was alive. "I'm coming." I splashed through the cloudy water, half stumbling and half swimming across the creek. I shoved debris and stones aside, until I finally reached the branch that held Bella in its clutches. I grasped her waist, holding her tightly against me, while using my other arm to tear away the foliage that held her down. "It's okay," I panted. "I've got you."

"I know." Dark strands of hair twisted around her face like an octopus. "And Mama?"

"She's lost a lot of blood. But the EMTs are with her now." I grunted as I peeled thick vines of undergrowth away from her body. "Take deep breaths."

When I finally freed her, I pried a muddy stone aside to make a landing for her to rest. "Here." I settled her safely down, moving my hands along her face to brush her hair aside. Impulsively, I kissed her, desperate to feel her quick, short breaths against my mouth.

"You saved me," she said softly, resting her forehead against mine.

"Are you okay?" I patted her all over, looking for injuries. "You made it all the way to the creek side."

"I know. I swam, and then I was going to climb up and run to Uncle Wolf's house to get his gun. But I tripped and slid back to the bottom." She frowned. "You're all bloody. You've cut yourself, Luke."

"I'm fine." I kissed her again. "I'm great now that I know you're okay." Although there were other words of endearment fighting their way to the surface, I said instead, "Madhawk is dead."

She nodded, as if she already knew, and then directed her sights to the helicopter swirling overhead. "Quite a posse for a rescue on the creek."

I pointed. "Look. There's your mom. And your Uncle Wolfheart." Several feet above us, we could make out their anxious expressions as they peered over the bluff.

"She's fine," I hollered. Bella and I chuckled as my voice echoed from inside the mouth of the creek.

Meadow, looking bewildered, waved and blew Bella a kiss before an EMT led her aside, presumably for a trip to Saint John's Hospital.

"She's stubborn," Bella quipped. "She probably wouldn't go until she had a look at me."

"Can't say I blame her." I kissed her again. "Were you scared?"

"At first. When Madhawk hit Mama, but..." Her expression blazed with confidence as she glanced at the woods on either side of the creek.

"But what?"

"I saw him."

I arched my brow, confused. "Who?"

"Hania."

"Your mamaw's wolf dog?"

"Yes. He was as magnificent as always. Regal. With that pure white ring of fur around his neck, and his glacier blue eyes." Bella glanced toward the cliff, where her mother and uncle had been standing moments before. "I wish they could have seen him."

"Was it really him?"

Bella's eyes glazed a bit, and she scanned the creek-side, suddenly mystified. "I don't know," she said. "And I don't know if he was even real." Her eyes swiveled back to me. "But maybe it doesn't matter. Maybe all that matters is that he gave me courage. When I saw him, I knew everything was going to be okay. That Mama was going to be alright. And that you were going to find me."

I tried to speak, but failed, so moved by this woman and her unshakable faith.

"His tranquil, steady presence reminded me to be brave. Even when the bridge fell, I had the most powerful sense of protection."

The churning blades of the helicopter interrupted our musings, yanking us back to the commotion amid the creek. When the pilots threw the rescue ladder, I caught it, securing Bella for her lift off. "This is exciting!" she yelled over the noise.

She flashed me a wicked, mischievous smile—only minutes after nearly dying. *God, I loved her.*

"Off you go." I watched the woman I loved airlifted to safety, thinking she was the most beautiful and courageous person I'd ever known.

After an EMT slathered a healthy amount of antiseptic over the cuts on my back, I lumbered over to the edge of the creek where Sheriff Rick and Wolfheart talked quietly.

"All these years," muttered Wolfheart. "Right under my roof—"

"Probably best you didn't know. It wouldn't have brought Axe back," the sheriff replied. "And knowing you, there's a good chance you'd have taken matters into your own hands."

Grim, Wolfheart shook his head, then turned to me with a worn smile. He shook my hand. "Thank you, Luke. I suspected I could count on you."

I nodded, a little embarrassed. "How's the boy? Fireman?"

The two exchanged looks before the sheriff said, "I reckon that's a problem for another day." The lines surrounding his eyes seemed more pronounced than usual, and I suddenly realized the toll being responsible for a town could take on a man.

They glanced at the coroner as he slowly approached. "Dan the Man," the sheriff said in greeting. "Heck of a few days, eh?"

"I heard that." The coroner considered the body bag as the EMTs carefully loaded it into the van. "At least we can sleep easy tonight."

Wolfheart's face lightened, as he obviously agreed. "What do you think killed him? The fall?"

Dan shrugged. "If not that, his ticker." The coroner clutched his fist into a ball, grabbing ahold of the front of his shirt. "His hand was tight against his chest, like that. Ain't exactly official, of course, but I often see that pose in fatal heart attacks."

"You don't say," muttered Sheriff Rick.

Wolfheart said, "If he had underlying heart problems, maybe that's why I didn't detect a pulse—"

"Could have been a number of things, but the autopsy will tell us for sure." Dan glanced at his watch. "Gotta run, *Dancing with the Stars* is on tonight. And it's tango night." The coroner demonstrated a jaunty jig as he hiked to his vehicle.

Night had fallen along the creek as Quietdove and Max worked with emergency personnel to set up a barricade with reflecting lights along the bluff. Another team had taken the long way around, toward Osprey Lake, in order to set up an equally vivid roadblock on the other side of the creek.

As the activity settled and the evening loomed, folks peeled off one by one, until only the sheriff, Bella, and I remained. "You did good today, Luke," he said as he walked with me to my car.

Bella sat in the passenger seat, her hair still damp, and a thick blanket wrapped around her shoulders.

"How ya doing, young lady?" The sheriff asked, "You still feel like singing tomorrow?"

"Of course," She nodded, the adrenaline keeping her wide-eyed and spirited. "I've waited for this all my life."

Sheriff Rick patted the hood of my car a couple of times before waving goodbye. "Mighty fine, then. Good luck."

"Any news on your mom?" I asked as I climbed in, and slowly followed the sheriff's truck out of the creek.

"She's doing better," Bella said. "Uncle Wolf is staying with her at the hospital tonight. The doctors said if she does well tonight, she'll be released early enough tomorrow to hear me sing."

"That's great news." I squinted at her, trying to get a read on the emotional toll of the evening. "Are you holding up okay?"

I could feel her eyes on me in the darkness. "I am." And then she added, "I explained to Uncle Wolf that you'd be sleeping on your couch tonight."

I chuckled. "And what did he say?"

"He said he'd see me at church tomorrow," she teased, sticking her head out the window, embracing the muggy Louisiana air.

"Bella." My voice cracked as I steered along the windy dirt road. "I love you."

"I know," she smiled. And then, "Listen." The faint echo of wolves serenading the moon drifted through the open window. She relaxed her head against my shoulder. "I love you too."

"Hey," I nudged her. "You never told me. What does Hania mean?"

"Hania." Bella set her mesmerizing blue eyes on the moon. "Hania means Spirit Warrior."

Chapter Twenty-Three

BUFORD AND GERTY
Sheriff Rick

As I stirred cream and sugar into my coffee, Gerty jumped on the kitchen counter for her morning trickle. I regarded her as I turned on the faucet. Tail high, eyes bright. As she swiveled in my direction, I shrunk under her scrutiny.

"It was a long night," I said in my defense. "I can't sleep ten hours a day like you."

She blinked. Licked her paw. Unmoved.

After I filled her bowl with kibble, I padded to my room and took a gander in the mirror. I'd nicked myself shaving, and my eyes were bloodshot, but I was hoping the khakis would tip the scales in my favor. The real wildcard was the button-down shirt—blue, to match my eyes—because I figured there was no sense playing around anymore.

When Robin asked if I'd pick her up for church today, I'd tried my darndest to play it cool. Maybe I'd overdone it, because she felt obliged to clarify, "You don't have to drive all the way to Osprey Lake, Ricky. I'll be in Shady Gully at Desi's."

I looked at my watch again. Counting down the minutes. I wondered if I should shave my mustache. Dean hadn't had a mustache, so maybe Robin wasn't into them. I placed a finger over my upper lip, trying to get an idea how I'd look—

The doorbell rang, shaking me out of my adolescent angst.

Gerty positioned herself in front of the door, flaunting her long, perfectly toned body for the benefit of whoever was on the other side. "Don't get comfortable," I told her gruffly. "I've got five minutes before I gotta go. Tops."

I swung the door wide open, discovering Fireman and Granny Lacey. Before I could say a word, the elder shoved the young hooligan inside. "My boys' got something to say to you. Is that coffee I smell?"

Once I had Granny Lacey settled with a warm cup of sugar and cream with a side of coffee, she eyed Fireman. "Well go on. Tell the sheriff what you told me."

The kid's eyes were swollen, undoubtedly from crying over the notion of growing old in prison. Or maybe he was allergic to Gertrude. He hadn't taken his hands off her since he arrived.

"I didn't mean for it to burn down." He stroked Gerty behind her ears and under her chin.

"What did you think was gonna happen then? And what if somebody had been in there?"

"Everyone was outside. Fighting. I knew I was alone."

"Sheriff," Granny said. "He knows what he did was wrong, but he's not a bad boy. His heart is good, and well, what would be the point in putting him in the legal system?"

"He's too young to actually do time, but arson is a serious manner—"

"He'll have a record," she said. "A Creek with a record, especially at his age, will label him for life."

I sighed, resisting the urge to look at my watch, while Gerty purred beneath Fireman's gentle fingers.

"It really was an accident," Fireman insisted. "I just wanted to set Jesse's papers on fire. I found some on his desk and put them in the garbage can. I guess I put too much gas in the can, because the flames shot up and caught on the curtains and I—" He dropped his head regretfully.

When he teared up, Gerty studied the boy for a long moment. She blinked at him a few times, and then stood and rubbed her body affectionately against his...

She then turned pointedly to me and glared.

"Okay. I'll see what I can do. But you're not off the hook. I'll expect you to do some kind of community service. Maybe at the station. And that's *if* I can get Jesse to drop the charges."

"Thank you, Sheriff." Granny Lacey tipped her head.

"Don't thank me yet. Jesse is…well, Jesse."

Granny Lacey asked Fireman, "What time is it?" She proffered her wrist.

Fireman cradled her scrawny arm and squinted at her ancient watch. "It's time to go. Everyone's going to see Bella sing. The whole creek is coming out."

Granny Lacey narrowed her eyes at me. "We had to set out at the crack of dawn. And go nearly all the way to Osprey. And then circle back. When are you gonna get that bridge fixed?"

I stood up. "That's next on my list."

Robin's son, Sterling, opened the door with a miffed expression. "You're late."

Bemused, I scrambled for a response.

He cracked a smile. "Just joshing with ya, man."

"Okay," I said. "Man." Over his shoulder I spied Lenny, holding a bagel dripping with cream cheese. "Morning."

"You want a bagel?" asked Lenny. "The girls are still primping."

I followed him into the kitchen where Petey sat at the table, his eyes glued to an iPad. "Hey Sheriff," he grinned. "Big night, eh?" As always, I was taken with the way Petey could light up a room. "How about that assist from my brother?"

I nodded in agreement. "He rose to the occasion, that's for sure."

"He's in love," Sterling said between a mouth full of eggs. "It gives you superpowers." I studied the kid, suddenly curious as to what lay behind his jovial manner and gifted musical instincts.

Chatty laughter rose as the scent of battling perfumes wafted in from the hallway. "We're ready!" Desi sashayed in a bright orange and yellow getup.

"Nice." Lenny, ever enamored, admired his wife favorably.

Micah, perky and petite, sported a short skirt and offered a sassy smile, while Violet, tall and pale-skinned, towered beside her, clearly uncomfortable with the attention.

"Ladies," I tipped my hat.

Robin's daughter avoided my gaze, focusing instead on the Papillion prancing at her feet.

"Hey, check it out, Ruby." Petey grinned, once again teasing Violet over her color-themed name. "It's the video Timothy showed at service today." He ambled over to the girls with his iPad.

When he hit play, Violet leaned in, engaged, while Micah ducked into the kitchen. She inspected the selection of bagels. "I wonder how many calories a bagel has?"

Desi gave her a loaded look before turning to Lenny. "Why didn't you wake me up early? I wanted to watch North Lake's early service online."

"It will be online all day, and you were tired last night," Lenny said. "I thought I'd let you sleep. Besides, we're going to an actual bricks and mortar church today. Imagine."

Desi pecked his cheek. "It is fun to dress up for a change."

"I don't know," Lenny remarked. "I was kind of enjoying worshiping in my pajamas."

Sterling quipped, "Let's just hope Luke gets Bella to church on time."

Petey's eyes widened. "Now that has a nice ring to it."

Micah snorted. "He's so gross. All moony-eyed over her. I hope he doesn't distract her. Ruin her focus."

"I'm sure she can handle it," Desi said, glancing at Lenny. "He texted me earlier about the shelter where we got Ginger and Mary Ann."

Lenny squinted, "Luke wants a dog?"

"Why would anyone want a dog?" Robin said as she entered the kitchen. "When they could have a cat. Right Sheriff?"

"Beats me." Buford tracked behind Robin, meandering over for a tour between my pants legs. Despite the black cat hair sullying my khakis, I stood tall with the victory.

When I subconsciously reached into my pocket for a celebratory taffy, Robin playfully whipped it out of my hand. "Grape! My favorite." She wore slim black slacks and a colorful silk blouse. Classy as always, with a pair of sassy red glasses perched on her nose. "Shall we go?"

"We shall," I answered, trying not to dwell on Sterling's shocked expression or the whitening of Violet's already pale face. Instead, I turned to Robin, suddenly finding the notion of escorting a beautiful woman to church thrilling in its novelty.

The mixed sounds of purses being zipped, and keys jangling came to a halt with the screech of my phone. A sense of foreboding flooded me when I saw Quietdove's name flash across my screen. "Just one minute," I muttered, stepping to the side.

"Oh Ricky," Desi fussed. "What could be so important?"

"What's up?" I asked Quietdove. "We're just headed to church."

"Uh, I don't think so, boss." Quietdove's ominous tone confirmed my apprehension. "There's been an…incident."

"Enlighten me."

"Jesse didn't like the idea of his brother having a monopoly on the town's worshipers today, so he took a page out of Fireman's book."

"What are you saying?"

"It's not burnt to the ground, but trust me, there won't be any services today. Or anytime soon."

Half the steeple smoldered on the ground. The other half was missing altogether.

By the time we made it to Shady Gully Baptist Church, aka James's church, folks from both across the creek and Shady Gully Proper pottered among the wreckage. Dressed in their Sunday finest, they wore dazed expressions. They'd hoped to be part of a fusing event, and instead faced the unlikelihood of unification.

Max had handcuffed Jesse to a bench in front of Dolly's Diva Dome next door, where Dolly stood next to her brother, holding her cell phone to his ear. Claire lingered close to Dolly, carefully gaging the winds of community reaction, which of course would determine where she planted her allegiance.

Patty and my high school classmate, Denise, were in attendance, scurrying about offering assistance wherever they could, as well as monitoring the shock and anxiety levels of the would-be congregation.

The fire itself had been contained, and with the help of Redflyer,

Big Al, and Moonpipe, some of the wooden pews and a number of items from the vestry had been salvaged.

I noticed young Fireman scanning the scene, plucking random hymnals and Bibles from the wreckage, and loading them into a red wagon. I watched as he purposefully tugged the wagon, curious as to its destination. Not surprisingly, it went straight to Father Patrick, who fanned himself under the shade of a massive oak tree.

I'd left Robin across the road at Luke's auto body shop, where she and Desi chatted intently with Meadow and Wolfheart. Meadow wore a white summer dress which matched the bandage on her head, and she'd even dawned a little lipstick for Bella's performance. Now that the adrenaline had run its course, she appeared softer, undoubtedly relieved that Madhawk was no longer a threat.

Daryl and Bubba moseyed over, their boots scuffed and filthy with rubble from the fire. "We saw the whole thing." Bubba boasted. "If you wanna get our statement."

Daryl added, "If you want us in two separate rooms to make sure our stories match—"

"No knuckleheads," I scoffed. "Just tell me. I promise you'll get your fifteen minutes of fame."

While Daryl looked offended, Bubba began, "Well, we were early on account of Bella's big debut. We were enjoying a cup of coffee under Luke's awning over there." He pointed at Luke's auto body shop. "Discussing the merits of blue or white button downs with tan slacks—"

"Bubba, please." I rolled my eyes.

Daryl nodded. "I know, right? Clearly blue is better."

As I sighed at their shenanigans, I spotted Quietdove, leading James my way. "Quick fellows, your time is running out. One of the suspects is on his way."

Bubba frowned. "What? No. James didn't do it. I ain't crazy about him, but he was the victim. Jesse was the one that done the burning. I can describe him if you wanna get a sketch artist—"

"Bubba," I said harshly.

"We watched him go inside," said Daryl. "And he and James started right up arguing. Jesse said he wasn't gonna stand by and allow this to happen—"

"Stand idly by," corrected Bubba.

"Yeah, that's right. Stand idly by, and he accused James of being part of the conspiracy to steal his church."

"Yep, he sure did," Bubba said. "Told James right to his face he was conspiring with the Creek People. They went back and forth like that for a while and then James started shouting. Like," he turned to Daryl. "What did he say?"

"He said, 'what are you doing? Are you crazy?' Stuff like that. And then we heard a pop. And then we saw the smoke."

Good grief.

"When Jesse went inside, did he have anything in his arms?" When they looked at me blankly, I clarified. "Ya know, like a gas can or dynamite or something?"

The knuckleheads laughed. Then took a moment to talk among themselves.

"Good gracious," I muttered, before turning to Quietdove and James.

"We'll be happy to provide written statements," Bubba said solemnly, arching his brow at James.

I cleared my throat. "Thank you. Gentlemen." Once they filed off with a great sense of importance, I turned my attention to James. "You okay? Have you been looked at?" He was covered in soot and had a minor scratch on his head.

"I'm okay." He glared at his brother and sister in front of the salon. "Just angry. And I don't want to be, but I guess they're not going to rest until I'm bitter and resentful like them."

"I understand y'all argued. Can you tell me how it escalated,"—I pointed at the ruined church—"into that?"

"He came in madder than a hornet. I honestly think he needs to be on medication. His eyes were bloodshot, like he'd been smoking, and he had a whiskey bottle in his hand. At first, I thought he'd fallen off the wagon again."

Quietdove and I traded looks. *Again?*

"But then I realized it was gasoline I smelled. And the bottle had a piece of cloth or something coming out of the nozzle. He kept waving it around. Had a lighter in the other hand."

"Sounds a lot like a Molotov cocktail," Quietdove narrowed his eyes. "Where did he learn how to do that?"

"He didn't," James answered. "Trust me, it didn't go well. He's lucky he didn't set himself on fire."

I stepped back, surveilled the area. Charlie Wayne and Sprite had backed up a truck to the four way stop sign. They lowered the tail gate to reveal soft drinks and the makings for burgers. As the crowd converged, Petey hopped up to help pass out refreshments. Soon he had the congregation laughing, and the horrors of the last few weeks seemed almost unthinkable.

I swiveled back to James. "I need to ask you one question, and I want you to be honest with me."

"Sure."

"Do you think your brother meant to do more than destroy the church?" I could see the confusion in James's face, so I elaborated. "Or were you the target?"

James considered his brother, who argued heatedly with Dolly at the Diva Dome. "I just don't know, Sheriff. I guess you'd have to ask him."

But Jesse had nary a word to say to me. He'd already sought legal advice, and by the time I formerly arrested him, his lawyer had made a call and arranged for a psychological evaluation. He'd likely end up with mental health treatment, an ankle bracelet, and community service.

Whether he meant to kill his brother, or burn down the church to keep Bella from singing, or keep the Creeks from assimilating, I had no clue. I was convinced he didn't know either. He'd always been mean and vindictive, but now, he was mean, vindictive, and dangerous. Not only to himself, but to others.

Once James left to be with his family, the rest of the community, including those that had supported Jesse in the past, like Thaddeus and Big Al, were left to deal with the destruction of their town and its churches. There was a sense we'd hit rock bottom, and hopelessness was as heavy as the humidity.

As the sheriff of Shady Gully, I felt a profound sense of failure. A noble, honorable woman had died violently, and after blowing time and resources trying to hunt down her killer, I'd failed. I'd allowed myself to be manipulated by said killer, and ended up foolishly chasing my tail. I'd also made things worse by turning up land that was sacred to the people across the creek.

Robin's home was ransacked on my watch. Wolfheart's property was destroyed on my watch. A bridge failed and Meadow was almost killed on my watch. Bella as well. And the cherry on top was the destruction of two of the town's three churches.

I ought to resign. I'd failed my hometown.

"Sheriff," Luke ambled over with his brother, Petey. "How ya doing?"

I took in the magnitude of the destruction, and struggled for a reply. "Just dandy."

"We'll rebuild. Shady Gully will be better than ever."

I regarded him, this earnest kid with ambition and integrity. "You were right, Luke. I need help. I need reinforcements. I'm not enough to protect this town. Certainly not enough to unify it."

"We'll get there," Luke said with more confidence than I'd ever seen. "It's a chance to start over, and this time, we'll include everybody in the renovation. Trust me, that in itself will help unify us."

"He's right." Petey agreed. "It's hard to see now, amid all the ashes and ruins, but adversity can help renew our faith. I promise you, this town's spirit will be restored, and when it is, we'll have us a good old-fashioned revival. You'll see, hope will bloom again. Real soon."

I almost believed him, this one with the light inside him.

"There they are, three of the best minds in Shady Gully." Father Patrick's Irish accent was immediately recognizable as he approached. "No doubt strategizing our recourse, and pondering our bright and brilliant future."

"Father." I shook the priest's hand. "Looks like you're gonna have a full house for a while."

"Perhaps," he scratched his red beard thoughtfully. "And that would be lovely. But for now, I was thinking a short prayer might do the trick."

I realized he was right as I scanned the crowd. Now that the burgers and sodas were gone, and the temporary respite from the destruction had passed, the folks had grown despondent. "Sure, Father. But I gotta be honest, it's hard to find God in all of this."

"Oh, God's here," Petey insisted. "And I believe He weeps with us."

Father Patrick regarded Petey. "My, my, son. Well done." He patted his shoulder, "Perhaps I should pass the baton on to you? Will you offer a few words of prayer?"

Petey didn't hesitate. As he made his way to the center of the four way stop, I felt a slight hand brush against my back.

Robin. Such a beautiful sight for my wretched, failure of a self.

"Sheriff." She pushed her glasses up her nose. "It appears there's going to be a little music."

I followed her line of vision.

Bella whispered to Sterling as he tuned his guitar, and the two nodded decisively as they made their way to center stage with Petey.

"Maybe afterwards," Robin said, "we should introduce Buford and Gerty. See how they get on."

Chapter Twenty-Four

Final Farewell
Wolfheart

Desi and I pondered the day's events as we drank sweet tea under the awning at Luke's auto body shop. "What a day," she said. "But at least we got to hear Bella sing."

"And Petey pray." I eyed her. "You think there's something there? He reminds me a little of Timothy."

"Wouldn't that be something?" She chuckled, "Shady Gully could do worse. Come to think of it, we have. Jesse is in jail and James is, well…" she trailed off.

"James is okay," I said. "But he's no Father Patrick. And no Petey."

We sat comfortably together, as neither of us had ever felt the need to waste energy with frivolous conversation. Desi, whose history would forever be tangled with mine, had become more than just a friend to me over the years.

In the beginning, she'd been nothing more than one of the many high schoolers I'd manipulated into lining my pockets, but over time, her combination of nonchalance and naivety wore on me. Even as I shamefully influenced her for my own practical reasons, her vulnerability aroused a fierce protectiveness in me.

While I hadn't been responsible for the ongoing flirtation between her and Adam, Shady Gully's smooth-singing homeboy, my negative influence had put her in the wrong place at the wrong time.

One nearly disastrous night, after we'd parted ways at Cicada Stadium, she'd been susceptible. Already weakened by the loss of her mother and a five-year split from Robin, she'd come close to stepping off a precipice with Adam that would not only have destroyed her marriage—but crushed what remained of her spirit.

To this day, she insists that I saved her that night, and perhaps I did arrive just in time to provide courage and moral support, but I knew for sure it had been the other way around.

Shamed by my part in Desi's near ruin, I began to consider the countless others before her—and how I'd robbed them of living their best lives. Megan included. And that realization haunted me. Changed me.

Quite simply, Desi's brush with regret had been the catalyst to my redemption.

"I worry about Lenny," she said finally. "Look at him out there, trying to do the things he used to." We both watched as Lenny helped Sterling, Redflyer, and Moonpipe drag a ruined pew to the burn pile. "I try to tell him. He won't listen."

"Looks to me like he's holding his own."

When Lenny caught us watching, he paused to flash us a dramatic muscle man pose. Desi batted her eyelashes.

Just past the burn pile, we witnessed Dolly hastily exit her salon, shut herself in her car, and sneak away from the day's action at a hurried pace. Her expression was blank, and she kept her eyes squarely on the road as she slipped past us.

"There are good people out here," I mused.

She squinted at me. "What an oddly timed remark, seeing as how the wicked witch of the south just rode off on her broom."

It felt good to throw my head back and laugh. "I'm serious. The truth is, there are good and bad people everywhere. On the creek. In Shady Gully. I think at some point in our lives we have a choice. Either we give the bad the power to root resentment and bitterness inside us, or we celebrate the good, plant it with exaltation, and pray it grows."

Desi studied me intently. "Now you sound like Timothy and Petey."

I shrugged. "Just look at everyone working together, helping clean up the mess that somebody else made."

Micah, Bella, and Violet tried to scrub some dishware they'd salvaged from the church hall, while Petey and Max chatted up Denise and Patty, seemingly interested in Patty's CPR technique.

"True. Working together being the key word. I hope the Bellas' and Lukes' of the town have their way and inspire assimilation and unity.

"Speaking of that," I wondered aloud. "If they get married, are we officially family?"

"We've always been family."

I nodded, my gaze naturally drifting to Meadow, who rested on the bench of a picnic table with Mrs. Shanna May, Granny Lacey, Bubba, and Daryl. "You worry about Lenny. I worry about her."

Desi knew who I meant. "She's been through a lot. And now the revelation about her father's murder." Desi looked pointedly at me. "You'll *all* have to process that."

I sighed deeply, still reeling at the extent of Madhawk's iniquities.

Desi remarked, "She looks good today. And did you see her when Bella sang? Brad, I'm serious. I think she was genuinely moved. Her daughter has the voice of an angel. How could she not be?"

I conceded the point, as a wave of grief for my sister swept over me. How Peony would have loved seeing Bella's shining moment. Aware of Desi's scrutiny, I focused on keeping my expression blank.

As Lenny sauntered over to take a break, the sheriff and Robin joined us as well. When the sheriff pulled out a lawn chair for Robin, she laughed. And then he laughed.

Amused, Desi, Lenny, and I exchanged glances. "Well, aren't y'all cute." Desi quipped, unable to restrain herself.

The sheriff attempted a frown, but failed miserably.

I tossed Lenny a towel and he mopped up the sweat on his face before kissing his wife.

We sat, relaxing into the afternoon, and I'd almost shaken some of the distress of the last several days when the sound of a clank and a clunk rolled our way. Father Patrick pulled a little red wagon with an ice chest. Fireman trailed behind him with another wagon, hauling a garbage bag.

Father Patrick stopped, teasing us with a wink. "I've got bottled water, cokes, and something a little more…spirited, if you're so inclined."

"But he has to see your ID first." Fireman stabbed a stray can on the ground, chucking it into his garbage wagon. A heavy breeze carried a few scorched papers by, and Fireman dashed after them, adding them to his trash collection. When he was done, he cocked an eye toward the Sheriff. "Father Patrick says I'm a good helper."

"Humph," Sheriff Rick guffawed. "Is that right, Father?"

"Most certainly," Father Patrick assured. "He'll be off probation in no time."

As Fireman beamed under the positive attention, he and Father Patrick clanked away as suddenly as they'd arrived. Off to recharge their flock physically or spiritually, as needed.

"That's a very constructive punishment for the boy," Robin said. "And Father Patrick will be a good mentor."

"I think so," Sheriff Rick said. "But he's not totally off the hook. He's gonna wash the deputies' trucks as well, and clean toilets at the station, and—"

"Don't be too hard," Desi remarked. "He's just a boy."

"A boy who burnt down a church," Lenny clarified.

"On accident," Robin rebutted.

When everyone looked at me, I shrugged. "It was me. I did it."

As the easy chuckles faded, Desi pressed me with her usual directness. "Now that it's over, and Madhawk is dead, why don't you tell us what happened the night Peony died?"

"Geez," Lenny breathed, stretching out in his lawn chair. "Way to be subtle, honey."

"Actually, I'd like to hear too," Sheriff Rick chimed.

As they all waited expectantly, I toyed with the idea of getting up and leaving. I had no legal obligation to wrap up the case in a nice bow for the sheriff, and I wasn't sure I could even verbalize the events of that horrible night. But as I considered their faces, even the sheriff's, I detected no suspicion, and no judgment. Only concern.

"It was my fault. I blame myself," I began. "I left Peony's a little before dark, and I sensed Madhawk's rage simmering just below the surface. He was twitchy and irritable. But I let—I let Hania follow me home."

"Hania?" the sheriff asked, leaning in.

"The older he got, the more he enjoyed the late nights in my garden.

238

Scurrying up squirrels and rodents was play for him. And I was tired. I didn't have the energy to force him to stay home at Peony's."

The sheriff dipped his head back in realization, closing his eyes. "The dog."

"I remember him," Desi said. "I thought he was more of a wolf."

"He was both. Born a wolf, but domesticated like a dog. But more than anything, he was Peony's beloved Spirit Warrior. He adored her, and protected her—from a number of threats."

"Like Madhawk?" confirmed the sheriff.

I nodded. "Hania was a deterrent. Madhawk was terrified of him. And on this night," I lowered my head, "he was with me."

"You aren't to blame," Robin said.

But I thought differently. Feeling lonely, I'd wanted Hania's company, needing the presence of another living, breathing soul. As aging males, he and I shared a special kinship. Ordinarily surrounded by females, our nights in the garden together were a reprieve from all the chatter.

Usually, he'd instigate a game of Hunt, which had always been his favorite. Nudging the back of my legs with a low growl, he'd swing his head from side to side, taunting me with the tattered blue wolf in his mouth. I'd start off pretending indifference, as was our ritual, and when he'd almost given up on a game, and loosened his grip on the stuffed animal, I'd wrestle it from his jaws and take off as fast as my old legs would carry me.

Hania rarely chased me. The appeal of the game for him had been the act of stalking me. The true wolf came out in him then, showcasing his instinct and cunning. Always the victor, he'd nip at my ankles until I grew tired, and finally tackle me with a celebratory romp.

After a rowdy game of hunt, we'd settle into a rhythm, just the two of us.

While I hoed and weeded, finding the steady movement therapeutic, Hania would rest his snout on his paws, keeping one eye open in case a random, daring squirrel ventured into his territory. Many an evening we'd pass this way, enjoying the companionable silence, while waiting for the cicadas to take possession of the night.

"On this night," I continued. "Bella came running for us. She could hardly breathe. She was in a frightened, panicked state. Hania, immediately alert, sensed her fear, and beat a path to Peony's ahead of us. You could smell the sweat, the urgency in him, to get to Peony. To protect her. His strong, muscular legs pushed as hard as they could, but I think—I think he knew."

"What do you mean?" asked Lenny.

"I don't know. Maybe I'm projecting, but in that moment, I believe he felt the weight of letting her down. Like he'd failed her." I sighed, weary with the memories. "I raced after him, and Bella raced after me. I'll never forget that journey to Peony. It seemed like it took forever, although it was probably only minutes. Behind me were the sounds of Bella's panicked gasps, and her tears, and ahead of me Hania snarled and growled, the fur on his back raised in fury. He was a warrior preparing for battle."

"I'm so sorry," Desi said thickly, resting her hand on my arm.

"While Meadow had done her best to fight Madhawk off, she couldn't match his strength. Both she and Peony were hurt when we got there, and as Hania exploded through the door ahead of Bella and me, he immediately went for Madhawk's throat. But it was as if Madhawk knew he had one last chance…to beat him. One last chance to break his heart."

"Oh no." Desi mumbled shakily.

"And he used it to lift Peony in his arms and"—I gestured—"slam her head against the mantel."

Robin stood, moved to my other side, so that I was bookended with support.

"Hania erupted with rage then, launching himself on Madhawk, nearly slicing clean through his arm and shoulder. Madhawk ran toward the back door, trying to escape Hania's wrath. Hania chased him, furiously ripping at his face and neck, and they both tumbled out the back door."

"What condition was Peony in at this point?" asked the Sheriff.

"Not good. But she was conscious enough to hear when Hania cried out."

My eyes coated as I relived those horrible moments. "Bella and Meadow were kneeling beside Peony, and my sister cried as Meadow held a cloth to her wound—with grief as much as pain."

"Oh man," Lenny commiserated.

"Hania stumbled in, and made it to my sister's side. He literally tucked himself along the length of her body. And she rested her hand on his head, near his ears. He was soaked in blood from where Madhawk's knife had cut him, and his eyes were heavy with agony, but they never left Peony's. Never. Until the end."

I blinked back the heaviness in my eyes as I considered Desi, Lenny, and Robin, and then the sheriff, who nodded as if he'd just found the corner piece of a puzzle. "Just before she died," I said finally. "My sister asked me, pleaded with me with every ounce of life she had in her—"

"What?" Desi asked.

"She asked me to bury him. Quickly. So that his spirit would meet her on the other side. She made me promise. And told me to hurry."

"So that's who you buried in the sacred grounds?" The sheriff asked gently.

"Yes," I breathed. "And Madhawk was dead on the back steps when I left."

Somewhere between late afternoon and sunrise, the atmosphere went from shocked and despondent to hopeful and festive. Once the volunteer firemen determined the grounds safe, the people of Shady Gully found their own unique ways to contribute.

Daryl, Bubba, Quietdove, and Youngdeer hauled the cross from the wreckage of the church, and once they deemed it restorable, chat bounced around as to which restoration company might be affordable. After the discussion, Redflyer got his hands on some sandpaper, and began sanding the wooden cross himself. Sterling and Petey, fascinated by his skill, quickly picked up his instruction, and pitched in on opposite sides of the cross.

Sprite sent Fireman to his store for more sandpaper, and within a few hours, the old rugged cross gleamed with new character, more distinctive now after its own distress. The act of raising the cross, and leaning it safely against a massive oak tree, sparked a sense of reverence among the crowd.

The spirit of harmony spread as Mrs. Shanna May, Meadow, and Granny Lacey salvaged some blackened silver trays, goblets, and candleholders from the church hall, and purposefully set about restoring them to their original shine.

Charlie Wayne enlisted Micah, Bella, and Violet to help him fry some fish Thaddeus had caught on Osprey earlier in the week, and as the smell wafted through the four way stop, it was impossible not to feel a spur of hope.

The bonfire of lost pews and other ruined material burned brightly as night fell over Shady Gully. Despite the length, and emotional drain of the day, everyone seemed reluctant to leave.

While Luke, Sheriff Rick, and I tended to the fire, we slid marshmallows on hangers for the kids, and then sent them to Robin and Desi, who finished them off with graham crackers and chocolate.

"This is what I wish for Shady Gully," Luke said, indicating the congenial atmosphere.

"Yeah well," muttered Sheriff Rick. "It would sure make my job a lot easier." He turned to me. "I've got a crew coming your way tomorrow to get that bridge fixed. Properly this time."

"Who's paying for it?" I asked, knowing instinctively it would come at a high price.

"Don't worry about it. I'll deal with the bureaucratic red tape later, but I ain't gonna wait around for the state. Let's just say we got an anonymous donor."

The three of us looked directly at Robin, whose colorful blouse was spotted with chocolate. When I turned back to the sheriff, his goofy smile made me laugh.

"Hey Luke!" hollered Charlie Wayne as he served a basket of fish and fries to a picnic table full of old timers, including the ornery Chester. "We just took a mock vote over here, and your incorporation passed unanimously."

"I'm still on the fence," countered Sprite. "But I'm leaning your way."

Bella dashed over, snaking her arms around my waist. "Uncle Wolf, guess who looks like she's not miserable?"

I chuckled. "Your mama?"

After a pleased smile, she left my side for Luke's, who puffed up with pride as she reached for his hand. "Guess what? Granny Lacey wants to register to vote, and Redflyer and old man BlueJay said they're not opposed to the idea of incorporation. If it means they'll have a voice in town."

"There ya go," Sheriff Rick nodded. "Luke, you're like a blind hog that found an acorn. I can't believe this thing might actually happen."

Luke eyeballed me. "You know, Mr. Wolfheart, uh…Wolf—"

"Go ahead and call me Wolfheart, Luke." I shot Bella a look. "For now."

"I was just going to say, you'd be the perfect person to champion them."

"I already do."

"I know you do, but this time, you'd have power. If you ran—"

"Okay," I avoided Luke's challenge as Quietdove trooped over with a dripping smore in his hand. "One thing at a time."

Quietdove wiped his chocolatey mouth with the sleeve of his deputy's shirt. "Hey Bella, the guitar boy with the funny name wants you. He's tuning up for another number."

"Gotta go," she pecked Luke on the cheek.

As I watched bold little Bella prance to the center of the four way stop with an air of confidence, a wave of joy swept over me. She'd broken barriers. She'd crossed lines. Even though Meadow had discouraged her, and I'd feared for her, she'd made her way.

Suddenly optimistic about the future, I moved in as Sterling strummed his guitar and Bella glided with the music. As they began to sing, it seemed all of Shady Gully closed in on the four way stop.

Desi and Robin sang ahead of me, holding up their hands with tearful praise and a rousing, "Hallelujah!"

After the intro, Sterling crooned the first verse, then faded into the background, allowing Bella to take center stage. As she moved her arms from side to side, Bella's expression erupted in joy as she mesmerized her audience with a rousing, emotional chorus.

I always appreciated that moment in worship music, just after the chorus repeats a few times, and the audience loses their inhibitions and belts out the melody.

Bella was there now, and as she sang out the first few verses, she opened her arms wide, and the gathering rewarded her with a resounding proclamation of faith.

On and on it went, worship songs, smores, fried fish, and a sense of community. As I stepped back from it all, roaming along the perimeter of the heady scene, I closed my eyes and welcomed the sounds of harmony and hope.

A familiar figure suddenly wrapped her arms around me.

"Meadow," I grinned into her hair, tugging her closer. "You're not miserable."

She laughed. "You've been talking to my daughter."

"I have. I admit it."

She looked over my shoulder, passed Luke's auto body shop, toward the patch of woods beyond it. "Guess what?"

"What?"

"He was here. I saw him." She scanned the trees again. "Just for a minute, while Bella was singing. But I know it was him. I'm not crazy."

"Who?"

"Hania." She squinted in the direction of the woods. "He didn't howl. He was just there, watching. Clear-blue eyes. A collar of pristine white fur. He was healthy. He looked…well."

I nodded.

"You don't believe me?"

"Of course, I believe you." I hugged her. "I believe in the middle of all this chaos and destruction, you've found your faith." When she started to interrupt, I went on, "Look at Bella up there. All that joy. That hope. She found it in Jesus. Look at her, Meadow. Just look at her."

Meadow paused, considering Bella who was singing with her arms outstretched, her face rosy with conviction.

Thoughtful, Meadow peered behind me once more. "I've gotta go. Just before I walked over here, Granny Lacey was giving Mrs. Shanna May her recipe for zucchini bread. I need to warn her."

My heart overflowing, I watched as Meadow hurried back to the festivities.

After a moment I turned toward the woods behind the auto body shop. I saw nothing but trees, thickets, and foliage. No matter. I didn't need to see to believe. As I walked back to the bonfire, I bid the great Spirit Warrior a final farewell—confident in the knowledge that he and my beloved sister, Peony, were reunited at the feet of Jesus.

Acknowledgements
& Thanks

T his book is fiction. That means I made it all up. For real.

As always, I'm grateful to Mike Parker and Wordcrafts Press for your expertise, your guidance, and especially, your patience.

A huge thank you to Jeff and Steve for the regular spit-balling sessions, the amazing publicity opportunities, and of course, pushing me to be fearless.

I'm forever thankful to the tech savvy genius in my life, Rachel Buettner.

And to my most treasured first-readers, Tammy Lynne Belgard and John Brothers, I'm forever grateful. You make my work better. You voluntarily scour for inconsistencies, mistakes, and typos; and even challenge me on seasonal foliage when necessary. You are better than all the thesauruses, encyclopedias, and farmer's almanacs combined!

I'd like to extend a very special thank you to Taylor Hatchell, who shared his in-depth experience and firsthand knowledge of raising a wolfdog. Cheers to you and your "best" dog, Ariel.

As always, my FRIENDS of HALLIE newsletter subscribers, my amazing Launch Team, and my Cozy Corner Chatters hold a very special place in my heart. Thank you, Jennifer Adams and Mark Cermak, for your dedication and constant support.

On a personal level, the transition from writer to published author has been overwhelming, exhilarating, challenging, and humbling. Thank you to my talented writer friends, Charly Cox, Janetta

Fudge-Messmer, Jeffrey Pentz, and Emma Lombard. I'm grateful to have you in my corner.

And finally, to my family, Bruce, Bree, and Phil—your genuine delight, your unconditional support, and your steady dose of reassurance means everything to me. You are, and always will be, my best people. I love you.

NOTE TO READERS
Hallie Lee

Thank you for spending time with me in Shady Gully. I hope you enjoyed Wolfheart's story. In *Paint Me Fearless,* he was initially a toss-in character, a mere villain to challenge Desi and Robin. But he had other plans. He evolved, became noble, and then insisted on his own book.

If you enjoyed *Paint Me Fearless* and *Wolfheart,* and look forward to Book Three in *The Shady Gully Series*, please take a few minutes to leave a review on Goodreads, Amazon, Barnes & Noble, Books-A-Million, BookBub or wherever you purchase your books!

And please, mosey on over to my website, www.hallielee.com, and sign up for my newsletter. When you become a FRIEND OF HALLIE, you'll get all the Shady Gully News FIRST, including release dates, cover reveals, contests, giveaways, recipes, and more! I'll see y'all back at the Cozy Corner in Book Three!

Until then—Stay Fearless!

https://www.facebook.com/HallieLeeBooks
https://www.instagram.com/Hallie_Lee_Books
https://www.twitter.com/HallieLeeBooks
Hallie Lee (@hallie_lee_author) TikTok

Also Available From

WordCrafts Press

In Search of the Beloved
Marian Rizzo

Little Reminders of Who I Am
Jeff S. Bray

Maggie's Song
Marcia Ware-Wilder

Oh, to Grace
Abby Rosser

The Mirror Lies
Sandy Brownlee

www.wordcrafts.net

Lightning Source UK Ltd.
Milton Keynes UK
UKHW041035121021
391908UK00018B/552/J